PRAISE FOR SHARON W...

Sharon Ward's IN DEEP is a stellar, pulse-pounding debut novel featuring a female underwater photographer. A heady mix of underwater adventure, mystery, and romance.

HALLIE EPHRON, NEW YORK TIMES
BESTSELLING AUTHOR

Pack your SCUBA fins for a wild trip to the Cayman Islands. *In Deep* delivers on twists and turns while introducing a phenomenal new protagonist in underwater photographer Fin Fleming, tough, perceptive and fearless.

EDWIN HILL, AUTHOR OF *THE SECRETS WE*
SHARE

How much did I love In Deep? Let me count the ways. Fin Fleming, underwater photographer, is a courageous yet vulnerable protagonist I want to sip Margaritas with. The Cayman Islands are exotic and alluring, yet tinged with danger. The underwater scenes and SCUBA diving details are rendered in stunning detail. Wrap that all into a thrilling mystery and you'll be left as breathless as - well, no spoilers here. You must read it to find out!

Breathtaking on two levels, Sharon Ward's debut novel IN DEEP will captivate experienced divers as well as those who've only dreamed of exploring the beauty beneath the sea. The underwater world off the Cayman Islands is stunningly rendered, and the complex mystery involving underwater photographer Fin Fleming, especially the electrifying dive scenes, will have readers holding their breath. Brava!

In Deep is a smart and original story that sucks you in from page one. Edge-of-your-seat suspense, a hauntingly realistic villain, and a jaw-dropping twist make this pacy read unputdownable until the very last word.

STEPHANIE SCOTT-SNYDER, AUTHOR OF WHEN WOMEN OFFEND: CRIME AND THE FEMALE PERPETRATOR

IN DEEP

IN DEEP

A FIN FLEMING THRILLER

SHARON WARD

For Erin, Taylor, Cam, and Scott. Pat, Colin, and our other Erin.
Josh, Jen, Isaac and Ryleigh. Thanks for being my family.
And for Jack, the best husband in the universe.
Maggie, I miss you.

FOREWORD

Grand Cayman is one of my favorite places on Earth. For those of you who also love it, please know that I took some liberties with the geography of the island and a few dive sites.

For example, I needed a convenient place to put the Madelyn Anderson Russo Institute, so I stuck one in.

In general, if something bad happens at any location, the spot is more than likely a figment of my imagination.

The restaurant where Fin and Lily have lunch is fictitious. Don't try to get a reservation.

For you divers, I added walls to a few dive sites where no walls exist, and I added some dive sites that aren't real.

And Fin and the other professional divers in the book engage in some very risky dive practices. They dive alone. They don't check their gauges. They dive too deep and ascend too fast. Unless you too are a pro, don't do as they do. Recreational divers should always obey the dive safety rules, and dive within the limits of their experience. Plan your dive, and dive your plan.

If you haven't been to the Cayman Islands, go. It's a magical place.

CHAPTER ONE

IT WAS JUST after dawn on the day of the first accident, and the scorching Cayman Islands' sun was already warm on my shoulders. Before starting to load my gear onto the *Maddy*, my stepfather's dive boat, I pulled on an old silver dive skin left over from one of the annual documentaries filmed by the Dr. Madelyn Anderson Russo Institute for Ocean Exploration. My name—Finola Fleming—was emblazoned in fluorescent pink letters down the right leg.

I was still in the first month of my new job and trying hard to make a name for myself. After finishing my doctoral coursework in oceanography, I'd rejoined the family business—the ocean exploration institute we call RIO for short—as marketing director and principal underwater photographer, work I love. Mostly because it requires me to dive every day.

My stepfather, Ray Russo, and his lifelong dive buddy, Gus Simmons, were sitting in the twin captain's chairs waiting for me to finish loading up. Today, they were training for a deep apnea dive that we wanted to include in this year's RIO documentary. My assignment was to film some of the training.

I tucked my dive bag under the bench along the side of the 36-foot Munson dive boat that had been custom made for Ray back when he was a champion freediver and a world-renowned treasure hunter. Despite years of hard use in every ocean on earth, his boat still gleamed like new. Ray made sure of it.

"All set, Ray," I said when I'd put my tanks and photography equipment away.

Ray gave me a devilish grin. "Is that all you're bringing, Fin? You sure you don't need any more stuff?"

"Maybe another camera, a change of dive skin, some lip gloss?" added Gus.

"Women never travel light, do they?" Ray said. "What is all that stuff?"

Gus chuckled. "I don't know, Boss. But there sure is an awful lot of it."

"Don't need it...," said Ray.

"Don't want it," finished Gus.

Ray and Gus both laughed, and I laughed along with them.

After a lifetime of friendship, the two men were so close they often finished each other's sentences, and to watch them dive together was like watching a single organism perform. I had been diving with them since I was a little kid, and they had trained me and taken care of me all that time. My heart swelled with love for them.

We moored the boat on the rim of a flat reef that dropped off into a vertical wall that went more than two miles down. Ray used a small portable winch to lower a heavy metal plate on a guide rope marked in ten meter increments. They would use the rope as a visual scale while they practiced.

Apnea diving can be tricky. Nitrogen narcosis, also known as rapture of the deep, can mess with your mind, making you forget which way is up. It helps to have the rope as a guide.

"Ready?" Gus asked.

Ray nodded. "All set. Let's suit up."

Ray and Gus wouldn't be using any gear except a small face mask and an aluminum noseplug while they made a series of progressively deeper breathhold dives. No scuba tanks full of life sustaining air; no fins for propulsion. Nothing but their frail bodies against the cruel ocean depths while training to freedive to 330 feet.

Down that deep, it's dark. It's cold. And it's lonely.

Not to mention treacherous.

Since Ray and Gus would be in the water all day, they pulled on thick neoprene wetsuits for warmth. Before stepping off the *Maddy*'s platform, they strapped dive computers to their wrists to track their depth. The powerful computers were just a little bulkier than a regular wristwatch, but they were technical marvels. My stepfather loved technology almost as much as he loved diving.

I entered the water to videotape their first dives. After filming their entries and exits, I'd have accomplished my assignment for the day, and I planned to spend the rest of my time working on the storyboard for a new promotional video I was planning for RIO.

"Let's start easy. Just 132 feet," Ray said.

Gus nodded. "You go first."

"One of us is up when the other one is down, right?" Ray said, repeating the safety rule for apnea divers. Although I wasn't a breathhold diver myself, I knew the rule's purpose was to make sure if the diver underwater ran into a problem, the diver keeping watch on the surface could come to the rescue.

In theory, at least, that's the way it works.

While Ray floated on his back, calming his mind and body, sipping air in preparation for his dive, I sank beneath the waves to get in position for filming. When he was ready, he made a head-first descent, using his powerful arms and bare feet to propel himself straight down. He was sleek, fast, and focused. A perfect visual for film.

At sixty feet, the ocean took over the work. Ray went still and relied on his body's own negative buoyancy to pull him down. I followed him until at 132 feet, his dive computer beeped. He turned and headed for the surface, kicking hard to break the ocean's hold on him. Shortly after he passed sixty feet, positive buoyancy propelled him to the surface with no further effort on his part. I followed him up, still filming.

He broke the surface and removed his mask. "I am okay," he said, while making the diver's traditional hand on head sign. This was the required protocol in competition, and the custom looked good on video. Ray was always well aware of the impression he made on camera.

For fifteen minutes after Ray surfaced, Gus studied him with care to ensure he wasn't suffering any ill effects from the dive. This was an important part of the after-dive procedure. The prolonged lack of oxygen sometimes makes divers forget how to breathe when they surface after deep apnea dives.

Once Ray's breathing normalized, Gus prepared for his own descent. I filmed him too, and like Ray's, his dive was perfect. Easy, even for Gus, who wasn't as experienced as Ray. But then again, these 132-foot dives had been a mere warm-up.

The human body needs time to adapt to freediving, and divers sometimes worked for months or even years to increase their tolerance by just a few feet. Soon Gus would be fighting to master every additional foot of depth, but for Ray, reaching the goal was a simple matter of reacclimating himself to the sport he'd once dominated.

Their next dives went to 140 feet. At these depths, divers were no longer visible to watchers on the surface. The designated safety diver above relied on the dive's elapsed time to decide whether to intervene. I climbed back aboard the boat to work on my video's storyboard while Gus and Ray kept diving.

By noon they'd progressed to 230 feet. Although Ray had gone much deeper on past dives, this was close to the maximum depth Gus had ever achieved. "One more dive before we break for lunch?" Gus said.

"Sure thing. I'm starving," Ray said. "I'm going to 260 feet on this dive." He inhaled several times and then disappeared under the water.

I checked my watch when he surfaced. Ray had been underwater for over three and a half minutes, still well under his personal best time.

Ray removed his mask. "I'm okay. In fact, I'm fine, and I'm more than ready to eat. No sense in waiting any longer than we need to for lunch since we're all starving. Fin can keep an eye on me. Why don't you dive now, Gus?"

"Okay, if you say so. I'm gonna try for 260 feet too."

"You sure? We're not competing here."

Gus grinned. "We're always competing, my man. And if an old guy like you can do it, I can do it too." He floated on his back for a moment, then swiveled beneath the water.

As we waited for Gus to surface, seconds slid into minutes. I checked the timer on my dive computer. He'd now been under water for three minutes. For Gus, that was a long time.

Gus wasn't approaching world record times yet, but then again, he was not a world class breathhold diver. I could tell from how uneasy Ray was that we both knew he should have surfaced by now, or at least we should have been able to see him making his way back from the shadowy depths.

At three minutes and fifteen seconds of downtime, Ray

peered through his mask into the water for any sign of his best friend. I put my camera away and lifted my scuba tank over my shoulders.

Just in case.

Three minutes and thirty seconds.

Still no sign of Gus. I could hear Ray's fearful panting even from my spot on the boat.

At three minutes and forty-five seconds, I saw growing alarm in Ray's deep brown eyes. His breathing was rapid and shallow, and his panic over Gus prevented him from catching his breath. He wasn't wearing tanks, and he couldn't freedive now even to save his friend. He wouldn't get past thirty feet before running out of air.

I donned my fins and stepped into the water. This was a problem.

A very big problem.

"Save him," he said. "Please." His voice was raspy, breathless, and full of terror.

I put my scuba regulator in my mouth and sank below the surface. While I descended, I turned in slow circles searching in all directions for any sign of Gus.

At first, I saw nothing.

At 100 feet, I spotted him, his foot tangled in the guide rope below me. He was very still, not even trying to swim for the surface.

I swam as hard as I could. I reached him at 130 feet of depth. He was unconscious.

I grabbed him and stuck my primary regulator into his mouth, switching to my spare for my own use. I clasped his torso with one arm, using the other to hold the regulator in his mouth in case he began breathing on his own. I began the long trek back to the surface, ascending as fast as I could and ignoring all safety stops.

The alarms on my dive computer went crazy at my rapid ascent. I didn't care. I had to save Gus, no matter the cost to my own health. My heart was pounding with fear and exertion.

Knowing every second could mean life or death for Gus, it felt like forever before we emerged from the water. Ray pulled Gus's limp body onto the *Maddy*'s dive platform.

I scrambled aboard and dragged the emergency oxygen tank over to where Gus lay immobile. I clapped the mask over his face and started the flow.

Meanwhile, Ray grabbed the radio and called RIO. "I need help. Get an ambulance and oxygen to the dock. Gus had an accident." Heedless of the tears running down his face, he gave our location and then began CPR, working to save his friend's life. "Please, God," he whispered, over and over again as he pumped.

I noticed the depth on Gus's dive watch, which showed he'd been down to 330 feet. I pointed it out to Ray and asked, "Why would he go down that far?"

Ray shook his head but didn't break his CPR rhythm. I was sure we were both thinking about the French freediving champion who'd blacked out and suffered lung barotrauma because the judges had set the guide rope a mere ten meters deeper than he'd planned. Gus had gone so much further than an extra ten meters. Still, that injured diver had been able to resume his freediving career soon after the accident. I prayed Gus would be as lucky.

Despite my desperate prayers, I was surprised when after a few minutes, Gus expelled a belly full of sea water, gasped, and at last, began breathing on his own.

Ray's sigh of relief was audible, and tears streamed down his face. He rolled Gus onto his left side to prevent him from choking. The color slowly returned to Gus's lips and cheeks, and his eyes fluttered open. He tried to sit up, coughing and spitting blood.

Ray put a hand on his shoulder "Just relax. Take a few minutes before you exert yourself."

Gus coughed again and nodded before he lay back down.

After a few minutes, his breathing steadied and once more, he tried to sit up. This time Ray piled several life preservers behind him to support his back.

"That diver tried to kill me," Gus said. "I'm lucky I made it."

Ray and I looked at each other over his head. "What diver?" Ray asked. "What happened down there?"

Gus took a deep breath and shuddered. "I was swimming hard but feeling good. I knew I could make it. Ears and sinuses were clear. I was going so fast I didn't have time to notice anything until I saw this other diver at around two-hundred-forty feet."

"There was no other diver down there, Gus,'" said Ray. "Fin and I were both on the surface. We didn't see any bubbles from a scuba diver."

"There was another diver," Gus said, spitting another mouthful of frothy blood into the cup I held for him. "Came out of nowhere. With a rebreather and a scooter. That's why you didn't know the diver was there."

"I think you might have been narc'ed, Gus." I said as I poured the cup's contents overboard.

"I wasn't narc'ed. It was real. As soon as I turned to go to the surface, the diver put a rope around my right foot and held me there. I tried to get away, but the more I struggled the tighter it got. I bet I have a mark on my ankle from the rope." He reached feebly for his leg.

"I'll get it." Ray rolled up the wetsuit leg. A red welt encircled Gus's right ankle. Ray's gaze met mine over our patient.

I shook my head slightly. "Your leg was tangled in the guide rope when I found you."

Gus tightened his lips and waved his hand in a dismissive gesture. "I wasn't hallucinating. That diver held me down there until I stopped struggling. By then it was too late. My lungs were ready to burst. I didn't have enough air to get back to the surface. Whoever was down there tried to kill me. I'd have been a goner if you hadn't come for me, Fin."

"Of course, I'd come for you." I wiped another trickle of blood from his lips. Bleeding lungs were a common complication of freediving, but the condition usually healed quickly without causing permanent damage. Even so, it was important to have a doctor evaluate Gus right away. I looked at Ray. "You stay with him. I'll drive the boat back to RIO."

He nodded. "Radio ahead that we're on our way in. Theresa will want to know he's awake."

I climbed the ladder to the flying bridge and started the engines. As soon as we were underway, I grabbed the radio to let the RIO team know we were heading to port. Their answer was nearly drowned out by Gus's wife sobbing in the background, and the sound broke my heart.

I raised my voice so she could hear me. "Theresa, he's awake, and he seems fine. We'll be there in ten minutes. Maybe less."

Cheers and applause greeted my words. Theresa shouted, "Thank you."

Theresa and I had met when she started dating Gus a few years ago. I always say she's my best friend, but the truth is, she's my only friend. You can blame my unorthodox childhood for my lack of friends, but I wouldn't have changed a thing about my life.

As a kid, I'd spent most of my time at sea on the *Omega*, RIO's research vessel. That's why I call my mother Maddy instead of Mom, because that's what everyone around me called her. Educated aboard ship by private tutors, I never went to a regular school until college. I was shy, gawky, and isolated, and to make matters worse, I was always visible on TV and the internet because of RIO's popular annual documentaries. Not a recipe for popularity, but I had experiences unmatched in any other environment. And now I had Theresa as a friend. On balance, it was all good.

I pulled the *Maddy* up to the dock at RIO headquarters where the entire staff was gathered on shore to assist Gus. He was popular with the team, and there was no shortage of people wanting to help.

Even before they'd secured the boat, the doctor, the EMTs, my mother, and Theresa all jumped aboard. The medics started preparing Gus for transport to RIO's infirmary. Theresa tried not to get in the way while still holding onto him as tightly as she could. Tears rolled down her face.

My mother went straight to Ray and wrapped her arms around him. "You're safe," she murmured. "I am so lucky." They stood together watching the medics strap Gus to a portable gurney.

A trickle of blood seeped from Gus's mouth and he grasped Theresa's hand. "Can't breathe," he said, clutching his chest with his other hand.

The doctor listened through her stethoscope. "Possible heart attack," she said. "Take him to Grand Cayman Hospital instead of sickbay." RIO's infirmary was the best in the islands for diving-related injuries, cuts, scrapes, stings, and barotrauma, but we weren't equipped for other types of medical emergencies. The medical staff lifted the gurney onto the dock and sped off toward the nearby parking lot to rush Gus away.

The doctor put her hand on Theresa's arm. "C'mon,

Theresa. You can ride in the ambulance with me." The two women hurried after the medics.

The rest of us stayed at RIO, willing Gus to make a full recovery. We couldn't focus on anything except Gus, so we closed RIO's aquarium and all our public areas. The entire staff gathered in the cafeteria, waiting for news.

Later that afternoon, the doctor came through the main entrance. She stood at the front of the room so we could all hear her. "I can't give you a lot of details, but I can say Gus will be fine. He did have a heart attack and he sustained some serious lung damage from the dive, but in time, I expect him to make a full recovery. He'll have to stay out of the water for at least six months, maybe more."

The crowd broke into cheers at the welcome news.

CHAPTER TWO

A LITTLE PAST sunrise a few days later—the day of the second accident—I was snorkeling alone in the warm waters at Rum Point on the north side of Grand Cayman. I was still trying to calm down after the drama of Gus's near drowning, and daily diving was part of my job.

Through my waterproof bone conduction headphones, I was enjoying the sweeping sounds of Ravel's *Une Barque sur l'ocean*. The rolling notes echoing the sunlight dancing through the clear seawater were tailor made for the moment. I aimed my video camera at the pile of sand where a stingray's hooded eyes and the telltale outline of his wings were the only hints to his presence.

I took a breath through my snorkel and dove, adjusting my camera to zoom in on the distinctive white scar above the stingray's eyes. As a kid, I'd named this stingray Harry because of the fictional wizard who bore a similar scar.

We were both a lot older now than when we'd first crossed paths. Recently, I'd taken hundreds of still photos and hours of video of Harry for a short film I was working on for RIO.

Since my playlist would end with the Ravel piece, I knew it was time to finish my dive and get ready for work. I surfaced and took one more breath through my snorkel, gently kicking a few times to bring me closer to Harry's position on the bottom. But when I dove back down, he rose, dipped his wings to brush off the sand, and glided away. Harry never let me get too close, although after all this time he must have known I was neither predator nor prey.

As usual, I was enthralled by the elegance of his gliding motion, and I followed his path with my camera's lens until he dropped behind a large orange brain coral. I lost sight of him just as my lungs signaled an urgent need to breathe. I hated leaving his mysterious watery world, but I couldn't stay any longer. I headed for the surface, while my gaze lingered on the clouds of slowly drifting sand indicating Harry was re-burying himself on the ocean bottom.

The top of my head had barely emerged from the water when something big and fast hit me hard, lifting my body fully out of the sea before I fell back. On the way down, I saw ribbons of blood swirling around me. Then, there was nothing but darkness.

CHAPTER THREE

SOMEONE WAS POUNDING on my chest, forcing me to spew out a stream of sea water that burned my nose and mouth as it emerged. I coughed and drew in a shuddering breath.

"She's awake." I didn't recognize the voice.

"Thank God."

That voice I recognized. It was Maddy. I opened my eyes and tried sitting up, but my aching head protested. I moaned and fell back to the sand.

Maddy's voice echoed through my throbbing skull. "Finola Newton Fleming, open your beautiful eyes right this minute. I know you're awake."

As always, I responded on cue. Even after I shook my head to clear my vision, I saw a double image of my mother kneeling in the sand beside me. Twice as much of her ice blonde hair, perfect skin, and steel blue eyes.

She's photogenic and undeniably beautiful, but that's not what made her famous. She's smart, and one of the most respected oceanographers in the world. Her drive and love of the ocean propelled her to create a multi-million-dollar oceanographic institute, and the annual documentaries she produced had made her a household name to anyone who cared for the planet and its oceans. She inspires many people, and although she never means to, she intimidates most people she encounters.

Except me. Because I've seen the tiny tattoo of a shark's fin on the instep of her left foot. She'd had the tattoo done the day I was born. She always said that was the day she truly fell in love for the first time. Even as an adult, I loved hearing the story.

I opened one eye. "Where am I?" My mother, three EMTs, and a handful of strangers stared at me.

Maddy took my hand before she responded. "Rum Point. We'll be taking you to Cayman Islands Hospital in a minute. I'm so glad you're awake. We were worried."

"What happened?"

"A joyrider on a stolen Jet Ski. He kept going. I guess he didn't even notice he hit you. Lucky for you, this young lady was on the beach and saw the whole thing. She swam out to get you and towed you to shore. But don't worry. We'll find the guy who did this."

While she spoke, Mom gestured toward a young woman standing near my feet. She wore a hot pink string bikini top and a pair of still wet cut off jean shorts. The polish on her fingers and toes matched the color of her bikini to perfection. Her huge brown eyes glowed with a fiery intensity, and her long dark hair was wet and shining in the sun.

"Thank you." I rasped out the words.

I tried to recall what I could about what had happened. "I don't think it was the Jet Ski guy's fault. I was outside the swim zone and wearing headphones, underwater without a dive flag, and I wasn't looking up when I ascended. I can't think of any other mistakes I could possibly have made. I broke every rule there is. I have to take responsibility for getting hit."

"You always take the blame whenever anything goes wrong, but this was not your fault," Maddy said. "And the person driving the Jet Ski broke the rules too, and then he just left you. You could have died."

"But I didn't. Everything turned out fine. The accident really was my fault."

"You were lucky. Again." Maddy sounded exasperated. Relying too much on luck was a frequent topic between us.

"We're both lucky. Lucky is good," I said.

Maddy laughed, and I laughed along with her. "Luck does make up for a lot of stupid. You and I have both proven that often enough."

She leaned down to whisper in my ear. "I agree you broke every rule, but that's no excuse for what he did. And what were you thinking? I know I trained you better than that."

I shrugged, wincing at the pain in my head. "Yes, you did. I was just snorkeling, and I wasn't deep enough to hurt my ears. Where are my clothes? And my camera?"

"I've got your camera, but right now, let's get you to the hospital. You need to be checked out and we'll want to have your face taken care of right away."

My face? I gulped and raised a hand to my head. "Mirror, please," I said.

Maddy pulled my hand away. "Leave your face alone. You'll be fine as soon as we get you to the plastic surgeon. Don't stress out in the meantime."

"I need a plastic surgeon? How bad am I hurt?" I tried to free my hand from her grip so I could touch my face.

"Hush, Fin. You'll be fine. You just need a couple of days of rest. I'm sure it's just a few cuts and some bruising." She moved aside when the EMTs wheeled up a portable gurney and loaded me aboard. "I'll get your things and then Ray and I will see you at the hospital." She brushed my long hair out of my face.

She turned to the young woman who had saved my life. "I can't thank you enough for rescuing her. If you ever need anything..."

The woman looked down at her feet. "It was nothing. I'm glad I got to her in time." She turned away and walked across the beach to the parking lot. The EMTs pushed my gurney through the deep sand.

Hours later, still at the hospital, I was more than ready to go home. I'd had X-rays, CT scans, eye exams, neurological tests, and stitches. The doctor came into my room where I was anxiously awaiting news.

"Hi, Fin. How do you feel?" he asked.

"Marvelous," I said. "Where are my clothes? I'm ready to leave."

His look was kind, but I could tell he was on to me. "Glad you're feeling feisty, but I'd like to give your body at least one night to recover, okay? And we'd like to do some additional tests. How's your vision?"

I told him the truth. "I was seeing double for a while, but I'm better now. I want to go home."

He scribbled some notes on his iPad. "I'll send a nurse in to make sure you're comfortable. We'll schedule the tests and maybe tomorrow or the next day we can let you go home." He stepped out of my room just as Ray came in, carrying my camera and laptop computer. He placed them on the table beside my bed.

Ray sat down and pressed my hand to his face. "Thank God you're awake. First Gus and now you. It's too much. I was afraid we'd lost you." His velvety brown eyes held tears. Ray and my mother married when I was two years old. I considered him my father in every way, just as I knew he thought of me as his daughter.

We sat together quietly until a nurse bustled in. "Visiting hours are long over," she said to Ray with disapproval.

He nodded. "I'll see you tomorrow." He kissed my cheek and he and the nurse left my room together.

I was bored and too restless to sleep so I booted up my computer and pulled the memory card from my camera. I slid the card into the computer to check for useable images or video.

The first files were all of Harry, the stingray I'd been watching before I was hit. This film was nothing special. I had hundreds of hours of footage just like it. The last few minutes were something else.

The camera had been trained on Harry, and his image grew smaller and more distant as I rose. I'd been intent on the stingray, and I hadn't noticed the dark shadow blocking out the sunlight filtering through the clear water. The shadow must have been the Jet Ski bearing down on me.

In the next images, the world spun and tumbled. Red streaks in the water floated across the frame. The camera had continued filming after my accident, making a record of its slow spiraling descent until the lens landed in the sand and everything went black.

The video was disturbing. The sight of my own blood in the water, the camera's crazy downward spiral, the world going dark. I couldn't watch it again. I pulled the memory card out of its slot in my computer and tossed it in the bag. I never again wanted to see the evidence of how close I'd come to losing my life.

The nurse returned with some pills and a glass of water. She removed most of my tubes and replaced the bandage on my face. Thanks to the pills, I was asleep before she left the room.

CHAPTER FOUR

I AWOKE to the silvery light that occurs just before dawn in the tropics. It was so early even the Cayman parrots were still asleep, although a solitary rooster was crowing in the distance. The hospital was as quiet as hospitals ever get. Clanging, banging, beeping.

I held up a hand to check my vision. Good. I wasn't seeing double. I slowly got out of bed. Aside from a slight headache and a little stiffness in my shoulders, I felt fine.

I'd been in a hospital three previous times in my life, and that was three times too many. Once was a childhood tonsillectomy. Next came a nasty burst appendix. The worst was the ciguatera poisoning I suffered after eating a grouper sandwich from a roadside stand when I'd been out with my ex-husband just before we divorced. Alec never even came to the hospital to see me.

Anyway, my experiences taught me that it was best to avoid hospitals, doctors, medicine, or surgery of any kind. Nothing good could come of more tests. It was time to make my escape.

I went in search of some clothes. In the closet, I found a

duffle bag of necessities Maddy must have brought while I slept. I rummaged around for a hairbrush, but when I looked in the mirror, I saw that half my shoulder-length brown hair had been shaved off. I'd been so fixated on my face I hadn't even noticed that happening.

Nothing I could do about my hair, so I pulled the bandage off to assess the wound on my face. A row of black stitches crossed the raised red line running from the crusty avulsion above my right ear, past the knot of scabbed flesh near my eye, across my cheek to the corner of my mouth. Yellowing bruises crowned my skull and scalp. I tried not to cry, but tears welled up anyway.

The early exposure in RIO's annual documentaries had cast an unexpected shadow over my adult career. Half the time people said I was riding on my famous mother's coattails; the rest of the time, recalling some of my wilder childhood escapades that'd been caught on camera, they said I was just another brainless girl with a pretty face. And Alec claiming my work as his own had started rumors of plagiarism, but the rumors had it backwards. He'd stolen my work, not the other way around.

Well, at least the accident would take care of one of these problems. After this, nobody would be able to say I was getting by on my looks. People might still think my mother was giving me a free ride, but my face wouldn't be pretty anymore. Meanwhile, I had to find a way to cope with my altered appearance.

I rummaged through the duffle until I found a bright silk scarf. I tied it pirate style around my head with the ends trailing over my shoulder along with what was left of my hair. I looked in the mirror and shrugged. Not bad. Pulled low on my forehead, the scarf emphasized the blue of my eyes and hid the worst of the fresh scabs on my head and face.

I slipped on a bra, some undies, a pair of shorts, and a RIO tee shirt from the duffle and stepped into a pair of flip-flops. I maneuvered my canvas cross-body purse over my shoulder with care, and then I crept out of my room.

Ray's car was parked at the curb when I snuck out the hospital's side door. He was leaning against the car's hood, arms folded, and face turned up to the sun. "Where to?" he asked with an impish grin when he saw me.

"How'd you know I'd be coming out now?"

"I know you," he replied, handing me a large Dunkin' coffee. "You're a rebel, and you hate hospitals. I figured you'd be trying to make a break for it, and I know you're an early riser. I went up to your room and peeked through the window earlier. I saw you fixing your hair so it was obvious you'd be out soon. And since you'd have to sneak by the security station if you went out the front door to make your escape, I knew this side exit was a better bet. Headed home?"

I nodded and we took off for my house on Rum Point. We were about half-way there when I saw Maddy's bright red Mini Cooper convertible headed to town. Ray tooted hello. She waved and kept going.

"She went over to stock your fridge this morning. Expect a lecture on proper nutrition next time you see your mother," he said.

We both laughed. My poor eating habits were legendary.

In another few minutes, we pulled into my driveway.

"Thanks for the ride, Ray. I owe you one."

"You can pay me back by coordinating the diving as well as managing the photography and marketing on the *Save Our Seas* documentary. Now that Gus won't be there to help, I don't think I can concentrate on my own dive and still do a good job coordinating all the other divers' logistics. I'm re-starting my training a week from Monday. Early. I want you there, but promise you'll take it easy in the meantime."

"Deal. I'll be there. Thanks for the ride." I kissed his cheek and slid out of the car.

"But wait, there's more..." he said in the dramatic voice of a TV announcer.

I gave a mock groan. "What?"

Ray stared at his lap, not meeting my eyes. "I want to bring on another photographer to help with the documentary filming. I'm thinking of Alec. It's a lot of work, and without Gus..."

I sucked in a breath as if I'd been punched in the gut. "But I'm the principal photographer at RIO." I'd never felt this betrayed, not even the day I learned what Alec had done.

"I'm sorry, but it's about funding our work," he said. "RIO needs money to keep operating, and a big-name photographer attached to the project can help us attract donors. It's not personal."

"It is personal. Bringing in another photographer will make it look like I can't handle it on my own. You know I'm struggling to make a name for myself. This will set me back. How can you ask me to work with another photographer, especially Alec?" I was upset and frustrated. Ray had been there for me through all my tears when Alec and I broke up, but this made me question Ray's faith in my abilities.

He looked away. "You'll still be in charge, and your name will come first in the credits. It's all about donations. Funding. The name of the game in non-profits. You know the way things work."

Trouble was, I knew, but I didn't have to like it. I got out and slammed his car door. "See you Monday," I shouted while I made my way down the walk, my thoughts reeling.

WHEN I FITTED my key in the lock of my front door, I breathed a sigh of relief. From the very first time I'd walked in, I knew I was home. I loved every detail of the house and its furnishings.

I hadn't seen Newton Fleming, my ultra-rich biological father, since I turned five, but a few years ago he had given me this fully furnished house as a twenty-first birthday gift. It was one in a long series of expensive birthday gifts, most of which were completely impersonal. I wondered why he didn't realize I'd have preferred a phone call or even a text to let me know he cared about me. I didn't want to be just some obligation penciled into his assistant's calendar. Anyway, the house was so perfect I suspected he had delegated the shopping for this gift to my mother rather than an assistant.

When I went inside, I headed straight to the kitchen where Maddy had filled my refrigerator with healthy foods. I grabbed a vanilla yoghurt and sat at the counter. Too restless to eat, I left the unopened carton behind and went outside.

In my backyard, I pulled a lounge chair under the shade of the pergola and tried to relax. I shut my eyes, hoping for a nap, but no luck. Within minutes, I was up, using the long-handled skimmer to sweep the surface of my already pristine pool. After a few passes, I tossed the skimmer aside and sat on the cool tiled edge with my feet in the water. That lasted no more than a couple of heartbeats before I was on my way back inside.

The sight of my face reflected in the glass door reminded me of my wound. This was a good time to assess the damages again, so I turned on all the lights in the bathroom and pulled the magnifying mirror close. The redness and swelling had gone down a little. I told myself the knot of flesh near my eye might just look like a bad case of crow's feet when I finished healing, and when my hair grew back, the scar on my head wouldn't show at all. I crossed my fingers, hoping I might be able to skip the dreaded trip to the plastic surgeon.

Meanwhile, I had to do something about my hair. One half was shaved to the scalp, the other was falling over my shoulder in long waves. I couldn't deal with lopsided hair in addition to everything else.

When I'm diving, I hate having my hair floating in front of my face or getting caught under my mask's skirt causing leaks. Getting back to diving was my highest priority. I'd once read a book where the female detective cut her own hair with manicure scissors. If it worked for her...

I grabbed my own manicure scissors, but they were so small it would have taken me forever to saw through my thick wavy tresses. Frustrated, I turned to my kitchen shears to lop off my remaining hair. As anyone but me would have expected, the choppy and uneven cut looked awful.

I like to accentuate the positives in any situation, so I chose to believe the haircut made me look fierce. Anyway, it would grow back someday. In the meantime, at least it wouldn't get in my eyes or under my mask. No long-term harm done.

CHAPTER FIVE

TWO DAYS LATER, I was back at work, heading down the hall to Ray's office when I saw my ex-husband Alec Stone knock on Ray's door and go inside. I lingered in the hallway just outside Ray's office, eavesdropping while pretending I was waiting for him to be free to review the copy for the invitations to the upcoming fundraiser.

"You wanted to see me?" Alec said to Ray.

"Thanks for coming. Have a seat."

When I heard Ray's footsteps approaching the door, I shrank back against the wall. The footsteps stopped and I heard his mini fridge thunk open. "Help yourself if you want something cold to drink."

"No thanks. But I'm a little curious why you asked for this meeting. As I recall, you were angry about what you believed I did to Fin. We didn't part on good terms. What gives?"

"Make no mistake. I'm still angry about what you did, but I've come up with a way for you to make it up to her and still save face in the industry. You're a good photographer, and we can use your skills, so I'm inviting you to join the film crew on our upcoming documentary." He paused a moment. "But before you accept, there are specific conditions attached to the offer."

Ray had made it sound like this was already a done deal, but it seemed he hadn't even asked Alec yet. It was all I could do not to storm into Ray's office in protest, but I bit my lip and continued listening. My whole body was shaking, but I tried to hold on to my faith that Ray would never hurt me.

Alec waited a moment before responding. "That's very flattering. Whatever the conditions are, I accept," he said at last.

"You'd better wait until you hear my conditions. You may not like them," Ray said. "And you have to know Fin's happiness and welfare are my primary motivations in this offer."

I swallowed the lump in my throat, but I was confused. Ray might believe he always had my best interests in mind, but how could he reconcile my welfare with forcing me to work with the man who had hurt me so badly?

"I'm listening. Fin's happiness is important to me too, you know."

I gagged. Alec sounded sincere, but I knew the only person he loved was himself. I could only hope Ray didn't swallow his lies. It was all I could do not to run into the office shouting for Alec to leave, but I swallowed hard and managed to stay quiet so I could hear more about Ray's plan.

"I still love her," Alec said. "You must realize that." His words seemed so heartfelt that if I hadn't known what a lying snake he was, I might have believed him.

"Sure you do." The disbelief in Ray's voice was clear. "Now cut the crap, Alec. We both know what you did, and why she kicked you out. Your behavior was despicable. The rages, the violence. That was bad enough. Stealing her work and publishing it as your own was the last straw for her. You need to undo the damage you did, and there's only one way you can."

"I don't see how I can fix it. Publishing her work was an honest mistake. I didn't know Fin's photos were in the same folder with my portfolio when I sent it to *Your World*. I swear that's the truth." *Your World* is a new high-end travel and photography magazine, like *National Geographic*. A spread in *Your World* could make a nature photographer's entire career.

Once again Alec sounded truthful, but I knew better. What he had done was no mistake. After our marriage, I had frequently caught him going through my computer, photoshopping some of my pictures, or commingling my work with his. I'd asked him not to touch my files, but it seemed like every time I left the house, he took the opportunity to rifle through my portfolio.

He'd been sweet, loving, and considerate while we were dating, but that changed as soon as we got married. I'd put up with his drinking, his bad temper, and his threats of violence. I didn't have to let him steal credit for my work too.

Ray paused a minute before responding to Alec's lie. "You can swear all you want, but I don't believe you didn't know what you were doing, and neither does Fin. And while what I believe doesn't matter, you still need to do the honorable thing. Step up and make things right for her. Tell Carl Duchette at *Your World* she took those photos, not you."

"I can't. If the industry found out, my career would be over. The spread in *Your World* was a terrific opportunity, and the photo montage opened doors for me. It was my big break. If Duchette knew I lied about who took those photos, I'd never work again, and you know I always wanted to be a famous underwater photographer."

"Fin always wanted to be a famous underwater photographer, too. Do you think it's right your lie cost her the opportunity to realize her own dream? Is that how you treat people you love?" Ray's voice shook with repressed rage, and I pictured him like a shark ready to ambush his prey.

"It's too late now. There's nothing I can do about it."

"Really? Or is the truth you're a selfish coward who's afraid to own up to what you did? I think we both know the answer to the question."

Ray's chair always squeaked when he leaned forward, and the familiar sound almost drowned out his next words. "So now, let me lay it all out for you. I think your ego is holding you back from doing the right thing because you know your confession will destroy your reputation. The reason I'm asking you to be on the documentary team isn't because I like you or even because you're a good photographer, because neither of those things is true. I'm throwing you a lifeline, hoping you'll do the right thing for Fin."

Alec's choked response was barely audibly. "What lifeline? Confessing is career suicide, and you know it. I can't..."

Ray spoke over Alec's whine. "Not necessarily. I know you'll never do the right thing unless there's something in it for you. If you act now, the documentary will come out about the same time the magazine prints their correction. The buzz about the documentary will help you weather the storm, and people will forget about the other thing."

Ray paused for a moment to snap open a soda can. "Look, Alec, I've given you a lot of time to come clean with *Your World*, but you haven't. Now with the documentary coming up, I can insist you do the right thing for Fin. And I expect you to do it, or when the news about you stealing her work breaks, I'll pile the stink on you along with everybody else."

Ray's solution was sheer genius, and I realized he must have spent a lot of time thinking of a way to get Alec to confess.

If I hadn't already known that Ray loved me, this act alone would have convinced me. I blinked back tears.

Ray opened his office door. "Call Duchette. Tell him you didn't take those pictures. Tell him it was a mistake and you never noticed, tell him you're a coward and I forced you to tell the truth, or don't give him any information at all about what happened if that's what you want. Just make sure he knows Fin took those photos. Ask him to compensate for the mistake by giving her a shot at a feature story of her own."

Alec's voice was a raspy near-whisper when he replied to Ray's ultimatum. "I can't. It would ruin me."

"Think about what I've said. I'm making it easy on you, Alec. I had to wait until we were ready to start filming to make this plan work, and it's your only chance. I'll give you two weeks to set this right. But know this. If you don't tell him the truth soon, I'll call Carl and tell him myself. Then you'll be on your own. No documentary. No lifeline."

"Please, Ray. Don't make me do this."

"The truth will come out. You might as well get in front of it. When you tell him what you did, I want you to ask Carl to print a retraction giving Fin credit for all the photos you stole. A big retraction, not a little paragraph in a tiny font hidden away on the back page. She deserves some glory for her hard work."

I sensed the moment when Ray grew tired of waiting for Alec to respond. "Do it, Alec. Don't put off telling Duchette, and don't think I'll forget about this. It's your one and only chance to keep your career from tanking. Two weeks. At most. You can go now."

The shrill sound of Alec's chair scraping across the tile floor startled me, and I dropped the papers I'd been holding. Alec stormed past me without a word, sweating, his face pale, and his lips tight. I bent over to gather the fallen pages, but my hands were shaking so hard I couldn't pick up the scattered sheets.

Ray stood in his office door watching Alec until he turned the corner toward the lobby. "Let me help you," Ray said, kneeling beside me. You know I'm always on your side."

The look in his soft brown eyes told me he meant it, and my heart swelled with love for my stepfather. He'd always been there for me, and after this, I knew he always would be.

I took a deep breath, struggling to control my voice. "Thanks. I heard what you said to Alec. I wish you'd told me your plan upfront. Then I wouldn't have been so upset. When you told me that you planned to ask him to join the documentary crew, I was floored. I couldn't understand why you would choose him, of all people, and then seeing him here surprised me. I'm sorry I doubted you." I shuffled the papers he handed me. "I'm here to go over the fundraiser invitations with you before I send them out. Do you have a minute?"

We went into Ray's office and I handed him a copy of the fundraiser invitation I'd been working on. It was full of cross outs and mark overs, but the mess didn't slow Ray down one bit.

"I'm not sure about putting Gus's name in the invitation. Will he be ready to go back to diving by then?" I asked.

He paused a moment. "I don't think so, but if he is, we can send out a press release. That'll bring us even more attention— and more donations."

He looked at the copy in his hand, crossed out a few words, scribbled a few digits, and handed it back to me.

"Thanks. I still have a lot to learn," I said.

"You're doing great." He smiled at me before going back to his spreadsheets.

CHAPTER SIX

I WAS HOME ALONE that evening, contemplating the vast empty space in my refrigerator. I was too tired to go out and too hungry to skip dinner. My doorbell rang, and I crossed my fingers hoping it was Maddy bearing food. I opened the door without looking to see who was there.

Big mistake. As soon as I saw who it was, I wished I'd ignored the bell. "What are you doing here?"

Alec pulled me into his arms. "I'm glad you're okay. I came as soon as I heard."

I broke away from his hug. "It's been several days, so I guess you didn't rush. And I'm fine. You can go."

Alec looked like a Viking god, but I'd learned to my detriment he acted more like a rabid weasel. Best to keep him at a distance.

"I needed to see you. I was worried." He tried to pull me into his arms again.

I stepped back before he could touch me. "As you can see, I'm okay. You can go now." I started to close the door, but he put out a hand to stop it.

Without touching me, one finger of his other hand traced the path of my wound. "Your beautiful face." His voice was low, as soft and warm as a whisper between lovers, but the way his finger traced my wound bore a taint like he was laying on a curse.

I shivered and moved further away. "I'm fine. My face is fine. In fact, the one thing in my life that isn't fine is you being here. Go away."

I tried shutting the door again, but he stepped inside.

"You shouldn't be alone after a serious accident. Let me take care of you, Fin."

"I'll be okay without any of your help. Thanks anyway."

He touched my lip with a gentle finger. I pushed his hand away, conscious I wasn't wearing anything except the old tee shirt I usually only wore to bed.

The soft cotton was so faded it was almost see-through, and although the shirt was long enough to cover the essentials, it wasn't by much. I might as well have been naked. I tugged at the shirt's hem. "I'm working. Go away."

"Have you eaten anything today?" he asked. "I bet you didn't even have lunch, so..." He grinned his devil's grin. "Cheeseburgers at Sunset House? I'll buy."

The cheeseburgers at Sunset House are thick and juicy, and the mudslides are to die for. My stomach gurgled at the very thought of a cheeseburger. My stomach and I held a quick debate, and my stomach won. I remembered Alec and I might be working together soon. Spending time with each other now would be a chance to see if that would even be possible. I gave in.

"Okay. Give me a minute to get dressed," I said. "You can wait in your car. I don't want you in my house."

I went to my room to throw on a pair of shorts and run a brush through what was left of my hair. While tying my pirate scarf to hide the scabs on my scalp, I debated putting on lipstick, but decided against it. I didn't want to give Alec the idea I cared or to let him pretend this was a date. I stepped into my flip flops, stuffed a credit card, a couple of twenties, and my Chapstick in the pocket of my shorts, and I was good to go.

We made the drive to Sunset House in Alec's red open-air SUV. As soon as we entered the bar, Theresa rushed over and gave me a hug. "I'm so happy to see you," she said. "I was worried sick when I didn't hear from you."

I grinned at her. "We're friends for life, Theresa. And it'll take more than a bump on the head to do me in. My skull is pretty thick."

"And don't I know it." She laughed. "Grab a table before the rush starts. I'll be right over."

"Sure. But not until you tell me how Gus is doing. I haven't seen either of you for a while."

"He's okay. Doc says it'll take some time, but we have our fingers crossed for a complete recovery." She spotted Alec standing behind me. "Girl, what are you thinking? Didn't you learn your lesson the first time?"

"Hungry," was the only response I could think of.

"I hope you know what you're doing." She glared over my shoulder at Alec. He stared right through her, a cold look in his blue eyes.

Before their interactions could get out of hand, I spotted an empty table in her section near the seawall. I hurried to claim the table and hooked one of the stools with my foot, spinning the seat around to face the ocean and what promised to be a stunning sunset.

Alec stopped at the bar to say hello to his friend Brian, whom he often proclaimed as the best bartender in the Caymans. It was possible he was right. When Alec joined me a few minutes later, he set bowls of pretzels and mixed nuts on the table between us before taking his own seat. "I put in our order with Brian."

I nodded and took a handful of nuts. We both turned our gazes out to sea to watch the sun set. We didn't speak, or even look at each other. We just stared at the water and the sky until Brian brought our drinks over. I cringed when his eyes lingered on the crusty scabs on my face, but at least he didn't recoil at the mere sight of me. "Hey, Fin. Glad to see you're all right. I heard things were touch and go there for a while."

"So I hear. But I'm okay now. Thanks for asking."

A few minutes later, Theresa arrived with our cheeseburgers. She placed mine carefully in front of me but slammed Alec's down hard enough that some of his fries popped out of the basket. "Oops. Sorry" She glared at him.

While we ate, Alec and I continued to stare at the horizon without speaking. When he swallowed his last fry, he turned to look at me. "Ray is resuming his training for the documentary. Are you still part of his team?" he said.

"I'm always part of his team. I'm lead photographer." I wanted to stick him with my plastic fork for even questioning that I'd be on the crew.

"He asked me to come on board, and I want to do it. We can work on the filming together. Switch off on alternate days or dives. Whatever works for you." His voice was soft, but he didn't quite meet my eyes as he spoke.

During our marriage, I'd learned that was a sure sign he was lying or trying to placate me to get his own way. No way was I letting that happen. I sipped my iced tea and took a deep breath for courage before I answered. "I said I'm the lead photographer, and I'll decide who does what. And I've decided I don't want to work with you ever again. Tell Ray you can't do it." I didn't want Alec to realize I knew Ray's offer was conditional.

"Look, I'm sorry for what I did. I can't change it now, but I want us to be close again." He touched my hand.

I pulled it away and stuffed it in my pocket. "After what you did, you're the last person I want to work with. I'm sure I'd see my work in your next exhibition or maybe under your byline in *Your World* magazine like last time." My stomach was roiling. No way could I finish my dinner. I pushed away the red plastic basket with the congealing remains of my burger and fries. "Tell Ray you changed your mind."

He reached for my other hand. "I won't quit. We used to be like two halves of a well-oiled machine. I'm sure we can be the same way again. The documentary can be our chance to try."

"No. That's final. Go home. I'll catch a ride with Theresa when her shift's over." I threw a couple of twenties down on the table to pay for my meal and walked away.

Alec rose to follow, but he stopped when Brian intercepted me.

"Hey, Fin. Someone here wants to meet you if you feel up to it." When I frowned, Brian continued. "I think you'll want to meet her." He waved his arm at a young woman sipping a mudslide at the far end of the bar.

I'd seen this woman before. She wore the same hot pink string bikini top, but this time with a coordinating printed sarong wrapped around her tiny waist. She had a stretchy bracelet of seashells on each wrist and big gold hoops adorning her ears. The mix of gold and silver chains around her neck sparkled in the light from the tiki torches. Each of her chains bore a different charm: a silver stingray, a gold shark's tooth, a painted silver sea turtle with green eyes, and a gold doubloon that looked exactly like the one Ray had given my mother when they got married. Her toenails and fingernails were polished a shiny hot pink. The overall effect of all the color and sparkle could have been garish, but she looked chic and stylish.

Brian said, "I can't stick around to talk, but I wanted to be sure you met. The rest is up to you. Fin, this is Lily. She's the one who rescued you when you had the accident." He made a flourish in the air and went back to his station behind the bar.

I held out my hand. "I remember you from the beach. I'm glad to have another chance to thank you. And I have a few questions about what happened if you have time to talk now."

She shook my hand but kept her gaze away from the wound on my face. "I've been worried. How are you?"

"Good. I owe you a big round of thanks for saving my life. If you hadn't come after me, I'd be dead now."

Lily made a 'no-big-deal' gesture. "I wanted to save you, and I wanted to see for myself that you're okay. I'm so happy we bumped into each other here tonight."

I laughed. "Sooner or later, everyone on Grand Cayman makes it to My Bar."

She smiled at me. "I was just leaving. I can give you a lift to wherever you're headed if you don't have a car. We can talk on the ride."

"Thanks, but I live all the way out on Rum Point. I'll grab an Uber. Or I can wait here for Theresa."

Theresa was wiping down a nearby table. "You might want to take her up on her offer, Girlfriend. With Gus racking up medical bills, I'm doing double shifts almost every day. I don't get off until the wee hours."

Lily smiled. "Then it's settled. It's no bother to take you home. I'm going that way. But would you mind...can we take a picture together first? I can't wait to show everyone back home I met Fin Fleming. I can get someone here to take the shot. Maybe you could..." She looked at Theresa.

I gestured toward my ex who was now at the bar chatting with Brian. "Let him. He's Alec Stone."

"Who?"

Her word made me laugh, and I laughed even harder when I saw the chagrin on Alec's face.. "He's a very famous photographer," I said, not even trying to hide the snark in my voice.

"Sure. I guess he'll do." She handed Alec her cell.

When he finished taking our picture, Lily thanked him and took back her phone. "C'mon. You must be tired. I'll get you home. And maybe on the way you can give me some advice on learning to dive..."

"My stepfather and I are teaching a class at RIO. Starts tomorrow morning at ten. I think there might still be a couple of spots open if you're interested."

"Are you kidding me? Count me in. Who wouldn't want to learn to dive from Ray Russo and Fin Fleming? You're two of the best divers in the world—living legends."

I laughed. "Living legends? Ray is legendary for sure. But not me. As soon as I get home, I'll log into our system and save you a spot in the class."

"Can you make it two? I'll be bringing a friend."

CHAPTER SEVEN

RAY and I leaned against the desk at the front of RIO's onsite classroom, waiting for the clock to strike the designated ten o'clock start time. The minute hand clicked, and Ray stood up. "Well, let's get this show on the road." He strode to the front of RIO's classroom, taking a last look at his notes for the first session of the Basic Open Water Scuba Diving class. Because Ray enjoys running the show, I was acting as his assistant even though I'm a certified dive instructor myself. I stood in the front of the room, but off to one side.

Strangers often stare at me. They think they know me because of my appearances in RIO's annual documentaries. Maybe that's all it was, but today, the students' stares made me self-conscious because of the wounds on my face. I tried not to fidget.

"Good morning, everyone." Before he could continue, the sound of running feet came from the hall outside the classroom. The door banged open.

Lily rushed in, with a young man close behind her. He was tall and rangy, with broad shoulders, long legs, and big hands

and feet. He wore a sleeveless tee shirt with a picture of the
shark from *Jaws* on it, and a plastic shark's tooth on a black cord
around his neck.

Lily and this man had the same dark, glossy hair, tan skin,
and shining brown eyes. They looked so much alike I knew
they must be siblings, maybe even twins. Lily smiled and
waved at me on their way to the back where they took two
empty seats in the last row.

Ray seemed startled by the entrance of the latecomers, but
like the pro he was, he recovered quickly. "Welcome. We're just
getting started." He introduced himself to the class and began
by asking everybody to tell us their first names and to explain
the reasons for their interest in diving. Most of the students
were vacationers from off island, hoping to attain their dive
certifications in the beautiful Caymanian waters. Having Ray
Russo, the world-famous diver, as the instructor was extra
buttercream icing on the cake.

When it was their turn, Lily and her brother Oliver
confirmed they were twins, here on an extended vacation with
their mother. After everyone finished introducing themselves,
Ray covered some of the basics of scuba diving, including the
most important rule: Always keep breathing; never hold your
breath.

Then he asked me if I would explain the diving reflex.

"Sure," I said. "It's sometimes called the mammalian diving
reflex because all mammals exhibit the same response. Whenever a mammal's face is submerged in water, this powerful
reflex kicks in and shunts blood to the central core of the body.
That prioritizes the heart and brain, conserving as much
oxygen as possible for the most vital processes. The rest of the
mammal's metabolism slows down, reducing the overall need
for oxygen. The diving reflex is the reason we're sometimes able
to revive people who have been underwater for far longer than

they could survive without air on land, and it's the reason why swimming doesn't raise your heart rate as much as the same level of effort on land does."

"Very good, Fin. Thanks," he said. "Class, you'll see the effects of the mammalian dive reflex as we progress in our training."

"And," I said, "if you're lucky, later this month you can see the mammalian diving reflex in action when we film Ray's free-dive to 330 feet for the annual RIO documentary. No scuba tanks full of air. No fins. Just a mask and a nose plug. One man against the sea. The event will be intense."

Ray grinned and wiggled his eyebrows at me. He gave them a few seconds to recover from their awe before continuing his lecture. After an hour of classroom work, Ray paused. "Any questions before we head to the pool?"

Lily raised her hand. "Will you tell us about the famous Russo treasure and why you never brought the legendary Queen's Tiara to the surface? I hear it's worth a fortune"

Ray laughed. "Nope. And believe me, you don't want to know the story. Once you hear it, it can't be unheard. And that's all in the past. Nowadays I'm just a humble dive instructor. This class is about teaching you to dive, not about perpetuating myths and fairy tales. Next?"

There were no further questions, so we went down to RIO's big pool for the water session.

Since he needed to be sure everyone in the class could swim well enough to dive safely, Ray asked the students to swim the length of the pool and back before we went any further. Lily and Oliver were slow but competent swimmers, and they were the last two to finish the laps. That meant they'd be my responsibility in the ocean. Although we'd all try to stick together, I'd have to keep a close eye on them to make sure they didn't get separated from the group.

To get started with the water sessions, I demonstrated how to set up the dive regulator—the parts that connect to the air tank and go in the diver's mouth—while Ray talked through the steps. He and I helped everyone to set up their own gear. When we'd checked out all the rigs to be sure they were right, Ray stood at the edge of the pool and reviewed three basic diving skills we were going to practice today: clearing your mask, clearing your ears, and how to breathe through a regulator. While he talked, I demonstrated the activities.

Oliver raised his hand. "I don't see any weight belts around. Don't we need weights while we dive?" He was smart and a good-looking kid, but he sounded cocky and over-confident—showing off for his classmates. I sensed he was used to being an alpha male in any pack he joined.

But I was used to answering this question. Students always loved the idea of weight belts. "Here at RIO, we use 'weight integrated' buoyancy control devices with special pockets for weights. They're safer and a lot more comfortable than traditional weight belts. Once you have your weights set up, you never have to worry you'll forget them on a dive because they're already in your BCD," I said. "And you don't have to worry they'll snag on anything or slip off at depth the way weight belts can."

He shrugged, looking disappointed. "Okay."

The class jumped into the shallow end of the pool to practice their skills while Ray and I offered help or advice to each student in turn. The novice divers shrieked and popped up when their masks filled with water, but one by one, we calmed them down and showed them how to adjust the mask for comfort and best performance.

Teaching beginning scuba students is stressful but fun, and the two hours flew by until Ray announced class was done for the day. "See you all tomorrow," he said. "Ten sharp." The twelve would-be divers straggled out while Ray and I gathered up the scattered equipment to take to the rinse vats.

While we were stacking the used scuba tanks on a cart for transport to the tank shack for refilling, I noticed two textbooks lying on the floor in a corner. "Uh-oh. Somebody isn't coming back," I said, pointing to the books.

"No, they'll be back. I'm sure of it." He grabbed two tanks by their valves and carried them to the cart.

I didn't know what made him so sure they'd be back tomorrow, but it sounded like he was. I decided if I could figure out who the books belonged to, I'd bring them to their hotel on my way home. That way the students could complete tonight's assignment and be ready for class tomorrow. I opened the books and saw the student registration cards they'd been supposed to hand in to Ray were still stuck inside the front covers.

One card said Lily Russo. The other said Oliver Russo. Both listed Ray Russo as the emergency contact person. I'd never heard Ray mention either name before, and he hadn't said anything about knowing them either before or during class.

"Ray, what's going on?" I held the cards up for him to see his own name and cellphone number written in the emergency contact space. "Are these kids your long-lost niece and nephew? Or is this a joke?"

"I'll take those and make sure they get them tonight." He took a deep breath. "Let's go to your mother's office. We need to talk." He turned to leave without meeting my eyes.

CHAPTER EIGHT

WE WALKED through RIO's halls to my mother's sunny corner office without speaking. I don't know what was going through Ray's mind, but mine was filled with dread. From his demeanor, whatever he had to say couldn't be good. When we got to Maddy's office, Ray stuck his head in her door. "Hey, Maddy. Got a few minutes? It's important."

Maddy looked up from her computer, and as always when she saw Ray, her eyes glowed. She closed the computer's lid and smiled at him. "Sure. What's up?"

Ray shut the door behind me, and we both took seats at the small round table in front of the window. Maddy left her desk and sat between us.

Ray's hands were shaking, and his face was pale. "You're not going to like what I'm going to say," he said, "but bear with me. I promise everything will be okay."

He paused and took a deep breath. "I don't quite know how to say this. I guess I'm just going to spit out the story." There was a long moment of silence while we waited for him to go on.

"I have two children."

My mother looked like she'd been punched in the gut. Her mouth dropped open, and she stared at Ray as though he'd spoken in Klingon. She stood up, turning her back to us. She picked up a picture from the credenza behind her desk.

I knew the photo well. In it, the three of us are standing on the bluff at Cayman Castle, gazing out to sea. Ray and Maddy are each holding one of my chubby two-year-old hands. The blue ribbons at the waist of my mother's simple long white dress dance in the playful breeze, and the famous gold doubloon necklace Ray had given her instead of a wedding ring shone on its delicate chain around her neck. She has flowers in her long, glossy hair and no shoes on her feet. Ray is movie-star handsome in his tuxedo, all dark eyes and shining smile. They look young, happy, and in love. The picture had been taken twenty-two years ago, on their wedding day.

Maddy looked down at the photo for a long time without speaking before she put it face down on the credenza. She kept her back to us. "Tell me about them." Her voice was so soft it was almost inaudible.

"Not much to tell. According to Cara, we had a drunken one-night stand years ago. I never heard from her again until she sent an email to tell me we had two children from our night together. To be honest, I don't remember the night, but she does have children, and she says they're mine. Twins, a girl and a boy. Lily and Oliver. I wish I had known them their whole lives, but she never said anything until a few days ago—just before Fin's accident. I meant to tell you about them then, but everything got so crazy..."

He looked at the ceiling and sighed. "I loved those kids from the moment I knew they existed. I saw them in person today for the first time. They look just like me."

Ray may have believed his explanation told the whole story,

but my mind was racing. I couldn't imagine what my mother was feeling.

Maddy turned to face Ray, leaning one hip against the credenza. Her face was as white as the papers on her desk. "Cara?" she said. "One-night stand? Was this before we met?"

"Mmhmm. Cara Flores. Like I said, I barely knew her. I remember being in a bar, drinking and kind of flirting. I'm sure I told her no, but the next thing I knew it was morning and I was in her hotel room. I don't even know how we got there or what happened, but I knew I'd made a terrible mistake. The one thing I'm sure about is you've always been the only one for me. You and Fin."

I noticed Ray's non-committal response to Maddy's question about when the tryst had taken place. But if my mother was prepared to accept it, so was I.

I could see her starting to relax. "You had no further contact with this Cara after that one night? And the twins? You never contacted them either?"

"I swear to God I never even knew about the kids. I wouldn't have just abandoned them. I love them now that I know about them. I'm angry at Cara for not telling me. Knowing about the twins wouldn't have made any difference in how I feel about you and Fin, but I still would have tried to be a good father to them."

"You were always wonderful with Fin," Maddy said. "But the twins must be almost her age by now. Too bad Cara didn't tell you sooner so you could have been a father to them too. How old did you say they are?"

"They're nineteen," Ray said, staring at the floor.

The tight lines of tension reappeared around Maddy's eyes and mouth. "So your one-night-stand actually happened after we were married. Not before we met or even while we were dating."

I was frantically doing the math in my head. Maddy was right. I'd seen their birthdates on the class registration forms. The twins were nineteen, and Maddy and Ray would have been married for more than two years before Ray slept with Cara. My heart broke.

Ray's face flushed. Maddy always was good at math. "It wasn't like that. The night together was just a one-time thing when I'd had way too much to drink. No big deal."

"You don't drink," I said to Ray.

"Nope. Not anymore." He looked at the ceiling. "I stopped after that night. I never want to be so out of it again."

Maddy didn't look at either of us, just stared out the window at the sea for a few minutes. "You said this night was no big deal, but we've been married twenty-two years."

His upper lip was sweating. "I told you I forgot all about being with her that night, and I honestly don't remember exactly what happened."

"I see. Perhaps you can find out for sure sometime." Maddy's voice was steady. Cold as an arctic wind, but without a tremor.

I was reeling from my own sense of betrayal. Ray had always been my rock. And now this. "I met them today," I said. "Lily and Oliver came to class. I didn't know who they were until just now..." My voice trailed off when I saw her flinch.

"Fin has already met them? Do I get to meet them too?" Her face hardened even more, and her eyes accused Ray. "I can't believe you brought your children to the institute I founded without telling me about them first. How could you embarrass me like this?"

"It's not like I put an announcement in the Cayman Compass. They just showed up. I didn't plan for you to find out this way." Ray's voice shook.

"Sounds like you didn't plan for me to find out at all," Maddy said.

"It's my fault they came here today, not Ray's," I said. "I met Lily the other night at Sunset House. She didn't tell me who she was, except to remind me she was the one who saved me after my accident." My mind reeled when I realized that Ray's daughter had saved my life. "She said she wanted to learn to dive, so I told her about the class. I didn't know she was Ray's...You'll like Lily, Maddy, she's..." My voice trailed off when I realized how unlikely it was my mother was going to like Lily. At least, not for a long time. Maybe never.

"I'm sure she's nice, Fin. And I'll always be grateful she saved your life, but could you excuse us, please? Ray and I have a lot to discuss right now." She opened her office door and waited for me to leave.

Out in the hall, I bit back sobs. I idolized my stepfather, but this cheater was not the Ray I loved.

As far as I knew, Ray and Maddy had always been happy together. They rarely argued. Although they both traveled a lot for their jobs, when they were in the same place, they spent most of their time together.

There was no doubt. I even counted on my fingers to make sure, but no matter how I did the math, I didn't like what the dates added up to. Lily and Oliver had been conceived after Ray and Maddy were married. I couldn't believe what he had done, and worse, that he hadn't told her.

CHAPTER NINE

OUR FORMERLY CLOSE family relationship changed after Maddy and I learned the truth about Oliver and Lily. I missed our family dinners, diving together, sharing our secrets and, most of all, the laughter and joy I felt when we were together. My happy family had been the bedrock of my life, and I felt like I'd been cast adrift without it.

Instead of the happy camaraderie the three of us used to enjoy, we now acted like strangers. We continued to do our jobs, but there was no laughter, no good-natured teasing, no sharing of thoughts and ideas. Ray and Maddy were polite, but cold and aloof to each other. I couldn't choose between the two people I loved most in the world. I didn't know how to ease my mother's obvious pain, and my anger at Ray's betrayal was a wall between us whenever I saw him. I was lost and alone. Utterly miserable. We all were.

After a few days, even RIO's employees could feel the strain. I don't think anyone outside of the three of us knew what caused the rift between my mother and stepfather, but the daily documentary production meetings were hour-long, ultra-polite ordeals instead of a creative, open sharing of ideas.

Chance meetings in RIO's halls were a brutal reminder of how things had changed, and I had taken to avoiding Maddy and Ray to escape the tension in the executive offices. So instead of working in my office, I was hanging out amid the noise and bustle of the public café at RIO, alone at a table in the corner while working on my film starring Harry the stingray.

I'd been so excited about this video. It was supposed to be my first big project in my new role at RIO, but now I was finding it hard to stay focused. I'd planned to use the piece as a teaser on one of the big screens in RIO's lobby to keep people entertained while they waited in line for tickets to the aquarium or events. Between Ray and Maddy acting like strangers and my dread of working with Alec, it was hard to care about a ten minute video that would play on an endless loop.

While debating the relative merits of two almost identical clips, I was sipping my lemonade and listening to music through my earphones. Ray and his friend Stewie Belcher entered the café. I turned my head to avoid catching Ray's eye while they stopped to pick up two iced coffees. Even so, they joined me at my table.

Since he'd told us about the twins, Ray and I had lost the ease in our relationship. I'd spent a lot of time exploring my feelings about his revelation and how it changed my image of him. To avoid confronting that feeling now, I tried to focus on Stewie, who leaned back in his chair, stretching the fabric of his bright Hawaiian shirt to its limits.

"Fin, I've decided I can't be Ray's safety diver when he freedives for the documentary. I'm nervous since Gus had his accident, and I don't want to do anything too dangerous. I'm not in great shape, and I'm getting older. You'll have to find someone else to dive with Ray."

I stared at the buttons of Stewie's shirt straining across his belly. He really wasn't in good shape. "I see. Ray, what do you have to say about this?"

Ray sipped his coffee. "I can't force the man to dive, Fin. His health and safety have to come first. As does his peace of mind." He didn't meet my eyes.

I nodded. "Agreed. Why tell me?"

"You're still the film's dive coordinator, aren't you?" Stewie took a sip from his coffee. "We all know your stepdad needs a designated safety diver for the documentary. I think you should do it."

I choked on my lemonade. "Why me? I don't freedive, Stewie. At least, not to any depth. It's strictly scuba for me. And I'm already the principal photographer and the dive coordinator this year. I think you both know I can't take on any more responsibility than I already have. What's really going on here?"

Stewie sipped his coffee. "Like I said, I think it's too dangerous for me."

Although freediving sounds like a crazy risk, with the proper training it's a safe sport. In fact, there have been fewer deaths or serious injuries during competitive events among professional freedivers than there have been in sports like tennis, football, or rugby. But I could understand his concern.

Despite the rarity of fatalities during competitive freediving events, Gus's recent accident had proven the sport still posed some risk, even for someone in great shape and with years of experience. But Stewie was not young or in great shape. Like Gus and Ray, he was now in his late fifties, and unlike them, he hadn't been a serious freediver even in his youth.

But Stewie's reluctance to dive didn't mean I had to take on the extra responsibilities myself. "Sorry, Guys. I can't add safety diver to my duties, at least, not this year. I've got enough on my plate already." I took a breath and wondered if my reluctance to take on the extra task was a side effect of the change in Ray's and my relationship or if I'd truly turned it down because of the added responsibility. "You must know someone else who can pitch in, Ray. You know everyone in diving."

Ray's face was stony and his voice was cold. "You have taken on a lot. But I didn't think I'd have to call in outside favors to get a dive buddy like I'm some unknown newbie. If you're sure you're not interested, I may have some other ideas. Give me a few days to flesh them out and then we'll talk again."

We all knew any serious professional diver would jump at the chance to dive with Ray during the prestigious annual RIO documentary. To me, Ray didn't sound as upset as his words implied. Maybe he was as uncomfortable working with me as I was with him right now.

"I'm sure as soon as you put the word out, you'd have qualified divers lining up for the opportunity. I mean, come on. You were a champion. Who wouldn't want to dive with you?"

"Well, you don't, for one." Ray said, swirling the melting ice in his cup. He sipped his coffee again. "I don't like the idea of asking outside people to dive with me. Makes me look desperate."

"Just call someone." I sighed with exasperation. This didn't have to be a problem. Ray's contact file was like a Who's Who of the dive world. Once divers heard he was looking, we all knew they'd be fighting for the chance to dive with him.

"You sure you don't want to dive with me?" he said. "You'll always be my first choice."

"Sorry. As gratifying as that is to hear, like I said, I've already got my hands full this time around." That was my story, and I was sticking to it, at least until I'd had a chance to sort out my feelings about Ray's shocking announcement.

"Okay. Thanks anyway. Let me work on a solution. I'll run any ideas I come up with by you and Maddy. See what you think." The men rose and headed back to their work. I returned to my video.

CHAPTER TEN

AS RAY HAD PREDICTED, Lily and Oliver had returned for the remainder of the basic scuba certification class. Ray was careful not to show any favoritism to the twins, treating them like any other student during class, although I'd noticed he joined them for coffee in the café after class each day. I tried not to be jealous of the attention he paid to them.

Initially, I'd felt awkward dealing with them in class, but after a while I began to think of them as I would any other students. Nothing special. The circumstances were not their fault. I had no reason to dislike them.

Today was the last day of their training. We were taking all the students out for the last of their required pre-certification open water dives. Ray and I met the class at RIO's dock where the *Maddy* waited, already loaded up with tanks and gear.

After Ray greeted everyone by name and gave a quick reminder about dive boat etiquette and safety, he invited the students to board. I checked each person off against the list on my clipboard as they stepped onto the *Maddy*'s deck.

Ray and I routinely verified our counts at the start of each trip and after every dive. Once we had completed this routine, Ray went to the *Maddy*'s flying bridge and started the engines. I pulled in the boat's fenders and untied the ropes, coiling them around the cleats on the dock.

Meanwhile, the divers set up their gear and turned on the air to check the tank pressure. If it will be a while before the dive, best practice is to turn the valve off after checking to eliminate the possibility of losing air. Divers then turn the air back on before making their entry.

We didn't have far to go to reach today's dive location. We reached Paradise Reef, an easy but much-loved site with about forty feet of depth dropping off to a vertical mini-wall that went to about fifty feet. The site had a wide variety of sea life, interesting corals, and little current. The combination made Paradise Reef an ideal place for the class to demonstrate their skills, and afterward, they could do a short wall dive for fun and experience.

I used a long gaff to snag the site's mooring line and tied the *Maddy* in place with ease. The twelve students were milling around the deck, reminiscing about what they'd seen on yesterday's dives and talking about what they hoped to see today.

Lily wanted to see sharks, but most shark species didn't often frequent this site. Maybe if we were lucky, we might spot a docile nurse shark hiding under the coral. A few divers were hoping to find a juvenile spotted drum with their long, elegant dorsal fins, and many of the divers wanted to see spotted eagle rays. Some of the other students were looking forward to a sea turtle sighting. We had a good shot at seeing turtles, common in the area because of the nearby Cayman Turtle Centre, although in the ocean, you could never predict what would cruise by.

Ray assigned the buddy teams. Lily and Oliver were buddied up, as they'd been throughout most of the classes. As I had predicted on the first day, Oliver and Lily would be diving with my sub-group. I shoved aside my feelings about the twins and resolved to make sure they had a positive dive experience. I might not be ready to welcome them to the family yet, but I was enough of a professional to make sure they had the necessary proficiency to dive safely.

Ray reviewed the dive plan and the emergency recall procedures before we helped each diver gear up. Ray went into the water first in case anyone had a problem, while I stayed on board until the last diver was in so I could do final gear checks.

The divers lined up at the *Maddy*'s rear platform, waiting their turn to enter the water. When they reached the head of the queue, I checked each one to make sure they'd remembered to turn on their air and had weights in their BCDs. One by one, they stepped into the water.

Oliver was the last in line. I checked to make sure that his tank valve was on, the same as I'd done for every diver before him. He'd made a serious error while setting up his gear—Oliver's tank valve was closed—so his scuba gear would not deliver air while he was under water. Because of residual air in the hoses from when he'd checked his tank pressure, it was possible he wouldn't have noticed the problem until he was at depth, and that could have caused a serious accident if he panicked under water. I stood behind him to turn on his air and reminded him his tank and regulator were life support equipment that deserved his full and careful attention.

Oliver had not responded well to any of my suggestions or corrections during the class pool sessions. He acted like I was singling him out for ridicule, although I'd gone overboard to be kind and to treat him with the same respect that I showed the other students.

As he usually did, Oliver bristled at my reminder. Nostrils

flared and lips tight, he said nothing—just nodded before stepping off the platform.

I did a giant stride entry off the boat and we began our
descents. At the bottom, Ray and I rounded up the student
divers near the mooring line and counted heads again to make
sure we had accounted for everyone. We hovered in a circle
along the top of the reef under the shadow of the boat. Ray
pointed to each of the students in turn and watched while the
novice divers performed the mandatory skills for diver certification. Ray wrote a few comments on his underwater slate to
share with the students later.

I was pleased that both twins performed all the skills flaw-
lessly since I'd been their primary trainer. I realized my feelings
went far beyond the satisfaction I usually felt whenever one of
my student's did well. Each time Ray gave Lily or Oliver the ok
sign when they'd finished their demonstrations, I could see his
eyes shining with pride behind his mask.

As we'd hoped, after everyone had successfully demonstrated the required skills, we still had time and air for some
diving fun. Ray, at the head of the group, checked the direction
of the current before starting to swim along the top of the reef.

I put my concerns about Ray, Lily and Oliver out of my
mind so I could focus on the task at hand. While in theory the
concept sounds simple, keeping a group of novice divers
together and safe is no easy task. The divers aren't comfortable
yet with their gear or how to navigate through the alien environment. They get distracted by the strange sights they
encounter. They wander away from the group. Most of all,
leading a class means being on the alert full time to resolve any
small problems before they escalate into bigger problems.

Most divers need some experience under their belts before
they realize how much longer their legs are with fins on than
they are without them, and the distortion of distance by the

water makes it hard to realize that objects may not be where
your brain thinks they are. Right away, Lily and Oliver ran into
that sort of problem. Oliver was swimming close behind Lily.
The tip of one of her fins touched Oliver's dive mask, knocking
it off his face. Since Lily didn't notice what she'd done, she kept
swimming with the group, leaving Oliver in distress behind her.
His mask slipped away and started to sink. He panicked,
flailing his arms and legs without purpose. I tapped his
shoulder and gave him the okay sign, signaled for him to wait
there for me while I chased after the sinking mask. When I
brought it back to him, I waited while he blew the water out so
he could see again.

As soon as he cleared the mask, he swam after Lily and
grabbed her arm from behind, startling her. Her regulator fell
out of her mouth, and she began to choke. Oliver shook her and
made angry gestures, letting her know how upset he was. Lily
shoved Oliver away, nearly driving him into a magnificent but
fragile elkhorn coral jutting from the nearby reef wall.

I swam between them, breaking up what might have esca-
lated into a nasty underwater fight. I put Lily's regulator back
in her mouth and pressed the purge valve to clear any water
inside to make sure she wouldn't choke again. Oliver reined in
his temper, and they both gave me the okay sign. The crisis had
been averted, but I was annoyed at their childish behavior.

Now that they'd calmed down, I hurried the twins along to
rejoin the rest of the group. The whole class swam along the
reef wall, following Ray's lead. In a few minutes, he found a
juvenile spotted drum in a tiny, almost-hidden grotto in the
coral. Each diver took a turn peering into the grotto to admire
the swirling black and white dorsal fins that looked like graceful
ribbons dancing in the current.

Next, he showed them a fish cleaning station, one of the
most amazing things in the underwater realm. A group of

cleaner shrimps made their home in an indentation in the reef. All manner of fish, including predators, would swim up to their location, and the shrimp would swarm the fish. They scurried about, removing—and eating—dead skin, parasites and whatever else they could find. The fish hovered passively while the shrimps did their work, then they would swim serenely away without bothering the shrimp. Today, the shrimp's "customer" was a six-foot moray eel. He bared his fearsome fangs without menace, while the shrimp gave him a thorough dental cleaning.

As we turned away, two turtles swam by out in the blue, and the class watched them with eyes full of wonder. By then it was time for me to lead divers who were running low on air back to the boat.

Because it was my job to help the divers get on board when they came up, I climbed the ladder first. Ray stayed below to manage any underwater problems and make sure no one went missing while completing the safety stop or awaiting a turn on the ladder. I checked everyone off on the class roster when they came off the ladder.

Lily and Oliver seemed subdued when they came aboard. They weren't talking to each other or interacting with the other divers, and they didn't meet my eyes. They clearly expected me to reprimand them for their bad behavior, but I didn't want to get into it publicly. If something similar happened on the second dive, I'd address it then.

When Ray reached the deck behind the last student, we did a roll call to double check we hadn't lost anyone during the dive. The worst thing that could happen would be to leave someone behind, so Ray and I were meticulous in doing roll calls.

When we finished the check-in, we passed around fresh fruit and ice water while we waited out the required surface interval—the time scuba divers need to off-gas excess nitrogen absorbed while under water so they can dive again without risking the bends. On training days, our usual practice was to wait about an hour between dives, but the surface interval could vary by the dive's profile. About ten minutes before we were ready to start the next dive, Ray went over the dive plan while I switched over everyone's used tanks to full ones, making sure the new tanks were snug in the Velcro straps that kept them in place. The second dives went off without any problems. It seemed Lily and Oliver had learned their lesson and made peace with each other. We headed home to celebrate our newly certified divers.

Whenever we completed a class, we always threw a small party with soft drinks and snacks. If RIO's research vessel, the *Omega*, wasn't out at sea, my mother tried to come by to congratulate everyone in person. Visitors were always eager to meet my mother, a celebrity diver and the founder of RIO.

The room was packed and the party was in full swing. Everyone was talking and laughing while chowing down on the refreshments. The new divers mingled with the staff, talking about the sights they'd seen and asking about taking more advanced diving classes. The staff told tales of their own diving adventures and sea life encounters. The new divers' eyes grew round with awe as they listened.

I noticed Gus sitting at a corner table. He looked fragile— tired and wan. Even from across the room I could see his hands shaking. But he was surrounded by novice divers, hanging on his every word. Before I could go over to say hello, Theresa swooped in. They walked out together, with Gus leaning heavily on his wife's shoulder.

Everyone still at the party looked happy and excited, bobbing their heads along with the throbbing beat of the Calypso music blasting from the wall-mounted speakers. Lily looked like she was enjoying herself, dancing with two men from class. Many of the people in the room had formed a circle around them, and they were clapping and cheering her on. Everyone seemed to be having a fabulous time.

Except Oliver. He was standing alone in a distant corner of the room, watching the party but not joining in the festivities. He looked bored, and the angry scowl on his face said, "Stay away from me."

I was still ambivalent about the twins. I wanted to like them for Ray's sake, but I resented their negative impact on my family. And I was jealous that they were Ray's biological children. He clearly adored them, and my own biological father hadn't been to see me in years.

But my responsibilities at RIO meant I couldn't just leave Oliver to his own devices, so I strolled across the room to chat with him. I knew my presence would attract some of the other new divers and he wouldn't be alone for long. "Hi, Oliver. Having fun?" I asked.

"No, I'm not," he said. "I was under the impression your mother would be here. I've been looking forward to meeting the woman who kept my father away all those years."

"That's not the way it was. Even Ray only learned about you a few days before class started. If we'd known about you, we'd all have welcomed you to the family." I crossed my fingers behind my back, because although I knew Ray would have embraced the twins with open arms, I still wasn't sure about my feelings for these new siblings. Or my mother's.

Oliver must have read my mind. "That's a lie. Your mother would never have accepted us. She kept Ray away from us our whole lives. And she's the founder of this place, but she can't even be bothered to come to her own party. Either she doesn't want to face us or she thinks she's some big-deal celebrity." There was no mistaking the anger and hurt on his face.

"Oliver, she's looking forward to meeting you. She'd be here if she could, but she's a busy person. She hands-on runs this place every day. She's in the middle of planning a major fundraiser and a complicated documentary.

"Yeah, right. She's much too busy to say hello to her husband's children. Before I knew he was my father, I used to look up to you all. I had posters of Ray on my walls, but I tore them all down and burned them when my mother told me he was my dad. I needed a father, but he couldn't be bothered with us because he already had you. I was just a kid. How could he do that? I never want to see his smug face again."

I knew Oliver was just striking out at me and Ray because he was hurt. I could understand how he felt. It's exactly how I would feel if my father suddenly appeared after all these years. I tried again to explain that Ray hadn't known about him. "Oliver, if that's true, then why did you come here to take diving lessons from Ray? It wasn't the way you think. Until a few days ago, none of us knew..."

"Yes, you did. Lily and I are the ones who just found out. You had to know. But all Ray and your mother cared about was their darling little Fin. I used to watch those stupid documentaries over and over again. Truth is, I was jealous of the way they doted on you. You aren't even his real kid—not like Lily and me are—but he loved you more than us."

"Oliver, calm down. Let's talk about this when the party's over."

"I bet you'd like me to agree to put it off, wouldn't you? That would give you a chance to forget all about your promise, just like Ray forgot we were his kids."

"I won't forget. I want to get to know you."

"Why, so you can show everyone how stupid we are?"

"I don't think you're stupid. What gave you that idea?"

"The way you acted in class. Treating us like we're idiots. 'Watch me demonstrate how to do a giant stride entry.' Like stepping into the water is so hard. 'This is how to clear a mask.' Like we don't know how to exhale through our noses. And your smirk when I forgot to turn on my air before the dive today. Big deal. You made me do it underwater in the pool so many times I could do it in my sleep. You had to show off and make a big deal out of a simple mistake."

"I'm sorry I made you feel that way. I never meant to embarrass you or hurt your feelings." I was horrified Oliver assumed I'd been trying to humiliate him. I hoped I hadn't ever come off like that to other students.

Oliver scowled. "I loved the RIO specials on TV. Learning about the ocean, seeing all the freaky fish, and watching the divers with their gear like something out of a sci-fi movie. I learned some incredible stuff from those documentaries. I used to have a crush on you. I watched those stupid shows over and over, hoping to catch a glimpse of you. You went everywhere, did everything. In every scene, you could see on their faces how much Ray and Maddy loved you. I admit I was jealous. So imagine how it felt to find out you were living the life that should have been mine. Taking all my father's attention and love.'

"Oliver, I swear we didn't know. None of us knew. Not even Ray. We just found out. But now that we know, we'll do our best to make it up to you. I promise. As soon as the crowd thins out, I'll come find you. We'll talk this through. I'll even take you to meet my mother. You'll see how nice she is.

Oliver started to walk away. "I'll be waiting," he said, turning back to look at me over his shoulder.

CHAPTER ELEVEN

THE CROWD STARTED TO LEAVE, departing in ones and twos. but Oliver must have slipped out earlier because he was nowhere in sight. I shrugged my shoulders and started helping Ray and the rest of the staff clean up the party debris. When we finished, Ray slung an arm over my shoulder. "Let's go talk to Maddy," he said. "We have a problem, and I have an idea I want to run by her."

On a list of things I didn't want to do, sitting in the same room while Ray and my mother talked about their problems would top the list. "Whatever you have to say, you don't need me as a witness," I said, trying to escape, but Ray wouldn't take no for an answer.

"I need you to weigh in on this, Fin" he said before opening Maddy's office door. "And I'd appreciate your support for my idea. It's a good one. If you'll both keep an open mind, I think you'll agree."

Maddy looked up when we entered her office. The sun was streaming in from the window behind her desk, making her blonde hair glow like a halo and casting her face in deep shadows that weren't quite thick enough to hide her scowl at the sight of us. "What?" she said. "I'm busy." I'd never known her to be short with Ray. Her pain was obvious.

Ray ignored her tone and sat at the small round conference table just as he'd done the other day. I shuddered at the memory of Ray dropping his bombshell about the twins. I never in a million years would have suspected he would cheat on my mother. They'd always seemed to be in love. I'd believed Ray was a standup kind of guy, not a cheat.

Ray and I were at the table, but Maddy stayed at her desk, staring at her computer screen, biting her lip. The silence continued while the air in the room grew oppressive, thick, and as heavy as the water down deep in the ocean. It was hard to breathe, and we all stared out the window instead of looking at each other. I started to fidget.

When the silence grew as brittle as the salty crust on an unwashed scuba tank, Ray took a deep breath. "Stewie refuses to freedive for the documentary, and I want Lily and Oliver to be my safety divers in his place."

I'd imagined more unknown of his kids coming out of nowhere, or hearing Ray wanted to leave us to be with Cara. Compared to those scenarios, this was benign. Still, it made me so angry I couldn't speak. I was sure Ray had been toying with this idea even before the day he talked to me in the café.

"Do they freedive?" Maddy asked, incredulous. "Didn't they just get their basic scuba certifications today?"

"It doesn't matter if they don't freedive, because you're right. They were both scuba certified today. We can have them do the job on scuba. It's not a competition, so we don't have to follow competition rules. It'll be a good experience for them."

I let out an exasperated sigh, but Maddy didn't look at either of us, just slid the gold coin of her necklace back and forth on its chain while mentally going over the pros and cons of his idea. I admired my mother's ability to compartmentalize business and personal concerns even while I was mentally berating myself for letting my personal and professional feelings mix.

She spoke at last, ticking off the points against using the twins. "Certified today, so not much experience. No deep diving certification or experience at all, so they can't go below sixty feet. No rescue training. What if something goes wrong? They wouldn't be much help."

"C'mon, Maddy. You know we just need the safety divers for insurance purposes. I'm an old pro at freediving. A champion, remember? Nothing will go wrong, but if something does, Fin and Alec will both be down there with me to help. The twins' presence will be just to introduce them to our audience and for them to gain some experience."

"Yes, I understand the gaining experience part of it, but until they've done more dives and obtained an advanced certification, they can't go below sixty feet. Fin will be filming near the surface, and Alec will be waiting at the bottom. Neither of them will be able to see you during the middle of the dive. You'll be on your own most of the time."

"I'll be fine." I could hear the determination in his voice.

"You okay with this, Fin?" Maddy asked. "You're the dive coordinator."

"I'm not making this decision," I said, standing up. "I've seen those kids dive, and this is not a good idea. But I don't believe this conversation is about their qualifications as safety divers anyway, and I don't need to be in the middle of your argument. I'll work with anyone you two decide to use." I left the office, not quite slamming the door behind me.

CHAPTER TWELVE

ON MY WAY HOME, I picked up some takeout at the chicken place on West Bay Road. It was a tourist trap, but I loved the food anyway. I'd just transferred the hot spicy meat to a plate—I do have standards—when I heard my mother calling my name outside my front door. I put down the plate to let her in. "What's up?" I asked. "Want some chicken?"

"No thanks. I just need to talk with you." She sat at the granite counter toying with her car keys.

With a sigh, I put my dinner in the fridge and poured us each a glass of iced tea.

"Honey, I know you don't want to be in the middle of what's going on between Ray and me, and I understand and respect your feelings. But God help me, I don't want anything to happen to him. Those kids just aren't competent to be his safety divers. They don't have the training or the experience. Maybe someday they'll be ready, but they aren't now, and we haven't even come to grips with the twin's existence yet. I don't want to make things worse between Ray and me by putting my foot down on something he feels so adamant about. But I also don't want to take the chance of anything happening to him. You're the dive coordinator. Can't you convince him to ask someone else to dive with him?"

"I don't see how I can if this is what he wants. There's no one here at RIO, and he wouldn't hear of bringing in an outsider. I already tried everything I could think of to get him to add a more experienced safety diver. He wouldn't listen. He's trying to make up for lost time with the twins. He's putting them ahead of everything—you, me, even his own safety. They're his biological children, and although I think of him as my father, I'm not his biological child. He wants them. They're certified divers. It scares me to rely on them. I'm angry he's putting this pressure on us, but it would feel petty for me to say no."

"How about this? What if you be the safety diver and let them do the photography?"

She had to know her plan wouldn't work. The cameras, lights, and other equipment are heavy and complicated. Nobody could just pick up a camera and be an underwater photography pro. It would be impossible if the person with the camera wasn't already comfortable diving. I'd been studying underwater photography for years, yet even I was still learning.

"No, we can't do that either. We wouldn't get the quality footage we need for TV, and you know it. But as the coordinator, I promise to make every detail of the dive as foolproof as possible. I'll watch Ray as closely as I can while he's in my sight. I'll ask Alec to do the same at the other end of the rope. I'll even ask Ray to wear a counterweighted lanyard like they do in competition now. That way, we can pull him back up if we need to. Will using a lanyard work for you?"

"He won't go for the lanyard plan. He'll think using such an obvious safety device will make him look scared. Or incompetent. It won't work."

I shook my head. "Then I don't think I can help you with this, Maddy. I'm sorry. But you're RIO's executive director and the film's producer. If you don't want the twins to be the safety divers, you have every right to say no. You'll have to work it out with him on your own."

She bit her lip in frustration. "Ray won't want more divers down there with him, and I can't say no to using Lily and Oliver. I don't want him to feel like I'm not welcoming his kids to the family and to RIO."

She paused a moment, making circles in the condensation on her glass. "Maybe that's all this is. Me resenting his kids because Ray sees this dive as a start to making up for neglecting his children while they were growing up."

Her words stabbed my soul. I couldn't remember a single day when Ray hadn't been there for me. I don't remember much about Newton Fleming, my own biological father. He dropped out of my life when I was about five. It still hurt.

I knew how lonely missing a father's love could make a child feel, so I could sympathize with Lily and Oliver's pain. But that didn't mean I wanted to share the man I considered my father with these two petty, immature strangers. On the other hand, I couldn't let anything happen to Ray, no matter what. "Don't worry. I'll find a way."

CHAPTER THIRTEEN

I TOSSED and turned most of the night before realizing the only real solution was to ask Stewie to reconsider his decision. We couldn't risk anything happening to Ray, even if he wouldn't like the safety measures we put in place. Around three A.M., I thought of a way to convince Stewie to dive with Ray, and I knew Maddy would agree to it. Now I could finally get some sleep.

Despite my late night, the sun had barely risen the next morning when I walked up the crushed shell path to Stewie's home. I knew he'd be up. Most serious divers are up early because it's best to dive before the wind and currents pick up.

Who am I kidding? The real reason we're up early is to beat everyone else to the best dive sites. Being first means a better chance of seeing something interesting or unusual cruising the reef.

Today's weather was typical for the Cayman Islands, warm but not too hot. The sun was shining and there was a slight ocean breeze. It was so beautiful I'd rather have been diving, or even working in the office instead of visiting Stewie at home. But I was on a mission.

Stewie's cottage was in a cute neighborhood, situated at the top of a rise in a nice middle-class neighborhood. I knew from prior visits the sea was visible from his front steps, although you had to look over a few rows of houses on the hill below the cottage to see it.

The nearby houses were well kept, all painted within the last few years. The yards had been xeriscaped with plants chosen to survive without much rainfall, yet hardy enough to make it through the occasional hurricane. Lush tropical flowers filled the yards, and neatly raked walks of crushed white shells gleamed in the sun. Most of the houses had brightly colored outdoor furniture gracing front porches and side patios. Some yards had swing sets in back or basketball hoops in the driveways.

In the entire neighborhood, only Stewie's house showed signs of neglect. No colorful flowers or shrubs grew in Stewie's yard. The landscaping was nothing but a few unidentifiable brown clumps that looked like they'd given up trying to make it against insurmountable odds. The one spot of color in the terrain was a dusty red and yellow pinwheel near the door, its ragged triangles spinning slowly in the gentle wind. His walk had dirty-looking bare spots where the seashells were worn down or scattered outside the poorly defined path. Lazy bees buzzed around a massive pile of empty beer bottles leaning against the side of the house.

The palm tree on the other side of his yard had been partially uprooted in last fall's hurricane. It tilted precariously over the neighbor's fence with most of its roots showing. Several garments flapped from a makeshift clothesline strung between the cottage's eaves and the tree.

Stewie's laundry consisted of two Hawaiian shirts in bright

prints, one pair of tan cargo shorts, one pair of red board shorts, a red Speedo bathing suit, three pairs of tighty-whiteys tinged with pink, and a faded and well-worn black diveskin that had split open at the seams after losing the fight to contain its wearer's girth. The ankles of the diveskin were brushing back and forth across the dry dirt as the clothesline swayed in the breeze.

I rapped on the door. "Stewie. It's Fin. Can we talk?"

Stewie opened the door wearing a dingy tank-style tee-shirt, stained cargo shorts resting below his belly, and a pair of low-cut dive booties instead of shoes. He tossed a cigarette butt out onto the dirt where his lawn should have been. "What's up?" he asked. He plunked down on his front step and took a swig from an open bottle of Stingray beer. "Hey, your face is looking better. The scar kinda makes you look like a badass." He patted the dusty step beside him. "Take a load off."

Mindful of the white shorts I was wearing, I asked "Can we talk inside?"

"Uhhhh, let's not go inside. The place isn't ready for company just now. Besides, it's a beautiful day." He brushed again at the top step with his bare hand, raising a cloud of dust but not making the step any cleaner.

I could see into the house through the open door. Empty takeout containers, newspapers, and dirty laundry covered every surface. The whole place screamed "I've given up." I sat beside him on the step. It was better than staring through the screen at the mess inside his house. "Is everything okay? Can I do anything to help you out?"

He took another long pull of his Stingray and tossed the bottle onto the pile beside the fence. "Nope. I'm fine Just I've been thinking about getting a real job."

"Diving is a real job," I said, "especially when you work at RIO. It's a scientific institute, for heaven's sake. We get thousands of job applicants every year. The job requires a lot more than carrying tanks for people on vacation. It's processing certification paperwork, collecting specimens, analyzing data..." My words trailed off when I realized Stewie didn't do any of these activities. A couple of times a week he and Ray went diving together. Stewie acted as divemaster for some of the advanced scuba classes, but that was about it. Pretty much all he did for work was hang around at RIO drinking coffee. He drank gallons of coffee.

And beer at home. The mountain of empties beside his house was the proof. It was still early in the morning, and he was already drinking. I was here to plead with him to be Ray's safety diver for the documentary, but now I wondered if I should even ask him. If he drank on the day of Ray's dive, he wouldn't be any more help than the twins if something went wrong. It could turn out to be a disaster.

Having with us could also mean the difference between life and death for Ray, so I asked him anyway. "Stewie, will you reconsider being a safety diver for Ray while we're filming? I'm sure it would mean a lot to him. It would mean even more to my mother and me."

"Sorry, Fin. No can do. Ray asked me to bow out. He wants those twins of his to have the chance to show their stuff. He thinks they have potential to be stars. Between his new obsession with those kids and me getting older, I think it's time to hang up my dive mask anyway."

I felt a pang of resentment that Ray's obsession was apparent to everyone around him. But Stewie's comment gave me an idea I was sure would make Ray agree to my plan.

Even though I was starting to feel as unwanted and unneeded as yesterday's newspaper, I put my jealousy aside to focus on the other part of what Stewie had said. "Ray asked you to step down?" It hadn't sounded that way in the coffee shop when Stewie resigned from the documentary crew.

"Jeez, I wasn't supposed to tell you or Maddy. Don't let Ray know I slipped up, okay? He'll kill me."

"I won't tell. Look, I understand if you don't want to dive because of what happened to Gus, but Ray needs a safety diver and that's not up for debate. To make it more palatable for you, we'll pay you a five-figure bonus to make the dive. Please say you'll do it, Stewie."

"Lemme think on it a minute." He got up and went inside. "Want a beer?" he said, over his shoulder.

"No thanks. I'm good," I said again.

He came back outside and sat beside me. He drained half the beer from the new bottle and gave a deep sigh. "Pay the bonus in advance, and I'm in." Stewie rose with a wobble, steadied himself and opened the screen door.

"Thanks, Stewie. I'll get the bonus paperwork rolling as soon as I get to the office."

CHAPTER FOURTEEN

WHEN I GOT TO WORK, I stopped by Maddy's office and stood in her doorway. "Problem solved. Stewie agreed to do the dive," I said. "For a five-figure bonus."

Maddy sighed in relief. "Thank you. I knew if anyone could bring him around it would be you. I'll cut him a check right now. Do you think twenty-five will be enough or should I go higher?" She opened her desk drawer for her checkbook.

"More than enough," I said, knowing Stewie would have done it for less but also knowing Maddy could afford to be generous. "I'll let Ray know."

Ray was sitting at his desk, but his back was to the door. He was staring out his window at the ocean beyond.

"Got a minute?" I asked. "I have an idea and some good news."

He swiveled his chair to face me. "Good news is always welcome."

"I convinced Stewie to be a safety diver during the documentary filming. Alec will be on the deep end. Stewie can cover the middle depths. The twins and I can handle the shallows."

He frowned. "I told you I didn't want another diver down there with me."

"I know. But we were worried about you, and Stewie diving with you is the best solution for everyone. But here's the best part of my idea. You'll like it."

"Really?" He sounded skeptical.

"Yes. I can rearrange the dive schedule so I go in before the Lily and Oliver. I can film their entry, and even film them while you're out of sight, since Stewie will be there to watch out for you. It's a good way to introduce the twins to our audience, and it'll give them plenty of screen time. I think they'll be excited about it." This was the idea I'd come up with last night.

"Hmmm. That is a good idea. The twins will be thrilled, but next time, run your idea past me before you make any commitments. I'm the one who needs to be comfortable during the dive. I told you I didn't want more people in the water. We don't need Stewie."

I took a deep breath. "Sorry, but you made me the dive coordinator, so it's my call, not yours. I hope you're okay with it, but either way, this is the plan. It only works if Stewie dives with you. Otherwise, I'd have to be hyper-focused on you and your dive time, so I wouldn't be able to spare any attention for filming the twins. You can't have both."

He was silent for a moment before he nodded. "I get it. Okay, so this'll be the new plan. Good work, Fin."

CHAPTER FIFTEEN

LATER IN THE MORNING, I was in my office, my head in the zone, working on a slide presentation that would run during the land portion of the fundraising event before Ray's dive. My brain was racing with the images I wanted to include to convey the message I wanted to send to the audience. This piece had to be enticing enough to convince them to make hefty donations to help keep us operational.

Between payments from the networks that aired them and promotional fees from equipment sponsors, that's where the annual documentaries really paid off. But running an institute like RIO is expensive. We had to pay for our research, including hefty salaries to the oceanographers and staff. We had to have the latest dive gear and equipment for rentals and staff, and we had the expense of keeping the *Omega* and RIO's other boats running. We brought in some money from the onsite aquarium and the dive and gift shops, but it was a pittance compared to our expenses. Even though I knew Maddy put in a lot of her own money, which she'd inherited from her parents, as a non-profit, we depended on donations and endorsements to cover most of our expenses.

To date, finding ways of attracting people who wanted to join us on the *Omega* to watch the dive had been easy. It was the donation part of the pitch I still needed to work on. My cell phone rang, causing the idea I'd been considering to evaporate. Between the visit to Stewie and the ringing phone, it was another morning wasted. I sighed before I hit the button to answer the call.

"This is Lily," the caller said. "Lily Russo. Remember me? Anyway, I hope I'm not disturbing your work, but I was hoping we could go diving together. Now that I'm certified and all. We are practically family."

"Uh, sorry Lily. I'm working now." I had mixed emotions about getting to know Lily. On the one hand, it wasn't her fault her father hadn't been able to be with her while growing up, any more than it was my fault my father hadn't taken the time to be a dad to me. On the other hand, her father was married to my mother. Lily's mere existence threatened to upset the very foundations of my life. And if I'd had a third hand, I would have to admit I didn't like either of the twins very much. Lily seemed to have nothing on her mind but a good time, while Oliver had shown he had a ruthless, angry side.

"Okay," she said. "But I didn't mean right now. When would be good for you?"

I wanted to be friendly for Ray's sake. He'd been nothing but kind and loving to me my whole life. I owed him at least this much. And then I remembered Lily had saved my life. I owed her for that too, even though her mere existence caused pain for my mother. And for me, if I were being honest.

I looked at my calendar. "I guess I could fit in a couple of dives tomorrow around noon. Does the time work for you?" I crossed my fingers, hoping she couldn't make it, but knowing if she agreed to my suggestion, a couple of afternoon dives would be a nice break in my day despite the company.

"Perfect," she said. "I'll meet you at the dock at noon. You can get tanks, right? Bye." She hung up without waiting for a response.

Yikes. Now I was stuck. But it was too late to back out. With a sigh, I went down to the dive operations office to reserve a boat and four tanks for tomorrow's dives. I signed the requisition at the tank shack. I returned to the office and my slide show, hoping the rest of the day would pass without interruptions.

CHAPTER SIXTEEN

LESS THAN A HALF HOUR LATER, Theresa and Gus walked into my office. She wore cut off shorts, a pink top, and pink flip-flops that matched the polish on her toes. Her caramel skin glowed in the sun streaming in through my window. She looked stunning. And angry. Gus just looked exhausted.

He dropped into one of the visitor's chairs in front of my desk. He was still panting from the walk between the lobby and my office, and he looked like he'd just run a marathon. Sweat beaded on his brow and ran down his cheeks. There were wet patches on his RIO tee shirt. He coughed for a long time, and when he finally stopped, there were flecks of blood on his lips.

Theresa gently wiped his face with a tissue from her pocket. Then she lit into me. "You gave Stewie a bonus? How could you do that to Gus and me?"

"Sorry, Theresa. I'm confused. How does this affect you two?"

She sighed loudly and sat in my other visitor's chair, crossing her long legs before she replied. "Of course, you wouldn't understand, rich girl. Gus deserves something to make up for his injuries. He was hurt on the job."

She leaned forward, putting her arms on the edge of my desk. "He can't ever resume his job as RIO's dive shop manager because he won't be diving anymore. He'll never be able to carry around heavy tanks, do boat maintenance, or any of his former duties. When his medical leave ends, he'll be out of work unless he gets a desk job. And not just any job. We need one that pays well. We can't live on just my earnings. Not if we want to buy a house or start a family."

Theresa's words hit me like a fist to the gut. It had never occurred to me that Gus wouldn't be able to come back to his old job at RIO. I'd known him since I was a child, and he'd always been strong and fit. I'd assumed after a few weeks of rest he'd be back to his old self.

When I'd agreed to give Stewie a bonus, I'd been focused on a short-term problem. I stood by my decision. I understood their concerns, but it wouldn't change anything. Ray's safety came first. And compensating Gus for his injuries was way outside my responsibilities.

"There were extenuating circumstances that I really can't discuss, but right now, Stewie gets a bonus. He shouldn't have told anyone about it, but that's Stewie. Meanwhile, I'll talk to Maddy and Ray about making sure there's a place for Gus when he's ready to come back. I promise."

"Yeah, right. While you're at it, talk to Ray about finally retrieving that treasure he's been sitting on all these years. Gus's share would sure come in handy. We've got medical bills to pay on top of everything else."

"You know the treasure isn't real..." I started, but Theresa helped Gus to his feet and they walked slowly out of my office. I could hear him coughing as he walked, and my heart broke for him.

CHAPTER SEVENTEEN

AT NOON THE NEXT DAY, instead of rushing out to meet Lily, I was stuck in a documentary planning meeting that ran long. The delay made me half an hour late arriving at the marina. Oliver was just leaving the boat I'd reserved.

He smiled and waved a cheerful greeting when he saw me. "They had the tanks you requested all ready when I came in. I brought them to the boat for you." He trotted down the dock toward me. "You should be good to go."

"Thanks for bringing the tanks aboard. I didn't realize you were working at RIO now."

"My dad hired me the other day to fill in while Gus is on medical leave. I'm here to do the scut work." He grinned. "But it's okay. I'm excited just to be here. This place is awesome." His dark eyes sparkled in the morning sun. Oliver was friendlier and more open than he'd been during class. He was over the moon excited about the job, and his resentment of Ray and me seemed to have disappeared.

"That's great news. Welcome aboard the RIO team. Thanks for loading the tanks. Such a treat to have someone else carry my gear. Since I usually do it myself, this feels almost like being a pampered tourist."

He laughed. "No biggie. All part of my new job. Lily's already on the boat. She's totally amped to dive with you. Maybe next time the three of us can go diving together." He jogged the rest of the way back to the tank shack.

What a change in Oliver's personality. He seemed so happy now. I shrugged and walked down the dock to the boat I had reserved. The 26-foot Zodiac had a rigid floor for stability. Its rugged inflatable hull tubes made it lightweight and easy to handle. This boat was sleek, fast, and all black with the RIO logo on the side. It had been customized with eight tank holders, but I'd only requested four tanks. Two tanks were already racked on each side of the boat. Lily's BCD and regulator were set up on a tank on the port side, in the slot next to the tank reserved for her second dive. She was sitting in the captain's seat, her feet up on the control panel.

"Ahoy, Lily. I didn't realize you had your captain's license."

She looked startled. "I don't. Aren't you going to drive the boat?"

"Since the boat belongs to RIO, I'd drive even if you had a captain's license. And I don't mean to sound grumpy, but it's customary to wait for the captain to invite you on before you board a boat."

"Sorry. I thought that stuff was just for dive class. I didn't know that's how it works IRL."

IRL—in real life—I translated in my head. "Yes, that's how it works IRL. Next trip I promise to be prompt if you'll promise to wait until I get here and invite you on board, okay?"

She beamed. "Next trip? You mean you'll dive with me again?"

"Uh, sure. Probably. Maybe. Let's see how it goes today." I slung my gear aboard. "Got all your stuff?" I asked, while setting up my rig on one of the starboard-side tanks. "Mask, fins, weights? Water, defogging drops? Snack?"

"Aye, aye, Captain. Everything I need is right here." She rose from the captain's chair where she'd been lounging and pointed to a brand-new hot pink dive bag stowed under the port-side bench near her tanks.

I started the boat's engine, and we glided away from the dock. Because I didn't want to spend the entire rest of the day diving with Lily, I just went around the point at South Sound to moor at the site known as Devil's Grotto.

I helped her into her rig and checked that she'd turned on her air and put weights in the BCD's weight pockets. I shrugged into my own gear, and we did simultaneous backward rolls off opposite sides of the Zodiac.

Right away, a green sea turtle swam by to investigate, and the schooling yellow jacks that always seem to congregate under a dive boat swarmed us looking for handouts. When we reached the shallow reef—a series of coral caverns and swim-throughs that led to the wall—we saw a school of giant silvery tarpon. Not even a minute later, a spotted eagle ray swooped by a mere few feet away. Seeing an eagle ray is considered a symbol of luck, and Lily's eyes behind her mask were huge with excitement at the rare sighting.

Although Lily did well on the dive, she burned through her air much faster than I did. A mere fifteen minutes had passed when she held up her computer for me to see how low her air supply was. I nodded at the numbers and turned back toward the boat.

My own air consumption had been minimal. The pressure gauge showed my tank was still almost full when I got back on the boat.

After helping Lily aboard, I slipped my rig into a tank holder on the starboard side. Lily rummaged in her dive bag for snacks. She pulled out an energy bar and a bottle of water to munch while she sat on the pontoon with her feet dangling over the side. When she finished her energy bar, she slipped into the water and floated on her back. She hadn't said a word since we got back to the boat.

She must have expected me to change over her tank for the second dive, because she made no move to do it herself. Well, she was used to tourist diving where service was the norm. This once it'd be easier for me to transfer her rig to the unused tank than it would be to explain why she should want to do it herself. She'd catch on soon enough.

I moved her empty tank to an open slot in the rack and attached her rig to the tank she hadn't yet used. But when I turned the tank's pressure knob, I realized it was already on. Sure enough, when I connected her pressure gauge, it showed the new tank was completely empty. All the air must have escaped while we were on our first dive.

Rather than skip the next dive, I decided to set up her rig on my unused second tank. Lily had sucked her first tank dry in less than 15 minutes, but the pressure in my first tank hadn't budged much below the full 3000 PSI mark. My tank still held plenty of air for me to use it. If I swapped my unused full tank for her empty one, I wouldn't have to ruin Lily's fun. I'd still be safe and comfortable on our second dive, with plenty of air. I carried my tank across the boat and set up her rig on it.

When I'd finished with her gear, I grabbed a bottle of water out of my cooler and sat on the bench next to my setup. We needed to wait out our required surface interval to allow our bodies to release the excess nitrogen absorbed during out first dive. Too much nitrogen can lead to the bends,

Lily climbed aboard and sat opposite me next to her own rig. We spent the remainder of the one-hour surface interval chatting about our lives. From our conversation, it was obvious

Lily and I lived in different worlds, but as the time passed, I found myself starting to like her better. Or at least, to understand her.

I learned that Cara Flores, Lily's mother, is an executive with a global financial investment firm. She made lots of money, and she frequently traveled to financial centers around the world, including the Cayman Islands. I guessed she must have met Ray on one of her business trips. Lily's upbringing included city life, nannies, posh private schools, designer clothes, and years of music and dance lessons. It was a lot different than mine.

Both Lily and I liked to read, and we compared our favorite authors and genres. Lily enjoyed mysteries, while I prefer stories of adventure. We both hated female protagonists who wait for a man to rescue them instead of acting on their own. After books, we segued to movies.

"The movies are always better than the books," she said. "You can get into the setting, and if the movie has a good cast, you can see the characters' thoughts on their faces."

"That's the problem," I countered. "There aren't many actors good enough to convey subtle emotional nuances without using words. But with books, the author puts it on the page for you."

Our next topic was shoes. We both loved shoes. I seldom had occasion to wear anything except flip-flops or sneakers, so I considered high heels to be like works of art. I admired their beauty, but I didn't wear them.

Lily was horrified by my attitude. "I have over one hundred pairs of shoes. I wear them all. The right shoe makes an outfit," she said. "Like the right purse or belt. It's a statement of self-expression."

I laughed, thinking of my wardrobe, which included raggedy shorts, faded tee shirts, and every color and style of bathing suit, but not much else. No shoes on earth were going to change the statement my clothes made.

I was surprised to find I enjoyed Lily's company. Somewhere during our conversation, I began to hope that Ray and my mother worked out their problems, so Lily and I could spend more time together. She was smart, funny, and a lot of fun. I'd always wanted a sister. Lily would be a good one.

Our surface interval was over, so I stood up to help Lily into her gear before donning my own BCD and tank. We did backward rolls off the Zodiac's pontoons and started our dive.

During our descent through the warm water, Lily had trouble clearing her ears. I slowed down to wait for her. I could tell by the expression on her face she was embarrassed, but sometimes even divers with years of experience had trouble clearing their ears. It's best to go slow and not try to force the pressure equalization, since forceful or inadequate equalization can damage the diver's ear drums causing dizziness, disorientation, or permanent hearing loss.

We finally reached the reef wall, but right from the start, Lily had trouble keeping up with me as we swam along the top of the reef. I stopped to wait for her. Diving can be deceptive. If you're doing it right, it looks easy, but it's hard work. At first, I thought she might just be overtired from the earlier dive. But this was more than mere fatigue.

She was sluggish and barely moving. I tried to take her arm because she didn't follow me when I swam. She pulled away, shutting her eyes, and sinking without seeming to notice. I tried to get her to turn around and head back to the boat, but she didn't respond to my hand signals.

I swam nearer to her to look at her up close. Her lips and fingernails had turned a deep cherry red, a sign of possible carbon monoxide poisoning. Carbon monoxide poisoning while diving usually only happens when using tanks carelessly filled by sloppy shops. RIO wasn't that type of dive shop, but accidents are always possible, and carbon monoxide poisoning could be fatal. I knew what to do, but every second counted. I tamped down my panic and swam for the surface towing Lily. This time, she didn't resist. I needed to get her back on the boat right away.

As soon as we surfaced, I verified her bright cherry red lips, flushed cheeks, and red fingernail beds. Now I was certain it was carbon monoxide poisoning. I pulled her onto the boat, and after removing her tank and BCD, I sat her in the bow. She vomited before slumping to one side and losing consciousness.

Now I was scared.

This was bad. Very bad.

I lifted the cover of the storage box in the boat's bow to pull out the small canister of oxygen all RIO's boats carried. I attached the mask to Lily's face before I radioed the Institute. "Lily's sick. She needs oxygen, and the hyperbaric chamber. I think it's carbon monoxide poisoning. ETA ten minutes." I used every bit of horsepower the powerful boat possessed to get us back to shore before Lily succumbed to the lack of oxygen and suffered brain injury or death.

Ray, Maddy, Oliver, and the RIO paramedics met us at the dock. Maddy and Ray tied up the boat while I lifted Lily into the arms of one of the EMTs. He placed her on a gurney and fastened the straps. They rushed her inside to RIO's hyperbaric chamber where they would increase the air pressure to two and a half times normal surface pressure. The extra atmospheric pressure would increase the amount of oxygen Lily's body could absorb, helping her to expel the carbon monoxide. Without the increased pressure, the human body has trouble eliminating enough carbon monoxide to make room for oxygen. That leads to death.

We raced behind the EMTs to make sure they treated Lily like family. "How could you let this happen to her?" Ray asked.

I was stunned by his words.

Outside the chamber, Ray stood with his face to one of the portholes, watching the paramedics work. "Sorry for what I said before. This was my fault, not yours." He reached down and clasped my hand. His was like ice.

After a while, the doctor came over to talk to Ray, who was still staring in through the port. "She's recovering well, but we won't know anything for sure until she regains consciousness. We'll want to do a complete cycle—that's three full rounds of decompression—so don't worry too much until we see how things stand after the third round. We won't be finished until tomorrow morning." She put a hand on Ray's shoulder. "Fin did a fantastic job recognizing carbon monoxide poisoning and rushing Lily here fast. Thank goodness she knew what to do. You should be proud of her."

"I am. I'm proud of both my daughters. I just don't understand how carbon monoxide got into one of our tanks. We're extra careful."

"Nobody doubts you, Ray, but accidents happen. Lucky Lily was with Fin. It might have been worse otherwise. Much worse."

"It's got to be my fault. Something I missed in the fill station design or procedures." Ray's voice trembled. "Accidents like this don't just happen."

I didn't think it was an accident. Someone was targeting us. Three near misses so close together was too much to be a coincidence. I didn't have any enemies I knew of, so I didn't think anyone had a reason to try to kill me. But still...

I didn't need to burden Ray with another worry while I worked out the problem on my own. I knew this accident wasn't Ray's fault. I owed it to him to prove it, so I had to find out how this happened. For my own safety, and for his peace of mind.

And for Lily. This had happened on my watch, and she was Ray's daughter. That made her my sister, whether I liked her or not.

Oliver was standing alone, staring into the chamber through one of the porthole windows. I walked over and stood beside him. "Was anyone else hanging around the tank shack today?"

"Sure," he said. "Lots of people. Stewie, your mom, a few of the divemasters. Ray. Your dad. Oh, and my sister."

"Anyone running a generator or compressor besides the fill compressor? Smoking? Motorbike idling nearby?"

"No, of course not," he said. "Why are you asking me all these questions?"

"No reason," I said over my shoulder. Oliver was the most likely suspect for deliberately poisoning the tank. He'd delivered the tanks to the boat, and he'd been the one who'd placed the poison tank away from Lily. I had to investigate.

I ran as fast as I could to the dive operations building, located all the way across the rolling expanse of lawn. We had placed it there to keep the tank fill compressor away from cars, smokers, and portable heaters, common producers of carbon monoxide. There was no way for carbon monoxide to infiltrate the tanks we filled there without intervention.

I made several loops around the building, examining every inch of the ground and every blade of grass. Finally, I saw what I'd been looking for. Just beyond the cement terrace surrounding the tank shack, the grass was bent over in two parallel tracks, about a foot apart. I followed the faint trail to the edge of RIO's parking lot.

The tracks that someone had brought a wheeled cart across the lawn to the tank shack. I went back inside the tank shack and hung the closed sign on the door. Then I took a powerful underwater flashlight from the rental equipment shelf and shone it at the floor, covering every inch with care until I found the proof I needed.

A single drop of gasoline glistened on the floor near the tank fill compressor's air intake valve. Now I was certain. Someone had wheeled a portable generator across the lawn, brought it into the tank shack, and set it up in the spot where it would spew its lethal fumes into any tank being filled. Lily's carbon monoxide poisoning had been deliberate.

Who knew how many tanks had been contaminated? After checking the log, I saw we hadn't rented out any tanks yet today. Luckily, today had been a slow day, so I didn't have to worry about more accidents. But the pile of full tanks waiting for divers to use during the next few days of dives was massive. Someone would have to test the air in every one of them to make sure none had a carbon monoxide problem. Gus was still on sick leave and Oliver was with his family. There was nobody available to do it except me.

I pulled the gas analyzer kit from behind the desk and attached it to the nearest tank. Then the next one. And the next. We had hundreds of tanks. It took hours to test them all. The gas analysis reading for every tank in the shed was perfect, whether filled with standard air or the oxygen-enriched air called NITROX.

When I had finished, I left the sun-filled dock to go into RIO's cool and shadowy interior. Ray and Oliver were standing shoulder to shoulder outside the hyperbaric chamber, staring through the porthole at Lily, who was still unconscious inside. This was the first time I'd seen the two men standing side-by-side, and they did look like father and son. They shared the same coloring, the same build. They even flashed the same weary but magnetic smiles as I approached.

I joined them at the porthole. My mother and RIO's doctor came into the infirmary, just as the medical team opened the door after the latest decompression cycle. Maddy came over to take Ray's hand, while the doctor went into the chamber to check Lily's vitals. She listened to Lily's heart and lungs, shone a light in her eyes, and drew a vial of blood. The doctor looked up at us watching through the porthole. She gave a slight nod. My mother nodded back.

"Another round of compression," the doctor said to the technicians when she exited the pressure chamber. "Then we'll see."

Ray's eyes filled with tears.

"Thanks, Doc," my mother said.

CHAPTER EIGHTEEN

THAT NIGHT I tossed and turned, trying to make sense of what had happened. I couldn't think of a single reason why anyone would want to hurt either Lily or me. Therefore, I concluded, it must have been an accident. But the tracks across the lawn and the single drop of gasoline told me otherwise.

My worrying accomplished nothing except to keep me awake all night. I rose before the sun to check on Lily before the day got busy.

I stopped at RIO's café to grab coffee for Oliver, Ray and Maddy. If I knew them, they'd have been standing watch over Lily all night.

Just as I expected, Ray was outside the hyperbaric chamber, his face pressed to one of its portholes. His weary stance and unshaven face said he had indeed been there all night. The unaccustomed deep lines in his forehead and beside his mouth communicated how worried he was. Oliver and Maddy were asleep in nearby visitor's chairs. A woman I assumed was Cara Flores, Lily's mother, stood alone near the door to the chamber.

Cara had the biggest melted-chocolate brown eyes I'd ever

seen. Her short, shiny dark hair was cut in a chic pixie. Her face was flawless. If she wore any makeup, I couldn't tell. She had on an expensive-looking bright pink sundress. The vivid polish on the nails of her hands and feet matched the dress to perfection. Gold hoop earrings, gold sandals, and a gold coin on a chain around her neck were the only accessories she wore.

"I'm so sorry about what happened to Lily." I handed her the coffee I'd bought for myself. Her hand shook when she grasped it. She didn't say anything—didn't even smile.

Ray took the coffee I handed him. "Thank you." He gulped half the cup's contents before speaking. "I owe you an apology. This was not your fault. I shouldn't have said that."

"You already apologized, and anyway, I understand. You love her. You're her father, and you were scared."

"I'm your father too. You're the daughter of my heart, and I love you. I'm sorry I was harsh to you, but I was so scared for her." He finished the coffee, tossing the cup into a bin near the chamber's exit door. "We okay?"

"Always," I said. I was still disappointed in him for the way he had treated my mother. And even though I understood he hadn't done it to hurt me, I was still angry because he'd invited Alec to be on the documentary team without consulting me first. But in the face of Lily's accident, these problems receded in importance. We'd have plenty of time to work things out once she was on the mend.

Maddy woke up and stood beside Ray. With our fingers touching, Ray, Maddy and I watched Lily through the hyperbaric chamber's port, until the doctor came by. She'd been monitoring Lily's vital signs from the feeds inside the chamber. We joined her, Oliver, and Cara near the chamber's door to hear Lily's prognosis.

"Things are looking good," she said. "She's regaining consciousness. I don't think there'll be any residual damage.

She was lucky we got her into the chamber right away. Outstanding work, Fin. Thanks to you, Lily should be fine."

Ray's face lit up like the sun rising on the East End of Grand Cayman. He closed his eyes and took a big breath. "Thank you," he said. He lifted my hand to his lips. "She's gonna be okay," he said, rocking a little from weariness.

We watched as they opened the door to the chamber and the EMTs wheeled Lily's gurney through the door. Cara and Ray both rushed to her side, but not before I saw the tears glistening on Ray's cheeks. "Thank God you're alright," he said, taking her into his arms for a hug.

Lily rested her chin on his shoulder and looked straight at me, her eyes like granite.

"Daddy," she said, snuggling against Ray's shoulder.

I felt a severe pang of late-onset sibling rivalry. I was happy Lily was okay, but hearing her call a man she'd just met "Daddy" seemed inappropriate and premature. Ray was the man who'd always filled the 'Daddy' role in my life, yet I'd never been invited to call him that. I was so jealous I couldn't see straight. My heart froze with sorrow. I might be angry at him right now, but I never wanted to lose the love of the man I considered my father.

Lily was scheduled to spend a few nights in RIO's infirmary. Ray, Maddy, Oliver, and Cara went along with the gurney to get her settled. I felt like a fifth wheel, so I didn't tag along.

I went back to my office, but I found it hard to concentrate on paperwork. I decided to work in the lab for a while until things calmed down. A visit with Rosie, RIO's resident Atlantic Pygmy octopus, was what I needed to get back on track.

Rosie is so cute and smart that she always cheers me up. I was working on an experiment for my doctoral thesis on the intelligence of octopuses, trying to prove they had the ability to differentiate colors and shapes. Rosie hadn't made a single mistake in the months we'd worked together, and she'd aced every test I sent her way.

No doubt. Rosie was a star.

I held a picture of a red marble to the glass of her aquarium. As always when Rosie performed, I was awestruck when she slinked over to her pile of treasures to pull out the matching red marble. She brought it to my side of the tank and put it next to the other items she had unerringly retrieved whenever I showed her a picture of what I wanted.

"Good girl," I said, dropping a raw clam into the water as a reward. Rosie turned pink for a brief flash, her way of saying thank you, and the reason for her name. As always, working with Rosie brightened my mood. Finished with her for the day, I put the cover back on her aquarium and cleaned up the lab before I returned to my office, much calmer than I'd been earlier.

CHAPTER NINETEEN

WHEN I GOT to the office the next morning, I checked on Lily's condition and learned that she was still in RIO's infirmary. I decided to pop in for a visit. I swung by the cafeteria and picked up a couple of sodas and some of RIO's famous chocolate chip cookies for her.

The infirmary was small—a mere three beds separated by curtains. The beds were seldom occupied except when someone on the staff worked late. Lily occupied the middle bed, sitting up playing Monopoly with Oliver. "Brought you something." I held out the bag of cookies and the tray of drinks.

She looked up with a frown but flipped it to a smile when she saw me. Or maybe when she saw the cookies. Either way, her face brightened, and she didn't seem as listless. She took the sodas and handed one to Oliver. "Thanks," she said, dipping into the bag of cookies. "I had one of these the other day. They're yummy." She passed the bag to Oliver but didn't offer me any.

"How are you today? Feeling better?"

She nodded, mouth full of cookie.

"How's the game going? Who's winning?'

Oliver laughed. "Don't ever try to compete with Lily. She's like a shark. Goes for the throat. Right now, she's killing me, as usual."

"I'll bear that in mind. Don't compete with Lily. Got it." We all laughed.

This was the friendliest and most open he'd ever been. I guess the job at RIO and our shared concern for Lily had melted the last bit of animosity away. Although I was still worried he'd had a hand in poisoning the tank in the first place, it was a relief not to feel like I had to watch every word around him.

After one more roll of the dice, Oliver was bankrupt. He stood up and stretched. "I'm out. It's time for my shift to start anyway. I'll see you later." He waved goodbye and left the infirmary.

Lily looked at me as soon as he'd left the room. "Dad said I can work in the gift shop part time when I get out of here. I'm pretty excited about it."

"That's great. Then we'll be seeing a lot more of each other." I hoped Maddy knew about it or it might set off another ice age.

Lily took another cookie and picked up the television's remote control from the table beside her bed. She turned on the TV and started clicking through channels.

Her silence made me feel I was imposing. I missed the easy camaraderie we'd enjoyed before her near fatal dive. I tried to think of a way to reconnect until I noticed the supermodel on the cover of the magazine on her bedside table. The woman was dazzling, beyond beautiful, with a blinding smile. "Do you think people who look like her exist in real life?" I asked, pointing to the magazine.

She glanced at the glossy photo. "Yeah, they do. I met her

once in New York. She's beautiful even when she doesn't have a full-time hair and makeup crew to help her out. Some people have all the luck."

"You're beautiful too, Lily. You won the genetic lottery. With your parents, you couldn't be anything but beautiful." Ray and Cara were good-looking people. Lily and Oliver combined the best of their parents' striking features.

She waved her hand in the air, making light of my comment. "Skin deep," she said. "And fades with age. Or after an accident."

I flushed at her reference to my scar. It was healing, but still very visible.

"Good looks are nice, but I'd rather be rich. Like you."

I was uncomfortable talking about money under any circumstances, and I was confused by Lily's comments. When we were chatting between dives the other day, I had assumed her family was well off. I had no idea how to respond to her comment, so I fell back on a cliché. "Money can't buy happiness."

"I'd like the chance to try." She pulled another cookie out of the bag and took a big bite. She chewed and swallowed before speaking again. "It's different for you. You've always had money. You don't know what it's like not to have it."

"That's true. I don't know. And although money can buy lots of things, it can't make people love you." It was odd Lily talking about not having money like she'd grown-up poor, when just yesterday she was telling me about tennis lessons and private schools with ivied walls. I wondered which was the true story.

I realized it didn't matter which account was true. What mattered was loving and being loved. Neither my father, Newton Fleming, nor Alec had cared about me anywhere near as much as they cared about themselves. At least I'd always had

Ray and my mother, who treasured me and each other. I'd been lucky. Despite my jealousy, I knew Lily was lucky too. Cara and Oliver loved her, and now she had Ray in her life

Lily swallowed the last bite of cookie and balled up the empty bag. She tossed it toward the trash bin and yawned. "I'm tired."

"I'll leave so you can get some rest, but before I go, I wanted to say how sorry I am about what happened to you. I'm glad you weren't hurt worse. I can't figure out how the tank got contaminated, but I'll get to the bottom of it. I promise you."

She brushed cookie crumbs to the floor. "No harm done. Just think. If you'd been using the bad tank, I never would have known what to do. You'd be dead by now."

Her words sent a shiver down my spine. The tank had been on my side of the boat. If I hadn't swapped it for her empty tank, the outcome would indeed have been different.

The filling station was set up to prevent accidental contamination of tanks, and I'd seen the faint tracks of the portable generator in the grass. The tracks' existence left no question in my mind. Someone had done it on purpose.

Since Oliver had been working alone in the tank fill station that day, he could have filled the tank with bad gas. But he was a new diver, and he'd only been working at RIO a few days. I'd have been surprised if he even knew how to introduce a lethal gas into a tank while filling it.

I knew Ray's training stressed being on the lookout for nearby sources of carbon monoxide, but was Oliver mature enough to understand how serious the warnings were? He hadn't seemed very mature in class. I was suspicious of him, but he'd been so friendly and open since class ended that I couldn't imagine him wanting to hurt me. But if not Oliver, then who? And why? I needed time to think this through, so I said goodbye to Lily and headed to my office.

CHAPTER TWENTY

I LOVE my office at RIO. It's small, but it has plenty of windows for light and a relaxing view of the ocean beyond the rolling lawn. I'd decorated the office myself. It was cozy yet businesslike, and full of my favorite things.

One of those favorite things covered most of the wall space behind my desk. It was a near-life-size photo of my mother free-diving with a great white shark. A mere few inches separated their faces. The shark's massive frame dwarfed her tiny fragile body. The shark had been about 18 feet long and weighed more than two tons. I still remembered the combination of awe and terror I felt when I took the photo, but Maddy's face, visible through her clear dive mask, showed no trace of fear.

This was the picture that had been on the cover of *Your World*, winning all sorts of awards for my ex-husband, who had sent the image to them on spec "by mistake." He never bothered to correct the error, and the shot had propelled him to the top of the A-list of underwater photographers. Meanwhile, the world still perceived me as a hanger-on. Alec's "mistake" had been the final straw that ended our marriage.

The world gave Alec credit for it, but the photo was my work, and I loved it. It hung there, in the place of honor behind my desk, no matter what anyone else believed about who had taken the shot. I admired its beauty and artistry every time I entered my office.

Except this time, a tall stranger stood behind my desk, blocking my view of the shark. He stared at my mother's image in the photo. He wore a bespoke Brioni suit, and his hair had the perfect taper only achievable after a lifetime of expensive haircuts. His shoes were Sutor Mantellassi oxfords, handmade, sleek, and polished to a high shine. A Patek Phillippe watch peeked from under the cuff of his shirt. I recognized these sartorial details from the accounts of his habits in *Human* magazine, not because I was a connoisseur of expensive status symbols.

He heard me enter and turned away from the picture. "She's remarkable." His smile was dazzling. His teeth were white and straight, the best expensive orthodontia could buy.

We had the same wide-set blue eyes, the same dusty brown hair, and the same pointed chin. We even had the same dimple in our right cheek. The one notable difference between us was the scar across my face. I knew who this man was despite the fact I hadn't seen him since I was five.

My father.

He held out a hand and strode across the tile floor. "Newton Fleming, in case you don't remember me."

He didn't seem like a long-lost father. He acted more like a business associate or a donor to RIO. This was not at all how I'd imagined meeting him.

I stepped back without shaking his hand. "Why are you here?"

"Madelyn called me about your accident. I came to talk some sense into you. Take you to New York. Get your face repaired. She said you wouldn't go, but we can't have you going around with that face." He pointed at my scar. Disgust seemed to leap from the tip of his well-manicured finger and drape itself around me like a foul gray mist.

"There's nothing wrong with my face."

"Yes, there is. You can't go through life looking like that. People see what's on the surface. Nobody cares about what's underneath. If you don't fix the scar, people will never see you —they'll only see your scar. They won't hear you when you speak—they'll only hear your scar. Don't give them something irrelevant to focus on if you can help it. Get it fixed. The sooner the better."

My mouth gaped open. It was hard to believe what I was hearing.

He continued his lecture. "I knew I should never have given Madelyn full custody all these years. She never did understand how the real-world works. All the 'save the earth' stuff she's into. Carrying on with that uneducated water buffalo husband. Now this. She let this happen."

"Ray's not uneducated. He has an MBA." It was all I could think of to say.

My father snorted and looked at his watch. "Let's go. My jet's waiting, and time is money. We can get your face fixed this week. I have connections."

"I'm fine the way I am."

He gestured at my head with two fingers this time. "We can get your hair fixed when we get there too. Extensions or something." His voice sounded like I was a little kid and he was offering me a pony.

"Not going," I said, turning away. "Nowhere. Not with you."

Before I could get away from him, Maddy rounded the corner at a brisk trot. "Fin, we need to talk right away. There's something you need to know..."

My father stepped out of my office and stood behind me. "You're too late. She already knows," he said.

I put my back to the wall and wished I could disappear.

My mother scowled at Newton. "I asked you to let me talk to her before you barged in. And don't try being a bully. It won't work with her. I told you she doesn't want to see a plastic surgeon, and she knows her own mind."

His laugh was full of scorn. "Get a clue about how things work in the real world will you please? You'd rather I act like you—a pathetic wimp," he said. "That may work here in your little Shangri-La, but it doesn't work in the real world. C'mon, Fin. Let's get you out of this backwater. You can stay with me in New York while you heal. See the sights. Go to a Broadway show. You'll learn what you've been missing all these years."

I ignored his bribes and focused on the fact he'd insulted my mother. No way was she pathetic. She was smart, strong, and brave. I admired her. She'd given me a good life, which was more than this gasbag of a father had ever done. Besides his genes, all I got from him were impersonal birthday cards stuffed with money. I could smell the guilt wafting out when I opened the envelopes each year.

"I said I'm not going with you, and that's final. And if you ever so much as whisper another insult at my mother, it will be the last thing you do. Do we understand each other?"

Both of my parents were staring at me in surprise. I'd even managed to shock myself. This outburst was not me. Like Maddy, I'm easy-going, quiet, and analytical, willing to let things go to get along. But nobody—nobody—talked to my mother that way in front of me.

I heard a slow handclap coming from the far end of the hall. Cara Flores stood behind Maddy.

"Cara, I told you to wait outside," Newton said.

"Pfff," she said. "I got bored."

Newton turned to my mother. "Maddy, do you know my friend Cara Flores?"

I swear both women's hair stood up like the fur on an irate cat's nape, but when my mother spoke, her voice was soft and calm. Nothing ever broke her cool façade. "We've met. Nice to see you again, Cara. Welcome to the Dr. Madelyn Anderson Russo Institute for Oceanographic Exploration. You've seen the infirmary, but would you like a tour of the rest of the place? I'm sure we can find someone to show you around."

I was proud of my mother. She didn't let Newton or Cara intimidate her. Her posture was perfect, and her voice was steady. I marveled at the way she'd made it clear she was the one in charge here. I loved the way she rolled out the full name of the institute—a subtle reminder that Maddy was the one married to Ray Russo. My mother's way of putting the other woman in her place was polite, subtle, and yet, oh-so-powerful.

Cara showed her pointed white teeth. "I'm sure it would be lovely to see your little set up here, but Newton and I have things to do. Newton?" She held out her hand to my bio-dad.

Newton ignored her extended hand, while Maddy and I both checked out her fingers for a ring. She noticed us looking, and her face flushed.

"Fin, would it help change your mind if I arranged a solo art show at a gallery in New York? I have contacts in the art world. I'll set it up if you'll come with me."

"Aren't you going to offer me a pony? An American Girl doll? A bag of my favorite candy? You can't bribe me to go with you."

"Please," he said. "I'm trying to do what's best for you. Let me help."

I wondered why my father was so anxious to help now, after all but ignoring me for more than twenty years. Whatever his reasoning, I wanted nothing to do with him. "No, thanks," I said. "Too little, too late. I have everything I need here."

I linked arms with my mother, and we sauntered away, heads high.

CHAPTER TWENTY-ONE

WE WENT into her office and sat at the round table. "Wow, that was intense," I said.

"Newton is always intense," she replied. "I'm sorry I didn't get to tell you he was here before he showed up. Are you okay?"

"Kind of a shock to see my father after all this time. What did you ever see in that man, anyway?"

"We grew up together in Pennsylvania. Our parents always expected us to get married. We just drifted into it. Then we drifted out of it." She had a pensive look on her face, and I wondered if she'd ever regretted leaving Newton behind.

Before I could ask her, June, her assistant poked her head in. "Call from the network. Can you take it?"

She looked at me and shrugged. "Duty calls. Talk later?"

Even though I was frustrated that we couldn't talk about my father—Maddy never made the time to answer my questions about him—I nodded and went back to my own office without a word. I spent the next two hours replaying the scene with Newton in my head. I'd just calmed down enough to concentrate on my work, so I wasn't happy to hear the words "Knock. Knock," in Newton's voice.

"Go away," I said. "I'm working." I looked up when I heard the creak of his body settling into one of my visitors' chairs.

I willed him to disappear. It didn't work.

He cleared his throat. "Fin, I apologize. I was insulting and a bully, to both you and your mother. I was scared to meet you again after so long. It was an awful way to introduce myself to the daughter I've loved from afar her whole life. Can we start over? Please?"

"Loved from afar, huh? What, has your private jet been in the shop for the last twenty years?"

His ears turned red, but after a pause, he said. "You're right. I deserved that. Neglecting you was unforgivable. But I always remembered your birthday and special events. I sent gifts."

"Yes. Expensive, age-appropriate, completely impersonal gifts. Did your assistant pick them out?"

He looked sheepish. "She did. I apologize for that, too. I see now I've been an even more rotten father than I supposed."

"True. You are a rotten father. But it's not like I didn't appreciate the gifts. I liked the house and the car when I turned twenty-one. Oh, by the way, I turned in the red Mercedes for a Prius. It's blue, which you obviously don't know is my favorite color. I used the difference in the prices to buy cameras and scuba gear. I hope it doesn't bother you."

I was having a hard time keeping my voice steady. My heart was beating like the ocean's surge in a hurricane. I hoped my words infuriated him because his very presence was annoying me. I put my hands in my lap so he wouldn't see them shaking, although I had the feeling Newton Fleming didn't miss much.

"Your choice, of course," he said. "Whatever you want is fine with me. I apologize for missing the mark and not taking the time to get to know you better. Will you give me a chance to make it up to you?"

His voice did sound regretful, but I could imagine him practicing the tone into a recorder, preparing to use it during negotiations. I didn't fall for it. "You're great at apologies, but short on real-world father skills. I'm too busy to take time to salve your conscience. Can you go away now?"

"No. Let me explain." This time I heard real regret in his voice. "Maddy wanted to move here to start the Institute and I was stuck in New York with my business. We separated, although I had hopes she and I would get back together. She was taking good care of you, and it hurt too much to see you knowing I'd have to leave you over and over again in a few hours or days. When she met Ray, it was all over for me. No more hope she and I could work things out." He paused and swallowed hard before brushing his hand across his eyes.

Were those tears I saw?

When he resumed speaking, his voice held a tremor. "After the divorce became final, they got married. I stayed away to give them space. My business was taking off, and it was hard to get down here for more than a few hours at a time. I hated seeing you cry whenever I left, so I started coming less often. Before I knew it, years passed without my seeing you. I know I'm a poor excuse for a father, and it galls me to know that all these years Aquaman has been a better father to you than I could ever be."

I couldn't help but laugh, despite my determination to dislike this man. "Aquaman? Ray would love it if he knew you called him Aquaman."

"Would he?" asked Newton. "I'll have to be careful never to call him Aquaman where he can hear me." He surprised me by chuckling.

"Sorry. I apologize again. I didn't mean to call him names. What I meant to say was Ray Russo, world's most incredible sailor, diver, treasure hunter, fund raiser, CFO. Star of countless documentaries and beefcake posters. A man of many talents, and a perfect match for your equally incredible mother. It killed me when she married him. I thank God he was a good father to you. To be honest, I admire him. A lot."

"Yes, he is an incredible man. And you owe my mother an apology. You were rude and insulting. And why would you bring Cara here anyway? After what happened between her and Ray, that's a dumb move, even for someone as emotionally clueless as you."

After a beat, he sighed. "It was pretty stupid, wasn't it? Cara's a good friend and one of my top executives. We spend a lot of time together for work. We had a meeting downtown today. That's why it took me so long to come back and apologize."

He sighed again "And I know I was rude to you both, so I'll apologize to Maddy, too." He looked up at me with beseeching eyes. "I can't expect to make up for twenty years of neglect in one afternoon, but I'll spend the rest of my life trying if you'll let me. All I can say is I'm sorry and I'll try to do better. And I meant what I said about the one-woman gallery event, or the Broadway shows. Whatever you'd like. You know, every year I scour RIO's documentaries looking for glimpses of you, but it's never enough. I'd like to get to know you in person." He stood and handed me his card. "Call me anytime." He left.

Leave it to my father to give me a business card but no hug. Not that I wanted him to hug me or anything.

CHAPTER TWENTY-TWO

IT WAS the end of the workday and I stood beside my car in RIO's parking lot trying to decide what to do. I'd always wanted to get to know my biological father, and our interactions earlier had left me confused. Was he the cold, unfeeling man he'd seemed at first, or the pleasant and reasonable one who'd apologized later? I wanted to know.

And I was curious about his relationship with Cara. It seemed too coincidental that he would be romantically involved with the mother of Ray's children. The more I thought about Newton Fleming, the more questions I had. While I waited for the notoriously finicky AC in my Prius to cool the car down to a livable temperature, I bit the bullet and called my bio-dad on my cell.

"Fleming here," he answered.

All business. This didn't bode well.

"Newton, sorry to bother you. It's Fin. I'd like to come by to talk. Are you busy now?"

"Always time for you, sweetie. Come on by. Do you know where I'm staying?"

Funny--he'd never had time for me before, but I didn't comment on the insincerity I found in his statement. "I bet you're in the penthouse at the Ritz Carlton, right?"

"Right. I'll let the concierge know you're coming."

The famous three bedroom, three-and-a-half bathroom penthouse at the Ritz cost $25,000 and up a night. I was appalled at the extravagance, even though he was rich. How much space did one man need?

"I'm still at RIO, but it won't take me long to get there."

"Good. I'm looking forward to it." He disconnected the call.

By now, the car's air conditioning had brought the inside temperature down to approximately the level of a blast furnace. I eased myself in, gingerly sliding across the scorching seat. Lucky for me, the Ritz was not far away.

When I pulled up in front of the hotel complex, a cute blond valet with a nametag proclaiming he was Liam from Sydney rushed over to open the door. "Welcome to the Ritz-Carlton, Miss Fleming. May I take your car?" Newton must have described my car to the concierge.

"Thank you, Liam." I said, handing him a twenty.

He waved it away with a smile. "It's been taken care of."

I walked into a cool, inviting lobby, where the concierge greeted me by name. "This way to the penthouse elevator, Miss Fleming." All the attention was creepy. I hoped I never got used to it.

When the elevator doors opened on the penthouse level, Newton was waiting for me. Although I was as stiff as a cardboard cutout, he pulled me into a hug. "Thanks for coming, Sweetie. Come in. Would you like something to drink?'

"Water, please." I looked around at the penthouse in awe. It must have been about 8,000 square feet, with an ocean view from every room. The floors were a mix of plush carpets,

Brazilian cherry hardwood, and gleaming tile. A balcony ran the entire length of the suite, with a dining table that would seat twelve people with room to spare, plus multiple lounging and conversation areas with comfy chairs and recliners. The suite's décor was stunning—every detail exquisite. I stared around like a rube.

Newton laughed. "It's pretty spectacular, isn't it? Most of the time I don't stay here when I'm on the island. But since Cara likes it, here we are."

"You and Cara come to the island often...?"

"Once or twice a year."

"So you're a couple?"

He laughed. "No. We were once, long ago. But now it's strictly business. That's why we come to Grand Cayman. It's one of the world's financial capitals, you know."

"So you came here once or twice a year, but you could never make time to see me." I couldn't stop the cracking in my voice. It was one thing to imagine him on the other side of the world or even in New York and not having time to see me. I could pretend he was too busy to pop over to Grand Cayman. But now he was telling me he had been right here, on my island, at least a couple of times a year. All my life. "That's unforgivable."

The color drained from his face. "It wasn't like that. I wanted to see you, but you weren't always here when I was. Remember, you were gone a lot yourself. Six months a year with your mother on the *Omega*. Ray and Maddy weren't too keen on having me drop in and out of your life if I couldn't make a regular commitment. With all our travel, it wasn't possible. It seemed easier on you for me to stay away."

"I see. Phone, texts, emails. All too hard to coordinate with a child's busy schedule."

He blushed. "You're right. I took the easy way out. I didn't think about how it felt to be you. I'll spend the rest of my life apologizing and trying to make it up to you. I didn't know what I was missing out on."

Newton handed me a baccarat crystal glass of spring water just as Cara opened the penthouse's boardroom door. She wore a pair of white raw silk shorts and a patterned silk top hanging off one shoulder. The pink in her top matched the fresh color of the polish on her fingers and toes. "Newt, I have the details on the Forthingham contract..." her voice trailed off when she saw me. "Fin, I didn't know you were here."

Newton didn't look up at her. "I'm not working now, Cara. I'm with my daughter. We can discuss the contract later. I'm in no rush. Forthingham isn't going anywhere."

She pivoted on her kitten heels and went back into the penthouse's boardroom.

"Hungry? We can celebrate our reunion downstairs at Bar Jack on the beach if you're free."

Cara emerged from the boardroom again. She carried a small white leather purse and wore a wide brimmed straw hat, her coin necklace, and huge Chanel sunglasses. "I'm going out to dinner with Oliver and Lily," she said.

Newton nodded. "Sounds fun."

All three of us rode down in the elevator together, but nobody spoke. The silence was uncomfortable until we reached the lobby. Liam was waiting with the keys to her car—a baby blue Lexus convertible. Before he opened her door, he winked at me. I blushed, hoping my father hadn't noticed.

Newton and I crossed the lobby in the opposite direction from Cara to reach the restaurant. Our table was on the sand of Seven Mile Beach, facing the ocean. We each sank into one of the plush, comfy couches flanking our table, shaded from the late-day sun by a huge, creamy-white market umbrella. The seats' brown cushions and the scattered throw pillows that matched the umbrella were cool and welcoming.

"Will you have a drink with me? The piña coladas here are the best on the island." Newton spread a cream-colored napkin on his lap and gazed out to sea, missing my frown at the reminder he'd spent a lot of time on my island without ever bothering to contact me.

I didn't answer him because the waiter hurried over just then. "Mister Fleming, sir. Good to see you again. The usual?"

"Yes, thanks. Fin, you want to try my usual or do you want to look at the menu?"

"The usual is fine." Whatever the usual was, it didn't matter. This latest demonstration of his lifetime of indifference to me made me angry enough I didn't think I would eat more than a bite or two of whatever his usual was anyway. Not to mention how mad I was that he seemed to be sharing his suite with Cara.

The waiter hurried away and was back within minutes with two frosty piña coladas and a small bowl of mixed nuts. I sipped my drink and waited for my father to carry the conversation.

I was still waiting when the waiter delivered two cups of steaming hot conch chowder. It was light, creamy, and delicious. We'd no sooner put down our spoons when the waiter brought fresh drinks, followed within minutes by two cheeseburgers and a huge basket of crispy truffle-scented fries.

"This is your usual? I expected a gourmet meal." I nibbled a fry.

He frowned. "I'm sorry you don't like it. If it isn't to your taste, you can get something else."

"No, this is perfect," I said. "It's surprising it's your usual, that's all." I eyed his flat waistline and narrow cheekbones. "You don't strike me as a cheeseburger kind of guy."

He laughed. "I'm full of surprises. And now that we've met and the ice is broken, we have the rest of our lives to surprise each other." He paused a moment. "Tell me about life with Aquaman. I've always been jealous of all the time he got to spend with you..."

I described our weekly fishing trips and how incredible it had been to have one of the greatest divers in the world teach me how to swim and dive. Newton seemed interested in the details of my life, and he asked a lot of questions. The hours slipped by like minutes.

The sun had gone down long ago by the time we were ready to relinquish our table by the sea. Although I hated to admit it to myself, I'd had a good time.

"Gotta go," I said rising from the comfy couch. "I have to work tomorrow."

"Let me get someone to drive you home," he said. "It's a long way and you've had a few drinks."

"I need my car in the morning."

"No problem. One of the valet's will drive your car and another can follow in mine. That way you'll have your car in the morning." He signaled to the maître'd. Newton told him what he wanted, and the maître'd hurried to the valet station to make the arrangements. I crossed my fingers that Liam would be assigned to drive my car.

A few minutes later, Liam held open the passenger door of my Prius. "Where to, Fin?" he said. "I mean, Miss Fleming."

"Oh, please. Call me Fin." I was thrilled that I'd be spending some alone time with the good looking and personable Aussie.

"Will do," he said. "Where to?"

"I live on Rum Point. Hit the home button on the navigation system. It'll take you right there."

"Good," he said. "We can concentrate on getting to know each other instead of worrying about directions. What do you like to do in your spare time?"

I hadn't been on a date since Alec and I split up, and my social skills—never good to begin with—were rusty. Thank goodness he started with an easy question. "I like to dive. Anywhere, anytime. I feel most at home in the water. How about you?"

"Back home I did Iron Man competitions, but I haven't since I've been on island. I'm a diver, too, but I'm not in your league."

"We should go diving together sometime," I said, before remembering how much I hated diving with people who weren't well trained. Then again, Liam was so nice it'd be worth making an exception to my rule for the opportunity to spend time with him.

"I've seen you dive in the RIO documentaries, and I guarantee I'm not as good a diver as you are. But if you're up for it, I'd like that. When can we dive? I'm off tomorrow unless that's too soon."

"Tomorrow's good," I said. A thrill of excitement shot through me at the thought of seeing Liam again. "Can you get to Rum Point early? It's my favorite time and place to dive."

"I can do that. I'll pick you up at six."

"Super. I'll introduce you to Harry."

Liam frowned. "Harry? I don't want to come between you and your regular dive buddy. Maybe we should do it another time."

"No, Harry won't mind if you're there. Or at least, not any more than he minds when I'm there. He's a stingray."

"Well then, I can't wait to meet him," Liam said. "Any friend of yours..."

I laughed like I'd heard the funniest joke ever. Liam joined in. We talked about our favorite dive sites the rest of the way home, but every few minutes, one of us would start to laugh and then the other would get the giggles too. It'd been a long time since I'd been this happy.

CHAPTER TWENTY-THREE

IT WAS a few minutes after sunrise the next morning. I waited for Liam at the end of my driveway. He pulled up in one of the ubiquitous open-air jeeps—the vehicle of choice for divers on Grand Cayman. Liam stowed my tanks in the back, and I dropped my dive bag on top of them.

At Rum Point, we laughed as we checked out the famous sign, with its colorful arrows pointing to places all over the world. When we were ready to dive, Liam set up his gear quickly and donned his equipment with ease. We waded into the ocean, and he gave me his hand to steady me and even held my camera while I tugged on my fins. All night I'd been worried he'd be a poor diver, but he had good dive manners. At least he seemed to be a thoughtful dive buddy.

We snorkeled to the swim area boundary ropes and ducked under, then descended to about 20 feet. Swimming side by side, we scanned the sand below for signs of Harry.

I caught sight of him watching us on our left. I touched Liam's shoulder to get his attention. He turned to look at Harry and a big, delighted grin swept across his face. He hovered without struggling to stay in place, watching Harry until the stingray rose and glided over the reef edge. Liam and I followed, but at the drop-off, we turned in the opposite direction so as not to spook Harry.

We swam at a slow pace, peering into all the nooks in the various colored corals. I was impressed with Liam's ability to control his buoyancy and his breathing. He was as good as a pro.

The site was teeming with sea life today, and I photographed it all. We saw two Queen Angel fish swimming back and forth in a grotto in the coral, looking as majestic as their name implied. A school of purple tang floated nearby. Every few kicks, we turned to look out into the blue, and we saw a hammerhead shark swimming far below us. Liam's eyes behind his mask sparkled at the sight. He reached out to take my hand, and we finished our survey of the reef hand in hand. We both hit the turnaround point on air at the same time, so we headed back to the top of the reef, still holding hands.

Keeping my gaze down and in front of me, I scanned the horizon and the sandy bottom for interesting sea life, just letting the ocean currents carry me along. I knew this site so intimately there was no danger I would ever get lost.

I spotted Harry and pointed him out to Liam. We both spread our arms and turned from a streamlined horizontal stance to a vertical position that provided more resistance to the slight current, waggling our fins just enough to stay suspended in the water about ten feet above the bottom and far enough away from Harry that we wouldn't frighten him.

I could sense Harry's caution, his hooded eyes following our every move. I exhaled, and through the glittering cloud of bubbles, I saw him rise out of the sand and glide away. I switched my camera to video mode to film him.

Behind him, a dark shadow rose over the rim of the reef's

drop off. When I realized it was a hammerhead shark, I pulled Liam with me and sank to the bottom to avoid attracting the shark's attention. I kept filming, and we both watched him. I was enraptured by his grace and power while marveling at his ungainly head.

For a few more seconds, Harry flew through the water, seeming to be unaware of the looming danger behind him. When at last he recognized the threat, he swam an evasive zigzag pattern.

The shark swished his powerful tail once and caught up to Harry. In two bites, Harry was gone. The hammerhead slipped back over the reef into the blue haze. I'd filmed the whole thing.

But after the awful scene, my breath came in ragged gasps and tears fogged my mask. I couldn't stay here. I turned to shore and Liam followed. When we reached the shallows, I pulled off my fins and trudged across the beach.

Though it was inadvertent, the weight of responsibility for Harry's demise fell to me. Harry had left his sandy sanctuary to put distance between us. That left him vulnerable when the shark cruised by. I'd never wanted any harm to come to him, yet he was gone all the same.

It was a constant concern for wildlife observers, and one reason many oceanographers were turning to freediving to interact with wild creatures. These naturalists weren't freediving in stylized events like those Ray had competed in, but they chose to accept the risks of diving in mid-ocean without air tanks to make the interactions less stressful for the sea life. Even if we didn't mean to interfere, the fact that we were an unnatural part of the environment still meant we changed the denizen's behaviors despite our benign intentions.

My emotions were roiling. I cried for my friend Harry, who died right in front of me. But even through my sorrow, I couldn't help but feel excited about how this piece of film would create a dramatic ending to my short documentary. I hated myself for thinking it, but instead of a short puff piece to play in RIO's lobby, now the film might even be prizeworthy. Special. Unique. Like Harry had been.

On shore, Liam removed his BCD. "I'm sorry about what happened to Harry, but thank you for diving with me," he said. "What an incredible dive. No wonder this site is your favorite. The coral is unspoiled, and the wall is mind-blowing."

"I liked diving with you too." I glanced at the time on my dive computer. "I'd hoped we'd have time for a second dive, but I need to get to work. Maybe we can do it again another day?"

"Name the day. I'll be here." He rested a hand on my shoulder while he removed his fins, then offered me his shoulder so I could do the same.

CHAPTER TWENTY-FOUR

THAT NIGHT, my dinner was a peanut butter sandwich eaten in front of my computer while going through the footage I had taken covering the weeks of Ray's training. The doorbell broke my concentration just as I was ready to start marking the best frames. I sighed with exasperation, knowing I would have to start all over again to reclaim my vision of the key segment. I popped the last bite of sandwich in my mouth and got up to open the door.

When I saw who was standing on my welcome mat, I slammed it shut and slid the deadbolt home.

"Fin, let me in. I want to talk to you."

"Go away, Alec. What you want is not my problem, and I'm working." I went back to my office, but Alec didn't give up. He rang the bell over and over again. Next my cellphone rang. I shut it off. After it became clear he wasn't going away unless I let him have his say, I opened the door. "What?"

"Can I come in?" he asked. I was surprised he hadn't fled at the anger in my voice.

"No. Go around to the back. I don't want you in my

house." I shut and locked the door again before going through the house to the glass doors that opened into my back yard. I had a small table with an umbrella and two chairs on the patio. On the table I'd placed two citronella candles in glass jars to keep the mosquitos away. A small pot of vibrant pink hibiscus in full flower stood nearby. It was a relaxing space, but I seldom invited anyone to join me there. Alec came through the gate at the same moment I sat in one of the chairs. "What was important enough you had to bug me while I'm trying to work?"

He sat beside me. "I want to apologize for what I did to you. I knew it was wrong when I let *Your World* think I'd taken the shot of Maddy and the great white."

"The lie paid off for you though. You're a big name now. You got what you wanted."

He was quiet for a moment. "No, I got what I thought I wanted, but at the cost of losing the most valuable thing I already had. Because of that stunt I lost the one person in the world I care about."

"Yep. Glad we're clear on that. You can go now." I rose to go back inside.

"Wait, Fin. I'll call Carl and tell him we were both shooting that day, and you deserve at least partial credit for the shot."

"Liar. You weren't even on the boat that day." I couldn't believe he thought this pallid gesture counted as a full apology.

He put a hand on my arm to hold me there. His face was red, and his lips were tight. He inhaled deeply before speaking. "Okay. Okay. I know I wasn't there when you took the shot. Would it make a difference if I tell him you're the sole creator? They're going to print a correction either way. Might as well be the whole truth. My career will be in the toilet now no matter what the retraction says." He glared at me, like this whole fiasco was my fault.

"I'm busy. I need to finish..." I gestured to my house, hoping he would take the hint and go.

He didn't. "I have a surprise for you," he said.

"Don't like surprises, and I'm busy."

"I've already been in touch with Carl. I told him about the mix-up with the photos. How your pix and mine were in the same portfolio. I told him he needed to make it right."

"I see. How nice of you to tell the truth. Or at least your version of it. Go on," I said, trying hard not to yell at him. My sarcasm didn't penetrate his thick ego.

"So, anyway. Good news. They're going to print a correction and offer you a multi-page spread of your own work. This could be big. Really big."

"That is big. And you did this for me? You came forward all on your own?" I was giving him the opportunity to tell the whole truth, although the Alec I knew seemed constitutionally incapable of truth telling.

He nodded. "That's right. And I'm willing to help you if you need it. Working with those sophisticated publishers can be complicated. You might want a little help from someone who's already been through it."

I wanted to smash the smug smile off his face. "Thanks, Alec. But I think I'll be fine."

"Okay. Do you want me to go with you to New York? The big city can be scary for a girl from the islands."

"Again, I'm good. I'm not naive. You forget I've traveled all over the world and I've been negotiating contracts for the Institute since I was eighteen. I'm fine."

He looked crestfallen. "Okay then. If you're sure..."

"Oh, I'm very sure. No question I'll be fine without you."

"Fin, I tanked my career for you. The least you could do is throw me a bone here."

"If your career is tanked, it's your own fault. You never should have stolen my work and claimed it as your own..."

"I didn't steal your work. It was an honest mistake..."

"Sure. An honest mistake you had ample time to correct before the issue hit the stands. My photo was the best one in that spread, and you knew it. That's why you didn't confess..."

"We can work this out if..."

"It's no longer a problem. Ray made sure of that."

He paused. "You knew?"

I nodded. "Goodbye."

"Wait," he said. "I'm sorry. I still love you. Can't we..."

"No, we can't."

He looked at me from under his long eyelashes, and his blue eyes held a sad and wounded expression. Too bad I'd learned long ago he could call up that remorseful look at will.

"I don't want to talk about this with you anymore. If you told Duchette about what you did, it was because you had no other choice."

"You're wrong. That's part of the reason, sure. But the most important reason I told him is because I want a chance for us to be together again. Doesn't this change how you feel about me?" His voice was a soft caress.

I resisted his pull. "No. This doesn't change anything between us. Now, go away." I felt nothing but anger and a little pity for Alec. He was learning a hard lesson, and the worst of it hadn't started yet. Wait until word got around the industry about what he'd done. His career would be toast.

"Won't you please give me another chance? I promise I'll never do anything like this again." He put on his sorrowful face.

I recognized that face from when we were married. I couldn't believe he thought this half-baked attempt at amends would win me back, but I realized I was finally free of his spell.

"Nope. You already blew your last chance. Good night,

Alec." I went inside, leaving him alone in the dusk. A few seconds later, I heard a crash, followed by another crash, and the slamming of the gate. I peeked out the door and saw that Alec had thrown the citronella candles at the fence, breaking the glass containers, leaving the shards strewn across my yard.

After I heard his car leave, I went outside to clean up the mess. I picked up the slivers of glass, thinking about how Alec's rages had been a daily occurrence in our marriage. I'd always had to walk a fine line between keeping him happy and being true to my own needs. It surprised me to realize Alec had done me a favor by stealing my work, because it'd made me angry enough to end our toxic relationship. A couple of citronella candles was a small price to pay for the realization that at last, I was over him.

CHAPTER TWENTY-FIVE

I WAS in the lab with Rosie when Lily came by after her discharge from the infirmary. "Hello, stranger," she said. "What are you doing?"

By now I was growing used to Lily's mercurial mood changes, so I grinned a welcome at her. "This is Rosie. She's the subject of the research for my thesis and the smartest octopus you can imagine. I adore her."

"Gosh, she's beautiful. But how do you know she's smart?" said Lily, rapping hard on the aquarium glass.

Rosie turned an angry black color at the noise.

"Please don't bang on the glass like that. It scares her, even more so if she doesn't know you." I moved Lily's hand away from the aquarium. "And she's astonishing. Let me show you."

Because Rosie is one of my favorite topics, I started explaining my research to Lily. After a few minutes I noticed her eyes glazing over, so I wrapped up fast. Then I had another idea. "Hey, are you free for lunch? I think Oliver is working filling tanks today, but maybe the three of us can go out together? My treat."

"Outstanding," she said. "I'd love it, and I'm sure he would too. Can you break away now?'

I went back to my office for my wallet and keys, then we went by the tank filling station to pick up Oliver. He locked the door to the tank shed and hung the 'Gone to Lunch' sign on the door. "Where we going?" he asked his sister.

"It's up to Fin," she said. "She's buying."

"How about Piñata?" I asked. "It's a little touristy, but you can't say you've experienced Grand Cayman until you've eaten there at least once."

"Sounds good to me," Oliver said.

Lily shrugged. "Sure. Whatever."

We piled into my Prius for the drive downtown. Because Piñata is located near the port where the cruise ships dock, the place can be a madhouse when the ships' passengers all come ashore at once. But there were no boats in port and it was still early for lunch. I figured we'd be fine. We paused inside the entry to let our eyes adjust to the dimness.

"Fin, lovely to see you. It's been a while since you've been in." Jeremy, the host, was an old friend of Alec's. "What can I do for you?"

"Hi, Jeremy. I need a table for three."

"I can do that." He grabbed some menus and led us to a table along the railing, under the awning, and overlooking the tranquil Caribbean. "This work?"

"Perfect," I said. "By the way, this is my sister Lily and my brother Oliver." Lily and Oliver both blinked when I introduced them as my siblings, but neither commented about it.

"PLEASED TO MEET YOU BOTH," Jeremy said without missing a beat. The news about Ray's kids must be common knowledge now.

Since Oliver and I both had to go back to work this afternoon, we ordered soft drinks to have with our burgers. Lily ordered a mudslide with hers.

She asked me what it'd been like to grow up living on the *Omega* half the year and on a tropical island the rest of the time. I told them about my childhood, and funny stories about Ray, Gus, and Stewie and the crazy antics they pulled. About the myth of Ray's fabled treasure, the Queen's Tiara, and how he always denied the stories were true. Tales of how Ray taught me to swim and dive and how patient and kind he'd been with me. I was growing misty-eyed at the sweet memories.

The twins seemed to be loving the stories as much as I was enjoying sharing them, so it was a shock when Oliver interrupted me just after Jeremy delivered our food.

"You stole my father, and now you're sitting here telling stories and gloating about it. That's mean, even for you." His face was red with anger. I was confused by the change in his demeanor. He'd been laughing a few moments before launching his verbal attack.

"I'm sorry, Oliver. I didn't mean to hurt you. I thought you were enjoying hearing about your father's life, that's all."

"Bragging about it, you mean. All about how much he loved you and how good he was to you. How do you think that makes us feel?" Oliver crumpled his napkin and threw it down on the table. Lily reached over and patted his arm. I noticed a tear rolling down her cheek.

I was so upset I could barely breathe "I wasn't bragging. I thought you'd like to..."

"Cut it out, will you? You think we like hearing stories about what a good father Ray was to you when he couldn't be bothered to see his real family? Ever. Not even once in our whole lives." His voice cracked. After taking a ragged breath, he gulped his soda. "You're just rubbing it in, trying to make us feel bad because our father loved you more than he loved his real kids." He pushed back his chair and rose.

"Ray didn't know you existed until just a little while ago. If anyone is to blame for you missing out on time with him, it would be your mother. She never told him."

"Don't you talk about my mother."

Lily stood beside him. "You honestly thought we would enjoy hearing about what a good father we missed out on, right, Fin?" She glared at me before turning back to Oliver. "Some people are clueless about other people's feelings. You can't hold it against them. It's not malicious. They don't see." Her eyes glittered and her voice dripped malice. She was deliberately turning the knife in Oliver's heart, and making me out to be too self-absorbed to notice his pain.

My face reddened with guilty embarrassment. I hadn't meant to hurt them. Maybe Lily was right and I was clueless. It wouldn't be the first time I'd missed social cues that were obvious to other people. I usually blamed my isolated upbringing when it happened, and sometimes I was blind to other people's feelings and had no idea how to have a conversation with people who didn't know me well.

Lily slung her purse over her shoulder. "Thanks for lunch. We'll grab a cab." They left their food untouched and stormed out of the restaurant.

Jeremy hurried over, a look of concern on his face. "Everything good, luv? Was something wrong with the food?"

I shook my head. "Everything's fine, Jeremy. Just a little family misunderstanding."

After Jeremy returned my credit card, I left Piñata. When I hit the bright sunlight on the sidewalk outside, it took a moment for my eyes to adjust. I jumped with surprise at a soft touch on my arm.

"Can we talk?" It was Lily. She looked contrite. "I didn't mean to spoil lunch."

"Didn't you go home with Oliver?"

"No, why would you think I left? I put him in a cab," she said. "I wanted to send Oliver home, that's all. Oliver's more sensitive than he seems on the surface. Our mother had always said our father died before we were born. It hit him hard when she told us our father was alive. Oliver was keen on getting to know his father, and it hurt him when he found out Ray had a whole other family. I thought he was over it, but, well...I guess not." She bit her lip. "Can we still have lunch? I'd like to hear more about my dad."

I nodded and we hurried back into the restaurant just in time to see Jeremy dropping our food in the trash. "Too late."

"No problem. We can reorder or go somewhere else. My treat this time," she said.

"We'll split it. And you can tell me more about what it was like growing up in a big city. Deal?"

Jeremy seated us at the same table out on the deck again. We ordered food, and Lily asked for another mudslide. We started talking, mostly about Lily's childhood this time.

She was funny, witty, and well-read. We'd finished discussing the summer's blockbuster beach read and we were still only halfway through our salads.

Jeremy kept replenishing our drinks, and we were having so much fun the afternoon flew by without my noticing. It was a shock when I caught a glimpse of my watch and realized how late it was. "Oh my gosh. It's after four. I should have been back to work hours ago."

"You needed the break," she said. "Life's been hard. Anyway, what good is being the boss if you can't take an afternoon off to enjoy paradise?"

"But I'm not the boss. I'm an employee like everyone else at RIO. I have to pull my own weight."

"Oh, please," she said, her voice cold. "Maybe you'd like to believe that, but it's not true. Head of marketing. Chief photographer. Marine biologist. Researcher. Do you think you'd have the job you do now if your mother wasn't RIO's founder?"

We'd been getting along well enough that the attack was unexpected. I didn't recognize the change in emotional temperature for a few seconds, but when I realized she was serious, my happy smile wilted.

Before I could respond, Lily's face turned a nasty shade of green. She clapped a hand over her mouth and raced away from the table, knocking over her chair as she left.

I picked up her chair, threw some money down to cover the bill, and followed her out. I found her standing over one of the restaurant's outdoor trash barrels still wiping her mouth with the back of her hand. It was clear she'd been sick.

I took a couple of tissues out of my purse and passed them to her before going back inside to get her some water. When I gave her the icy bottle, tears appeared in her deep brown eyes.

"I'm sorry, Fin. I didn't mean what I said. Everybody knows how talented you are. I don't know what got into me."

"I do," I said. "Too many mudslides. Let's forget it ever happened and call it a day."

She nodded and followed me to my car.

A few minutes later I pulled up in front of the Ritz.

Liam opened my door. "Welcome back to the Ritz, Miss Fleming. Miss Russo. Can I help you ladies with anything?" he asked.

"Just dropping Lily off," I said. "Will you see she gets to her room, Liam?" I handed him a few bills for taking care of her, hoping she wouldn't get sick on him.

He handed me back the cash. "Thank you, but Mr. Fleming takes care of all the tips for his family and guests. This way please, Miss Russo." He took her elbow and walked her through the glass doors.

CHAPTER TWENTY-SIX

A FEW DAYS later I was scheduled to work with the twins to be sure they were ready for their roles during Ray's dives. After our disaster of a lunch, I wasn't sure they'd show up, but they arrived at RIO's classroom a full five minutes early. They were all smiles. My head was spinning from their continual mood changes, but I buckled down to work as soon as they took their seats.

I explained how critical the timing of everyone's dive was. Ray and Alec both had very tight constraints on their ability to stay underwater—Ray because he wouldn't be breathing at all during his dive, and Alec because he would be breathing compressed gases at great depth. When I questioned them, they proved they understood the concepts.

Next, I drew a diagram on the classroom's white board that showed where everyone would be positioned during the dive. Lily would be stationed at thirty feet and Oliver at sixty feet. Alec would be at the bottom of the dive trajectory at 330 feet. I would start at fifteen feet to film the twin's entry, then hover there until Ray started his dive. I'd follow Ray to 100 feet so I could film him, and on his return, I would pick him up on camera again as soon as he was visible. One and a half minutes after Ray started his dive, Stewie would dive to 200 feet, and wait for Ray so he could follow him back to the surface. As Ray passed the twins on the way up, they would start their own ascents beside him. Because they were breathing compressed air from their scuba tanks, they'd do a safety stop at fifteen feet while Ray would go straight to the surface. I would stay deeper below to film their ascents before beginning my own.

The twins said they understood their roles. When I quizzed them, they knew where they were supposed to be during all points of the dive, and they grasped the need for pinpoint timing. We had crossed one hurdle. Now for the open water training.

I led them onto one of RIO's Zodiacs for the practice dives. We went to the same location where Ray would be diving, and I moored the boat. I had each twin gear up and enter the water, but I asked them not to descend until I had checked their weights.

To check for proper weighting, a scuba diver stays at the surface with a full tank and no air in their buoyancy control device. If the diver sinks, they are wearing too much weight. If the diver's head is fully out of the water, they aren't wearing enough.

I carefully added and removed weights a pound at a time until each of the twins was weighted properly. Then we dove, so they could become familiar with the site and accustomed to the new weights they carried.

We would repeat the entire sequence—classroom lecture, weight calibration, and site familiarization—every day for the two weeks until Ray's dive day to be certain they were ready. But so far, so good.

CHAPTER TWENTY-SEVEN

THE NEXT TWO weeks passed in a frenzy of training and preparation, but at last the big day arrived. We would be filming Ray's dive later in the morning, and the RIO building was hopping. Since Ray needed to rest and relax for the deep apnea dive later, Maddy had recruited me to take his place as co-host.

About fifty guests thronged RIO's huge lobby. Every person here had paid at least $15,000 a ticket, even more if they'd also attended the dinner last night. In exchange for their donations, RIO had given everyone a bucket hat, a long-sleeved tee-shirt with built-in sun protection, a small bottle of sunblock, and a personalized insulated steel mug in a tote bag. Each item was adorned with RIO's logo and SOS: *Save Our Seas*, the title of the documentary.

Except for Ray, RIO's whole staff was on hand, mingling with the people who'd paid big bucks to be on the *Omega* during Ray's exhibition dive. Stewie, Gus, and Theresa were eating breakfast at a corner table. Gus still looked pale and shaky, but Theresa was taking good care of him. Stewie was scarfing down a massive plate of pastries and bacon. I hoped his meal didn't weigh him down. He'd need to be alert and on top of his game if anything happened during Ray's dive.

Newton was here too, with Cara Flores, Oliver, and Lily. The twins would be diving with us later, but for now, they were gawking at all the celebrities. I assumed Cara was here to see the twins dive—and I knew Newton was here because he'd made a very big donation.

Cara's white dress clung to her curves, and the light color complemented her dark hair and eyes. Her shoes were white open-toed stilettos. She carried a hot pink handbag that matched her lipstick and nail polish. Her only jewelry was the gold coin necklace like my mother's.

I hoped Cara's necklace was a knockoff. Maddy's coin was rumored to be part of the loot from Ray's fabled sunken treasure, the Queen's Tiara. If Cara's had also come from Ray's treasure, there might be unplanned fireworks on today's program.

We were projecting a series of photos on the big screen behind the stage. The attendees oohed and aahed over the brilliant colors and exotic sea life we'd captured on film. Most of the photos had my byline in the lower right corner, although a few had credits reading Alec Stone or Madelyn Russo. The shot of my mother facing down the great white was in the mix, and of course, my name was on it. Take that, Alec.

Maddy smiled as she strolled across the stage to begin her speech. She looked stunning in a turquoise sheath dress that brought out the unique color of her eyes. Her white-blonde hair was coiled in a complex twist at the back of her neck. She wore a string of pearls, her gold coin necklace, and simple leather sandals that showed off her pedicure and the shark fin tattoo on her instep. Her favorite white gold Omega Seamaster dive watch was on her wrist.

The room lights dimmed, and she began to speak. "Here at RIO, we don't think there's anything more important to future generations than ensuring the Earth's oceans can continue to support their role in the environment. I assume you're all here because you too love the sea and recognize the importance of clean oceans to the health of our world."

As Maddy spoke, the images behind her switched from healthy happy sea life to a grimmer theme. It started with a shot of once-vibrant coral reefs now bleached and dying. Then a giant pile of trash floating across the Pacific. A banana peel and a sandwich wrapper floating in the water under a dock. Coils of fishing line wrapped around a double-crested cormorant's wings. A slick of oil spreading across waves. Uprooted mangroves along a tropical coastland.

Each picture told a story of greed, apathy, and sorrow. A story of death. The coming death of the ocean, and unless something changed, the death of the Earth and everyone on it.

While the images flashed behind her, Maddy talked about where the shots had been taken, and what the RIO team was doing to bring the ocean back to health. Her presentation was powerful, and I was proud of her. After she finished, people thronged around her to ask questions, make additional donations, or just to congratulate her. When it was time to leave for the *Omega*, she clapped her hands in the air. "Let's head out to the dive site. If you look on the back of your nametags, you'll see whether you're scheduled to be on *RIO One* or *RIO Two* for the trip out. I'll escort group one, and Fin will take group two."

There were a few moments of confusion while people sorted themselves out, then we rushed down the crushed shell path to the dock where *RIO One* and *RIO Two* waited. We'd polished the boats until they gleamed. Red, white, and blue streamers attached to their handrails waved in the soft breeze.

"Permission to come aboard, Captain." Madelyn slipped off her sandals.

I was surprised when Vincent, one of RIO's senior staff members, helped Maddy aboard. I'd thought Gus would be piloting this boat.

Once Maddy was beside him, Vincent helped the guests board. Most people who lived on the islands were familiar with boating, and they automatically removed their street shoes before boarding. When my father and Cara stepped aboard with their shoes on, Vincent pointed to a rack near the ladder to the bridge. "Sorry. No shoes on the boat. They mar the deck. You can stow them over there."

When Newton slipped off his shoes, I noticed he had a small tattoo of a shark's fin on his instep, identical to my mother's tattoo. I wondered if they'd gotten those tattoos together, right after I was born, way back when they were still married.

The tattoo told me he'd loved me back then. He claimed he still did, but I couldn't reconcile his words with the years of neglect. Maybe someday I'd understand why he'd stayed away all that time.

While the guests were boarding *RIO One*, Theresa tapped me on the shoulder. "Can we talk?" She took my arm and guided me to a quiet spot away from the throng of people waiting to board.

"What's up? And where's Gus?" I said when we'd moved far enough away to have a little privacy.

Theresa bit her lip. "Gus had a dizzy spell, so I sent him to the infirmary and asked Vincent to take his place."

"Thanks for taking care of that. Is Gus okay?" I asked

"He'll be fine. But I thought I should warn you. Stewie isn't coming today. He won't be diving with Ray."

"What? We paid him a lot of money to dive today. What happened?"

"He said Ray asked him not to come because he wants to dive alone, with just the twins as backup. I wanted you to know before you got to the *Omega*."

"When did you find this out?"

"This morning at breakfast. Stewie left during your mother's talk. And before you ask, I don't know where he is."

"What am I supposed to do now? Ray shouldn't be diving with just the twins. I can't believe he'd do this. We had a deal."

Theresa shrugged. "I couldn't stop him, but I thought you should know before you got out there. At least now you have a little time to think of another way to handle the dive." She walked away and boarded *RIO One*.

When everyone had found a seat on his boat, Vincent tipped his hat to the people in my group who were still waiting on the dock for the next launch to pull up. "See you there," he said. Then he was gone, leaving a spray of shining droplets glistening in the sun.

I ushered my donors to the *RIO Two*. I didn't see anyone on deck waiting to greet us, and the flying bridge was empty. I was furious at Ray and Stewie.

Stewie was supposed to be the captain, but now that he'd gone AWOL, I didn't know who would be handling the boat. In a pinch, I could do it, but I was angry that one more task was now on my plate. We couldn't leave our guests waiting in the hot sun on the dock for long. I was just about to climb up to the bridge when Alec emerged from the hold, wiping a wrench on an oily rag.

I didn't like being on a boat with Alec, especially after our last encounter, but we were shorthanded. "What are you doing here?" I hissed. "And do you know where Stewie is?"

"He asked me to cover for him. I assumed he was going with Ray on the *Maddy*." He put the wrench down.

There was nothing I could do about Stewie now, but I

wasn't happy with Alec either. He should have let me know about Stewie right away. Gesturing behind me to where the guests were lined up waiting, I said, "You ready for us?"

He hurried past me to welcome them, helping everyone aboard with a smile. He showed them where to stow their shoes and find seats. When the last guest was on the boat, Alec climbed nimbly to the flying bridge and started the engines. We glided away from the dock like the ocean was made of glass. I had to give him credit. He'd always been an accomplished boat captain.

The *Omega* floated above the reef at the planned dive site. The cluster of boats looked like a scene out of *Waterworld*, with *Omega* playing the starring role. Ray would be diving from the *Maddy*, and he'd moored it beside the *Omega*.

Alec idled his launch behind the *RIO One* until all its passengers had transferred to the larger boat. When Vincent pulled away, Alec tied up in his place, and we helped our guests join the party. Most people stayed on the *Omega*'s main deck enjoying the sun and salt air while noshing on snacks and drinks from the trays passed by the waitstaff.

Despite being over 220 feet in length, the *Omega*'s deck was cramped with the caterers, the guests, the dive team, all our usual underwater exploration equipment, plus the winch we'd installed to manage Ray's guide rope. We'd also added new sonar capable of tracking Ray's dive, but we'd decided not to use it today

Since watching a freedive is an odd combination of boredom and excruciating tension, we hoped not knowing how Ray's dive was progressing would make the live show more dramatic. From the surface, it's impossible to see anything going on at depth. As each second ticks by, the tension ratchets up a notch. The three to five minutes of a dive feel like years to those watching and wondering when—or even if—the diver will make it back. Now I was rethinking my decision not to use the sonar, but there was no one to monitor it now anyway, since we were so shorthanded.

We'd put up a small, gated barrier around the winch to keep people from tampering with the controls. Gus had been supposed to stand guard to prevent people from touching the controls and explain how everything worked. Vincent couldn't do it. He was the *Omega*'s captain. But with no one to stop them, a trio of people stood inside the gated area, playing with the switches like they were at an interactive exhibit in a museum.

That could be dangerous for Ray, so I went below to Maddy's onboard office and made signs reading 'Do Not Touch' and 'Do Not Enter.' I used duct tape to attach them to the barrier's gate and the winch's control panel. Before going back to my hosting duties, I reset the depth control for the planned 330 feet.

When everyone had something to eat or drink, Maddy split the guests into smaller groups for a tour of the *Omega*. She took the big-money donors below to see the captain's quarters. Alec took his group to the bridge, and Vincent headed to the engine room. My group—Newton, Cara, and a few island dignitaries—started our tour at the gated area around the winch.

I described how the equipment worked to raise and lower the plate that would mark the target depth for Ray's dive, and how he would need to detach a depth verification tag from the plate and bring it back to the surface with him. Everyone had a lot of questions for me. Most of them were about how freedivers could hold their breath for so long.

I told them about the mammalian dive reflex and its effect on slowing metabolism. "But the reflex is only part of the reason Ray can do this. The rest is training and practice. It takes an unbelievable amount of preparation, dedication, and discipline to be good at deep breathhold diving."

Half an hour later, I'd finished leading my tour when I noticed with exasperation that the gate to the winch was open and several people were in the area. I saw the governor, two bartenders, my mother, three financiers from big Cayman Island banks, Lily, several donors whose names I didn't know, Alec, Oliver, the Cayman Islands Police Superintendent, Newton, Theresa, and Cara in the crowd. It seemed the only two people within a nautical mile who hadn't gone in there were Ray and me. I shooed them all away and re-verified the depth setting.

I went in search of Vincent, to ask if he could assign a crew member to watch the winch. He agreed to send someone over right away. I didn't relax until I saw a member of the crew standing near the gate.

A few minutes later I was chatting with the governor when Alec caught my eye and pointed to his watch. It was time to start the show.

I rounded up the twins and joined him in the prep area to get ready for our part in filming the dive. As we began our preparations, Gus and Lily's accidents were heavy on my mind. Diving is safe if you obey the rules and take the proper precautions. Today, the responsibility for all those safeguards rested on my shoulders.

I swallowed my anger at Stewie and called everyone into a huddle. I explained that Stewie would not be diving with us today, but that everyone else should continue with their original assignments. Even though we weren't expecting anything to happen, I cautioned them to be vigilant.

Alec and I wiggled into our dive suits. Since down deep the water is much colder than it is near the surface where I'd be, he needed more insulation, so his suit was much thicker and heavier than the colorful Lycra skins the twins and I wore.

Each diver had a vital role in the event, and the entire plan revolved around Ray and Alec, who had the most complex and dangerous assignments. I'd set up each dive plan to ensure we could complete our missions within the technical limitations and precision timing required by Alec's and Ray's dives. It was like a dance, with every move choreographed to a specific beat.

Next to Ray's, the timing of Alec's dive was most critical. The blend of air diluted with helium he'd be breathing allowed him to dive deeper and longer than he could on regular air, but the extreme depth would still limit his bottom time to a mere few minutes. The schedule called for Alec to be the first one in the water so he could be in position early—just not too early, because he had to be able to be there filming when Ray arrived.

Ray, the only person associated with the documentary not on the *Omega*, was waiting alone in the cabin of the *Maddy*. It was a given that he had to stay calm and relaxed to control his body's oxygen consumption and to help make his single precious breath of air last as long as possible once the dive began. Nothing could be allowed to interfere with his prep.

Ray would be making the entire dive on that single breath of air, with no breathing equipment or even dive fins to help him swim. The event would have to move fast once it began. We had no room for error.

Ray's dive would last four to five minutes. Once Ray began to ascend, Alec would begin his own much slower return. Alec, breathing compressed gases, would have to make a series of decompression safety stops or risk triggering an embolism. Ray wouldn't be breathing at all, so he could ascend faster, and without stopping for decompression.

As part of the preparations for his dive, Alec had already checked the proportions of the mixed gases in his tanks, but I double checked to make sure everything was perfect. Even a small variance in the mix could be dangerous for him. I might not love Alec anymore, but I didn't want anything bad to happen to him.

Satisfied all the gas blends were correct, I helped Alec into the heavy double tank setup on his buoyancy control device. Then I attached tanks of pure oxygen and NITROX to the side mounts.

Last, I clipped a 'pony bottle' of regular air to a D-ring on the front of his BCD. Altogether, Alec was carrying about 250 pounds of tanks. He shuffled over to the edge of the dive platform where I steadied him while he put on his fins. He made a giant stride entry and gave me the okay sign before starting his lonely descent.

Before I made my own entry, I rushed over to the winch to check the depth. It was still set for 100 meters—330 feet. The sailor stood at his post near the gate. I'd never met him before, but I smiled and thanked him for watching the winch while I double taped the 'Do Not Touch' sign back over the controls and returned to the dive area in the stern of the boat.

While I'd been helping Alec and checking the winch, Lily and Oliver had donned their diveskins, and now they were helping each other into their buoyancy control devices. When they finished, they walked to the dive platform with their fins.

I went over to give them a few last-minute pointers. "Remember what I told you. Don't take your eyes off Ray and pay attention to how long he's under water." Once he's out of sight, stay focused on the rope. That's where he'll reappear, and bang on your tank to get my attention if you think there's a problem."

Oliver scowled at me. "Quit ragging on us, will ya? How many times are you going to repeat that crap? We've got it."

Lily patted his arm. "Fin's just doing her job. We all want Ray to get back safely."

I smiled at her, grateful for her intervention with the more volatile Oliver. I needed to start my dive, but before I entered the water, I checked their tanks to be sure they'd remembered to turn on the flow of air.

Oliver scowled when he realized he'd forgotten to turn his air on again.

"Hey, it happens. That's why we double check everything. See you below."

I didn't want to upset Oliver just before the dive, so I tried to sound calm. Inside, I was seething. This was another rookie mistake on Oliver's part.

The plan called for me to go in after Alec so I could film the twins' entry. Ray had said it was a super idea, and my suggestion was the only reason he'd agreed to have Stewie dive with him. I was livid he'd reneged on our deal. But Ray was experienced and well prepared. Nothing would go wrong.

The twins stood aside while I shuffled to the edge of the dive platform to make my entry. Neither offered me a steadying arm, so I held onto the boat's gunwale while I put on my own BCD and fins. I took a big step off the boat's edge. As soon as I was in the water, my stress faded away. I was at peace.

For me, breathing underwater is as natural as it is on land. I can use my breathing to perfectly control my depth and buoyancy. I exhaled and descended until I hovered motionless at exactly fifteen feet below the ocean's surface. I was at least a mile and a half above the ocean floor.

The twins were late making their entries. I was fuming at the delay. They'd been ready to dive when I went in, so there could be no reason for them not to have been in the water on time. I'd been in position for ten minutes, and we had used up most of the safety margin I'd built into Alec's dive time.

I was about to surface to find out what the problem could be when Lily and Oliver made their shaky giant-stride entries off *Omega's* dive platform. What could they have been doing that was so important they would risk the whole dive for it? They knew the timing of everybody's entry into the water was crucial, yet they'd stayed on the *Omega* long after they should have been at their posts. They gave the okay sign as they passed me on their way to their assigned depths.

Lily seemed to be having trouble managing her buoyancy and keeping to her assigned position. The rhythm of the bubbles from her regulator told me she was breathing too fast. I knew just by looking at her she was wearing the wrong amount of weight, although I'd calibrated it with her just yesterday. Together, the two problems were making it hard for her to stay in place. She kept bobbing up and down with each breath. Instead of holding a stable position, she was swimming in circles around the boat to try to stay close to the right depth. Even worse, more than half the time her back was turned to Ray's planned travel line.

Oliver wasn't paying attention either. He was hovering over the drop off, arms spread wide like a kid pretending to be an airplane and staring out at the blue haze, his gaze also turned away from Ray's guide rope.

It's time for Ray's entry. When I look up, the golden Caymanian sunlight cast a flickering glow around the *Maddy's* dive platform. Ray is standing on the edge of the *Maddy's* dive platform, staring at the water, ignoring everything around him, a calm center in the flurry of activity. He sits down on the edge of the dive platform, dangling his feet in the water. He buckled the flexible weight around his neck. Then I saw him remove his dive watch and place it on the bench under the gunwales.

I was annoyed. We had discussed his wearing the watch several times, and we always came down on the side of safety over appearances. Ray wanted to look sleek. I wanted him to be safe. It looks like Ray figured how to get his own way after all.

Relax, Fin, I told myself. *Everything will be fine. All he has to do is swim and stay parallel to the rope.*

The visibility is super for filming—probably a couple of hundred feet horizontally, but of course, nowhere near that looking straight down. It's so clear I can see the *Omega*'s crew and all the documentary donors waving and jumping around trying to get Ray's attention so they can get a picture. Ray has the discipline to ignore them, which is good, because he can't afford to get excited or nervous. He needs to keep his metabolism low to make optimum use of every molecule of air he can pack into his lungs.

Ray pulls on his low-volume freediving goggles and slides into the water. I watch him as he tightens the aluminum nose clamp that makes it easier to equalize the pressure in his ears. Then he eases back, floating on his back, sipping air, and packing it into the deepest recesses of his lungs. His chest swells as he takes one final deep breath and jackknifes under the crystalline water.

I took a deep breath through my regulator and forced myself to relax. It was a perfect day for the dive. In just a few seconds, depending on his swimming speed, Ray would be spending over four minutes underwater without breathing.

CHAPTER TWENTY-EIGHT

AN AGONIZING TWO minutes after he'd disappeared, Ray emerged from the depths on his way back to the surface. He was swimming fast, his powerful arms and legs working hard to propel him upward against the pull of the sea.

Ray's two safety divers were not watching his ascent. Lily had joined her brother over the drop off, and they were both looking out at the blue forever, gawking at the beauty of the Cayman waters as though they'd never been diving before.

I swallowed my annoyance and swung the camera to follow Ray's trajectory. Everything would be okay. It had been a model dive.

Until it wasn't.

Ray was still twenty feet below me when his back arched, and his arms and legs began to twitch in the random, uncontrolled movements freedivers call the samba. His chest spasmed so hard it looked like he'd been kicked by a mule. He stopped swimming and his body began to sink. His eyes rolled back into his head. His mouth gaped open and a bubble of blood and air escaped.

As an experienced rescue diver, I didn't have to think about what to do. I reacted as Ray had trained me. When I reached him, I wrapped one arm around his torso, holding him close to my body. With my other hand, I shoved my primary air supply regulator into his mouth and cleared it of water before putting my octopus—my auxiliary breathing device—into my own mouth. Because Ray was having a seizure, it was hard to hold on to him, but I kicked my way to the surface holding him with one arm and keeping the regulator in his mouth with the other.

When I reached the *Omega*'s dive platform, two crew members helped pull Ray out of the water. Vincent herded the guests below deck away from the rescue efforts. The caterers served snacks and drinks to keep them occupied.

The *Omega*'s medical team placed Ray on a stretcher, propped on his left side in the recovery position. The doctor cleared Ray's airway and administered pure oxygen. When Ray didn't resume breathing right away, the team flipped him on his back and two of the medics started CPR. Vincent was on the radio begging for an air ambulance. The Medevac chopper wouldn't arrive any time soon, but *Omega* couldn't leave the area with Alec and the twins still below. He shook his head in frustration at the delay.

"We'll take him on the *Maddy*," Vincent shouted. "She's the fastest boat we have anyway." He jumped aboard and started the *Maddy*'s engines.

At the edge of the *Omega*'s dive platform, I pulled off my swim fins and slid them under a bench where they'd be out of the way. I clambered up the ladder and wiggled out of my buoyancy control device. I used the underwater siren located near the dive platform to sound the emergency recall alarm for the divers below before I threw myself across *Omega*'s deck to be with Ray. I was just in time to hear the medical team yell "Clear."

My mother stood near the low-slung gurney, her hand at her mouth. Her elegant face was tight and drawn, and she was biting her lip while tears seeped from her luminous blue eyes.

I took her right hand when we knelt beside Ray. Maddy grasped his limp hand in her left. Blood from his ruined lungs seeped out of his mouth. His eyes were wide and staring. His body convulsed, went still.

CHAPTER TWENTY-NINE

THE MEDICAL TEAM moved Ray's stretcher onto the *Maddy,* continuing to work on him even while the stretcher was on the move. One EMT held an oxygen mask to Ray's face while the other kept up chest compressions. The doctor monitored Ray's vitals with a stethoscope plugged into her ears. Maddy got aboard just before the boat sped off.

On the *Omega,* the rest of the crew huddled together. I crouched off to the side, alone with my guilt.

"Hey, I could use a little help here." Lily's petulant whine broke the stillness. "I want to get in on the celebration too, ya know." She tossed her fins in my direction. One stopped in the middle of the deck, while the other one skidded to a halt in front of me. I rose and trudged to the dive platform.

Lily stood on the ladder waiting for me to lift her heavy BCD with the attached tank off her shoulders. I carried it the few feet to the tank rack and slid it into an empty slot, then went back to spot her as she climbed aboard.

Seconds later, Oliver's flying fins almost struck me in the

face. "Oops. Sorry," he said, his expression telegraphing he was not sorry in the least. "Take my tank, will ya?" He turned his back to the ladder to give me easier access to the lift strap on the back of his buoyancy control device. I said nothing, just lifted the heavy bundle and slid the tank into the rack next to Lily's setup. I went back to my perch on the port side, leaving Oliver to climb aboard on his own.

"Aren't we having champagne? Ray said there would be a big celebration," Oliver asked. He and Lily stood together near the edge of the dive platform, looking at the somber crew.

"No celebration," I said. "There was an accident. You would know that if you'd been doing your jobs."

Oliver kicked the empty syringes across the deck. "Adrenalin. Epi. Somebody have an allergy attack?"

"What happened? Where's Ray?" Lily turned her head from side to side, craning her neck to look up at the bridge.

I turned to the stern, facing Lily and Oliver. "On his way to the hospital aboard the *Maddy*, but he wasn't breathing when they left.

Lily put her head on Oliver's chest and started sobbing, but Oliver clenched his fists. "You're lying. Where's my father?" He glared at me defiantly as he drew Lily to the bench along the *Omega*'s side.

I walked away without a word and sat near the dive platform to wait for Alec to surface. Because I had no idea how his ascent was going, I decided to use the sonar on the winch control panel to check his progress. Stuck on with a single layer of duct tape, my handmade sign was covering the controls, but I gasped when I lifted it and saw the depth gauge. It read 122 meters—four hundred feet—much deeper than Ray had planned and a full seventy feet deeper than his training had prepared him for. That meant he'd had to travel 140 feet more than he had intended. I blinked, but the numbers stayed the same. If Ray had gone that whole depth without training for it, it was no wonder his lungs had failed.

And I knew he had done the full depth. The verification tag from the metal plate was on the floor, mixed with the detritus from the resuscitation attempt.

I wrapped my arms around myself, trying to control my shivering. Praying that Ray had not been taken from me, I lifted my face to stare out at the sea. It looked tranquil and inviting, but I knew it was an alien environment, hostile to human life. Let your guard down for a second, and you never could know what might happen. While focused on this bleak thought, I saw the sailor who was supposed to have been watching the winch chatting on deck with a few of his crew mates.

I stormed over to the group. "You, there. What's your name?"

"Stefan Gibbs, Miss Fleming," he said, smiling.

"When did you leave your post?"

"When you told me I was done," he replied.

I drew in a deep breath. "Well, Stefan Gibbs, you're fired. I never told you to leave your post."

He blanched but recovered quickly. "You can't fire me. I work for Vincent."

"And Vincent works for my mother, and you may have just killed her husband by leaving your post. She'll back me up. Clean out your bunk."

Gibbs had gone pale. "When you came over to thank me, I thought that meant I was done. If something went wrong after that, it's as much your fault as mine."

"Did I say you were done? And anyway, like you said you don't work for me. Vincent told you to stand watch. You left your post, and now Ray is injured—possibly even dead. If it's anyone's fault, it's yours." My voice had gotten louder, and people around us heard me. The entire crew was staring. Well, too bad. Stefan Gibbs deserved to feel the shame.

He gulped, and I could see his throat working as he tried to speak. At last, he gave up on making a response. He turned and walked slowly away toward the crew quarters without another word.

I went back to the winch area and flipped on the sonar. It showed Alec about fifteen feet below the surface, making his final decompression stop. It wouldn't be long now. Once he was aboard, the crew could take *Omega* back to port and we'd learn how Ray was doing. I waited for Alec on the dive platform.

After a short while, he rose to the surface and gripped the ladder's rails. He unclipped the tanks on his side mounts and passed them up to me. I stowed them in the tank racks and went back for his fins. He handed them to me before he climbed the ladder. He lumbered across the deck and sat on the bench to guide his rear tanks into empty slots. "Where is everyone?" he asked when he'd removed his mask.

"How deep were you, Alec?" I grabbed the console that held his dive computer and pushed the button to show the data for his last dive. The depth showed 408 feet. It should have read something close to 330 feet, at most a few feet below Ray's planned dive depth.

Alec should have aborted the dive as soon as he realized the metal plate was at the wrong depth. I shook the console at Alec. "Four hundred feet! What were you thinking? Why didn't you stop the dive?" My voice cracked, and tears leaked from the corners of my eyes.

He looked sheepish. "I didn't look at my gauges. I was using the metal plate as my depth gauge. It wasn't until I started my ascent that I noticed the discrepancy. Where is Ray anyway? Celebrating?"

"Cayman Hospital ER, or maybe the morgue by now." I

could hear my own heartbreak under the angry tremor in my voice. How could Alec have gone down that deep without once looking at his gauges? My ex wasn't a fool, and he was a good, safe diver. He knew better.

CHAPTER THIRTY

THE FUNERAL WAS A NIGHTMARE, and the church was a madhouse. All the well-known faces and recognizable names in the global dive community were present. The presidents of all the major dive organizations—USA Freediving, DEMA, PADI, NAUI, SSI, and AIDA—attended. Members of the environmental and diving press were there in full force. The entire RIO staff was in attendance.

Gus and Theresa were there, sitting next to Stewie. Despite the tears in his eyes, Gus looked a little healthier than he had the last time I saw him—but compared to his old self— he looked awful. He cried during the service, and it broke my heart.

Lily, Oliver, Cara, and Newton sat together in the front row. I'd invited the twins to join Maddy and me in the receiving line after the ceremony.

Maddy was a basket case, staring out at the world through wounded eyes. I was sure everyone blamed me for Ray's death. Even I thought it was my fault.

Because Ray had wanted his ashes to be scattered at sea,

there was no coffin, just a large brass urn on a table in front of the altar. Maddy and I had chosen to display two recent photographs of Ray. We'd originally planned to use these new photos in publicity for the documentary.

One showed Ray on the deck of the *Maddy*. He wasn't wearing shoes or a shirt, and his blue printed board shorts hung low on his hips. A floral tattoo I hadn't known he had until the day of this shoot was peeking out of his waistband. He was looking at the camera over his shoulder while holding the ladder to the *Maddy*'s flying bridge. He looked happy, vibrant, and alive.

The second photo showed him in his RIO diveskin climbing aboard the *Omega* after a dive. His smile was as bright as the Cayman sunshine.

I'd included an enlargement of the photo of the three of us on the day Ray married my mother. Tears welled up whenever I looked at any of the pictures. My head spun with the constant refrain of "ifs" running through my brain. I'd failed in my role as dive coordinator, and Ray had paid the price for my failure. I couldn't wait to get out of there.

By the time the church emptied, I was drained. I must have hugged or shaken hands with the entire Who's Who of the diving community and every inhabitant of the Cayman Islands. We were holding a reception at RIO, but first, Maddy and I had to scatter Ray's ashes as he'd requested.

After scattering the ashes at a few of his favorite dive sites, we docked at RIO. We were still on the pier when two members of the Cayman Islands police force approached me. "Finola Fleming?" asked the older of the two men.

"That's me, Officer. Don't worry. We had a permit to scatter the ashes. Hold on. I'll get it for you." I started back down the dock to fetch the paperwork.

"That's not why we're here," he said. "We'd like you to

come to the station for a few questions about Ray Russo's death."

I turned around. "Why? I admit Ray's death was my fault. I should have checked the depth meter again. I should have made sure the controls weren't accessible and that Stefan knew he had to stay at his post until Ray finished diving. I should have made sure Alec would watch his own depth and that he knew it was his responsibility to call off the dive if he saw any problems. I should have insisted on better trained safety divers. My fault. All my fault. Any other questions?"

The two police looked at each other, looking surprised at how easily I took the blame. "Okay. But right now, we just need you to come with us."

We walked off the dock and over to their car. My brain was still buzzing when we arrived at the police station in East Bay. The cops left me alone in a locked room and went off to do whatever it is cops do while they soften up a suspect. When they returned, the questions began.

"Can you tell us what happened on the day of Ray's death?"

"Who had access to the depth setting?"

"Are deaths common in apnea diving?"

"Did you know of anyone who had a grudge against Ray? Anyone at all?"

"Why was Newton Fleming on the *Omega* that day?"

"Did Ray eat or drink anything unusual that day?"

"Why didn't you have safety divers with him the whole dive?"

"Were you aware of any financial problems Ray might have had? How about your mother? RIO? Yourself?"

By this point, I was exhausted.

"Just a few more questions now, Miss Fleming. We've heard Ray recently became aware he had children with another woman, not his wife. How did you feel about that?" asked the older of the two detectives.

"The twins made Ray happy, so I was happy for him. I was getting to know them, and I liked them. Everything was fine between Ray and me."

I was surprised to realize I'd spoken the truth. I was glad Ray had been able to meet his kids before his death. I'd seen how happy it made him, and I'd worked hard to let go of my jealousy.

"Mmhm. How about your mother? Was she happy for him too?" the younger detective asked.

"You'd have to ask her, Inspector. She was surprised at first, but I think she was happy for him."

They'd been at it for over an hour when the Detective Constable, head of the Criminal Investigations Unit, entered the room. "I think we've heard enough. Right now, Ray's death sounds like an unhappy accident, but we'll let you know if anything changes. Thank you for your time and cooperation. You're free to go, Miss Fleming. Your lawyer is in the lobby." He waved his arm toward the open door and my path to freedom.

Since I hadn't hired a lawyer, I was confused, but I wasn't about to hang around to protest. When I scurried out of the interrogation room, Newton and Alec were standing in the lobby.

"C'mon," Newton said. "I'll drive you home." He took my arm and walked me out of the building. Alec trailed behind.

The dazzling sunshine was blinding after being inside the police station, and I blinked several times to give my eyes a chance to adjust. I looked around. "The Detective Constable said my lawyer was here?"

"Right here. I told them I was your lawyer." Newton

grinned and pointed the key fob in his hand at a red Mercedes roadster convertible parked in the no parking zone.

I didn't question his lie, just opened the door, and sat in the passenger seat. Newton slid behind the wheel and the car started with a throaty roar. The vehicle was so smooth we could have been rolling on a cloud instead of the busy road. In the car's side mirror, I saw Alec watch us leave before trudging to his own car to follow us.

Newton shut the engine off in my driveway. "May I come in?" he asked. "I believe Maddy is inside waiting for you."

"I guess I owe you. How did you get me out of there, anyway?"

"It wasn't hard. They'd already decided Ray's death was an accident. I told them I was your lawyer. They don't need to know I don't do criminal law. I won't be able to hold them off for long if they change their minds about his death being accidental, but I don't see that happening."

Once inside my home, Newton paced around, picking things up and putting them down in the wrong places. I followed him, putting everything back in the right spot. Maddy and Alec perched at the kitchen island watching our strange dance.

After a while, Maddy got up and wrapped her arms around me. She was crying silent tears. Alec stood up like he planned to join us, but the hard glares Newton and I both sent his way stopped him in his tracks.

"Are you okay?" Alec asked instead. "What can I do?"

"I'm fine. Thanks for stopping by. You can go now."

To my surprise, Alec left without any protest.

Maddy and I sat on the couch, while Newton leaned against the kitchen island.

"I don't think Ray's death really was an accident," he said. "We need a plan in case we have to prove Fin didn't deliberately set him up to die in case they decide it was murder. That means we need to find out who did it."

Maddy said, "Ray's death was an accident. The police know it."

"Do you want to bet our daughter's future on that?"

Maddy's shoulders tensed. Newton was being his usual overbearing self. Ray's death, coming so soon after the news about the twins, had been hard on her. I didn't want her any more upset than she already was. The best way to stop the tension was to separate everybody.

"Look, I screwed up a lot of things on the dive, and my cascade of errors led to Ray's death. But I never intended him any harm, and I don't need either of you to step in. I just have to be able to explain how the torrent of mistakes happened if the police decide to question me again. How about you both leave me alone to work on that? I'll let you know if I need help."

"Aren't you coming to the gathering at RIO? All Ray's friends will be there, and I'm sure you'd feel better if you had something to eat," Maddy said.

"Nope. I'm good here. I'd rather be alone," I said. "Please. You can go. I'm fine."

Maddy and Newton shrugged before they each took their keys from the table near the front door. Before she went out, Maddy turned back to me. "Call if you need anything." But she knew me better than that, so she left without another word.

CHAPTER THIRTY-ONE

A WEEK AFTER HIS DEATH, we held the formal reading of Ray's will. The will was simple. Newton had drawn it up for Ray, and Maddy and I already knew what was in it. He'd left me the *Maddy* and all his dive gear, charts, and logs. Disposing of the rest of Ray's things was straightforward, since he'd held most of his assets jointly with my mother. The will held no bequests for Lily and Oliver because he hadn't gotten around to changing it after learning about their existence.

My mother was planning to set up trusts for the kids out of her own money. Cara had been bugging her for a cut of Ray's assets, so Maddy gave her Ray's car just to keep the peace. Maddy didn't need the car and she was happy to avoid the hassle of selling it. She didn't care about the monetary loss, but I didn't think it would hold Cara off for long.

Because I'd always loved being with Ray on the *Maddy*, I was thrilled he had left her to me. I'd rather have Ray, but the bequest told me he too had valued our good times. What I hadn't counted on was the onslaught of calls from people looking to help me find Ray's legendary treasure.

The treasure was rumored to include a fabulous, jeweled tiara, supposedly once owned by a Spanish queen. Along with the tiara, there were alleged to be chests full of gold doubloons and loose gemstones—enough loot to rival the fortunes of modern-day tech entrepreneurs. And of course, as legendary treasures always are, the lore says the treasure is cursed, and that's why Ray never brought it to the surface. Ray always said the stories were nonsense.

Even so, Stewie called as soon as he heard the news about Ray's bequest. "I'll come with you when you go after the Queen's Tiara," he said.

"Thanks, but I won't be going anywhere. There is no treasure, Stewie."

"Everybody knows there's a treasure. You just need to find the map. I'm sure Ray left you his boat and his logs because he wanted you to go after the booty. The map must be on the *Maddy* somewhere. In exchange for my share of the treasure, I can help with..."

"There is no map on the *Maddy* or anywhere else, because there is no Queen's Tiara, Stewie. It's just a story he liked to tell. Like a myth. I'm sorry if you were counting on something that doesn't exist, but I can't help you."

"Then I'll quit my job at RIO. I'll go after the Queen's Tiara myself."

"We'd be sorry to see you go, Stewie, but if it's what you want, you should go for it. Let me know how I can help."

I hung up, but the phone rang again. "Fin, it's Theresa. How are you holding up?"

"I'm fine, Theresa. How's Gus doing?"

"That's actually why I'm calling. I think you should split the treasure with Gus and me. Gus and Ray dove together nearly all the time. It was just a fluke he wasn't there the day Ray found the treasure."

"There's no treasure, so there's nothing to split."

I could feel her anger through the phone. "I should have known you'd keep it all for yourself." She hung up.

Five minutes later, the phone rang again. "Fin, it's Alec. I wanted to volunteer my services as photographer when you go after the Queen's Tiara. You'll be too busy diving and leading the expedition to waste your valuable time with cameras, and..."

"There's no treasure, Alec. And even if there were, I wouldn't take you on in any capacity." I hung up.

The phone rang again. "Leave me alone," I barked.

After a moment of silence, a tiny voice came through the speaker. "Fin, it's Lily Russo. I heard about my dad leaving you his treasure map. We were hoping you'd take me and Oliver on the expedition when you go looking for it. We'll do anything that needs doing...cooking, swabbing the decks, scraping barnacles. Please, please let us come along."

"I'm sorry, Lily. There's no map, no Queen's Tiara, and no expedition."

I fielded call after call from local divemasters, chefs, bartenders, bankers, friends, distant acquaintances, and total strangers. Everybody except me was convinced the key to untold wealth was somewhere aboard the *Maddy*. I needed to get away from the calls and constant reminders of my failure.

Ray had trusted me to keep him safe, and I'd failed. I'd made lots of mistakes when planning his final dive, and many of them were foreseeable.

I should have fought harder for adding better-trained safety divers instead of using the twins. If only Stewie had kept his word and been with Ray during the dive. If I'd placed an additional diver besides Alec at the bottom, they would have called off the dive as soon as they realized the depth setting was off. I should have foreseen the donors on the boat would be interested in the winch, and I should have found a way to make it impossible for anyone to touch the controls. Barring that, I should have made sure the crewmember assigned knew not to leave it unguarded for any reason—not even for a second.

The 'if onlys' and 'should haves' kept coming on an endless loop through my head. I'd made one mistake after another, setting up a domino of disasters.

I was angry at Stewie. I was angry at the twins. Angry at Stefan Gibbs. And at Ray. But most of all, I was angry at myself.

Ray was dead, and it was my fault. I'd loved him with all my heart, and I missed his wisdom, his ready laugh, and his bright smile.

My fault. All my fault.

On the open water I might find some peace, and with luck, a way to live with Ray's death. To get away from the echoes in my head, I decided to take the *Maddy* out for a short cruise, hoping the sea would help me find the peace I craved.

Ray had always used the *Maddy* instead of one of RIO's boats when we went out together, and the happiest times of my life had been spent with him on the boat. He taught me to swim and dive, and we would go out to practice buoyancy management or do diving skill drills every few days. Sometimes we fished, and later we'd pull up to a sandbar and cook the fresh fish over open coals for our lunch. We could talk for hours about everything while we fished or sat out the surface intervals between our dives. He never talked down to me the way many adults talk to children.

When I got older, we practiced rescue diving hundreds of times, with Ray always playing the part of the victim. Ironic he became a victim in need of rescue in real life.

Ray had taught me how to run the boat and often let me helm her, but it wasn't like being in charge. Now she was mine,

I was her captain, and I wanted to spend a few days living aboard the *Maddy* and remembering Ray.

I packed a duffle bag with bathing suits and clothes for two days at work, then put a bottle of water into a soft sided cooler along with some orange slices. I stowed everything in the trunk of my Prius and set out for RIO. I stopped on the way to buy a chicken sandwich, some cereal, more fruit, a few cartons of yogurt, and a quart of milk. On an impulse, I added some lavender scented candles and a paperback book to my purchases.

When I arrived at the marina, I stowed my food in the *Maddy*'s fridge, set out my candles, and put my clothes in the drawers. I started the engine and headed out to dive at Fish Tank. It was one of my favorite dive sites, and a spot where Ray and I used to love to swim.

Once I'd tied up at the mooring and changed into my bathing suit, I walked along the gunwales to the bow to enjoy the last bit of sunshine. I ate my sandwich and contemplated my life.

Here I was, twenty-four years old, and with only one friend in the whole world. I already had a divorce under my belt. I did have a wonderful job I loved, but as Lily had pointed out, most people assumed I had the job because of my mother, not because of my own abilities. I'd been working on a PhD in marine biology, but although I loved working with Rosie, buckling down to writing my thesis was another story. I didn't know when or even if I'd ever get back to it. My biological father was kind of a jerk. My hair was still a wreck and I had a big honking scar on my face. Worst of all, my beloved stepfather was dead and it was my fault.

No doubt about it. I needed to change my life. Since being underwater quiets the noise in my head. I put on my dive gear and stepped off the platform for a dive.

Fish Tank is a wonderful site. It's not very deep, and it teems with sea life and beautiful coral growths. I watched two Queen Angelfish sailing like royalty across the top of an intricate formation of staghorn corals, while three turquoise parrot fish with their big funny teeth chomped on the nearby coral. Sargent majors watched me from arm's length, and bright yellow jacks swam alongside me. A large school of tiny blue chromis hung nearby.

I slowed my breathing to a trickle and let the current take me to the chromis while I stayed as motionless as possible. Within a few minutes, the schooling fish made room for me, and I was one of them. I swallowed my delighted laugh. Joining a school of fish was one of my favorite things to do.

Maybe it was because I had finally stopped beating myself up, but while I was hovering with my 'schoolmates,' I realized the 'Do Not Touch' sign covering the winch controls had been carefully taped back in place with a single layer of tape from the roll I'd left nearby. I knew I'd double taped it before I entered the water that day.

An innocent guest might have lifted the sign and changed the setting out of curiosity, but if that were the case, they'd have done one of two things. They'd either have reset it to the original depth, or if the person was clueless, they'd have left the sign loose or at most pressed down on the original layers of tape that had held the sign in place. But whoever changed the depth setting had gone out of the way to cover the evidence of tampering by neatly securing the sign back in place—with a single layer of tape.

The sudden change in my breathing scared the chromis enough that they shot away from me as fast as they could. I didn't care. I had just realized Ray's death was not my fault at all. It was murder, as Newton had said. I'd been so busy wallowing in guilt I'd almost missed an important clue.

I climbed aboard the *Maddy*, unhooked the mooring and started the engine. The boat glided into her slip at RIO like she knew she was home. I tied her off and shut down the engine before heading below for the night.

I was awakened by sunlight dancing on my eyelids. I hadn't slept well since Ray's passing, but this morning I was relaxed and ready for the day. I threw on the kind of outfit I wore to work most days—shorts and a RIO-branded tee. I slipped on a pair of sandals and raked my fingers through my hair until it looked presentable. That was one big advantage of the short haircut I'd given myself. Since my hair always looked disheveled, I didn't have to bother with it much. Ready to face my day, I set off across the parking lot for work—and to start my investigation into Ray's death.

CHAPTER THIRTY-TWO

I HAD a hard time keeping my mind on work that day, because I was constantly making lists of potential suspects in my head. My thoughts were spinning, and I accomplished nothing. At 5:00 P.M., I gave up and went right to the *Maddy* to make a written list of everyone I suspected.

While plenty of people had been angry at Ray over the years, he was likable enough nobody ever stayed mad at him for long. In fact, I would have said he didn't have an enemy in the world, until I started looking for people who might have a grudge against him. By the time I went to bed, I had several sheets of paper with names I'd written down, crossed out, added back, crossed out again. It was a mess, and I was no closer to having a manageable list of suspects at the end of the night than I'd been when I started.

The next morning, before the sun was even up, I was already sitting slumped at my desk. I was looking at the crumpled, scratched, and ink-stained pages that constituted the progress of my investigation so far. I opened a spreadsheet for a more organized approach.

I labeled the left column suspects, and made a heading row with types of relationships, including business, personal friends, treasure hunting, family, publishing, donors, casual acquaintances, memberships, fans, and diving rivals. I added a total column for the number of areas a person intersected with Ray's life. I would rank the suspects by priority, using the number of relationship types they had as my starting point. My suspicion scale went from one to ten, so people who intersected in all ten columns would become the highest priority suspects.

Even though he didn't intersect in all ten aspects of Ray's life, I put Newton first on my list. I didn't know what had gone down all those years ago between Maddy, Newton, and Ray, but I'd caught vibes that Newton still had feelings for her even after all this time.

Maybe he'd hoped to win her back by getting Ray out of the picture. Except it didn't make sense for him to kill Ray now after more than twenty years. I had to admit, even though I still distrusted him, Newton would have acted before this if he'd been jealous. I changed his rank to a five.

Next, I added Stewie's name to the suspect list. Stewie and Ray had been friends forever, but Stewie needed money. He was convinced Ray had a treasure buried somewhere. The way he figured it, at least a third of the treasure was his. Except Stewie didn't know where the treasure was. Maybe he'd killed Ray hoping the will or Ray's logbooks would uncover the location of the Queen's Tiara.

Theresa was worried about her future if Gus couldn't work. Maybe she too hoped to find the treasure. Although with Ray gone, they had even less hope of finding the missing loot. Ray had kept its location hidden for twenty-five years, and nobody had a clue where it was. I didn't even believe the treasure was real.

I gave Stewie and Theresa each a five in the priority column, ranking them as unlikely killers.

Cara was on the list because she believed Ray had money. She was open about wanting a shot at his presumed wealth, and she claimed he'd promised her a share of the Queen's Tiara treasure. Her kids would be heading to college, and she'd have hefty tuition costs to pay. Maybe that's why she'd told Ray about the twins now, after having been silent for all those years. But as a highly placed executive in Newton's firm, Cara wasn't destitute. He was rich and generous, and I suspected he paid her very well. I rated her a five too.

Alec and Ray had words back when we split up, and Ray had still been upset over what Alec had done to me. I'd heard him threaten to tell *Your World* what Alec had done if he didn't own up to it on his own. But Alec had the weakest motive for murder, and he was the first one in the water.

On the other hand, I couldn't believe an experienced diver would go down that deep into the ocean without looking at his dive computer even once. That was an unnecessary risk and beyond foolhardy, yet Alec claimed he'd done just that. Alec had said he was too excited for Ray to remember to look at his gauges, but that seemed suspicious to me. Since he was the first one in the water, it would have been impossible for him to change the depth setting. Maybe he had an accomplice. I gave him a five too.

Lily and Oliver at least thought they had a reason to be angry with Ray. In their minds, he had neglected them their entire lives. It was Cara's fault, not Ray's at all, but they didn't know the whole story.

I knew how hurtful it was to think your father couldn't be bothered with you, since it was the same thing Newton had done to me. Ray had always treated me like a much-loved daughter, while they'd had no one.

They were excited about getting to know Ray, and their excitement didn't jibe with murder. Changing the depth for Ray's dive was simple, but would the twins have known it could be lethal? Maybe they'd just wanted to scare him.

Was I letting my jealousy cloud my judgement? I didn't think that was the case. I had a lot of legitimate questions about those two. They stayed on the list, but I ranked them as unlikely suspects.

I hesitated before I could bear to enter the final name. Madelyn Russo. My own mother. She and Ray had been married for twenty-two years, and she had every reason to be angry at him. She was knowledgeable enough about freediving to have planned her revenge this way. She knew the extra depth would be hard for Ray to traverse, but if she'd done it, she would have counted on the team's ability to save him. Maybe that's why she was so upset about him diving without competent safety divers.

On the other hand, Maddy was one of the calmest, sanest, most reasonable people in the world. If she'd had an issue with Ray, she'd have talked to him about it. And in the last days before the dive, they seemed to have worked things out between them.

I was torn. Thinking of my own mother as a suspect was impossible. And yet...she had motive and opportunity. I added her name to the list but left the rank column empty.

I'd simply ask her point blank, and then I'd be able to cross her name off with a sigh of relief. But how could I ask my mother if she'd killed her husband and was letting me suffer by thinking it was all my fault? What kind of mother would do that? Certainly not the Madelyn Russo I had known all my life. But I had known Ray all my life too, and I would've staked my life on him being faithful to my mother.

I'd confront her with my question as soon as I could so I

could get on with the list of real suspects. I was sure she'd laugh it off.

No time like the present. I printed my spreadsheet and took off down the hall toward Maddy's office.

I was about twenty feet from her door when I heard shouting and stopped short.

"He promised me half of everything. You owe me at least that." I recognized Cara's voice.

"Do you have the promise in writing? I'll be happy to have my lawyers review the document." Maddy sounded calm.

"No, I don't have it in writing. It was a verbal promise he made when I told him about the kids. You know how he was. Always living for the moment. But I shouldn't have to pay the price of his negligence. I've done my share. I raised those kids alone their whole lives."

"I understand, and if what you say is true, I'm willing to do what's right. I just want to see this promise in writing before we start negotiating."

"But he swore to me..." she wailed.

"You do realize no matter what he said, Ray didn't own much. I already signed his car over to you. Besides the car, he owned his boat and his dive gear, and he wanted Fin to have those. That's about it for Ray's assets, and your half of nothing is still nothing. Everything else you see is mine."

"That's ridiculous," Cara said. "The house, the cars...this place? You're saying none of it was Ray's?"

"Correct. The house has been in my family for generations. I started the foundation with money inherited from my mother. Ray was on the board of directors, but he didn't have any ownership."

"But he must have had savings, investments, something?"

"He earned a salary, but he wasn't much for saving."

"What about the treasure?" Cara said.

"There is no treasure. Look, I'm willing to work with you if you give me a copy of any documents that support what you say."

"And I said I don't have any documents," said Cara.

"In that case, we have nothing further to discuss."

To stop them from realizing I'd been eavesdropping, I scurried back down the hall, but I could still hear the anger in Cara's voice reverberating off the walls and high ceilings.

"You're hiding something. I know it. I'll find out what it is and then I'll be back to make you pay." She stormed out of Maddy's office, slamming the door behind her.

She brushed past me. "Get out of my way," she snarled.

I drew in a deep breath and walked to Maddy's corner office. "That sounded intense. Are you okay?"

Maddy waved a hand in the air. "She's a gold digger. But I can handle her. What do you need? I'm pretty busy, so make it quick if you can."

"I wanted to ask you something."

"Can it wait?" She didn't look up from her computer.

"No, it's important to me." I ignored her sigh and shut the door behind me. I settled in her guest chair and crossed my legs, waiting for her to look up.

"Well?" she said at last. "I have to tell you I'm in no mood for..."

"Ray's death wasn't an accident. Did you kill him?"

Her mouth dropped open. "Are you kidding me? I loved that man."

"People kill people they are supposed to love all the time. Maybe you were trying to pay him back. You'd just learned about Cara and the kids. That had to hurt."

Maddy slammed the lid on her computer. "Oh yes. It did. It hurt a lot. But we worked it out. I would never kill anyone—and especially not Ray. No matter what, I loved him." There was real heat in her voice.

"And, for your information," she continued, "I don't believe Ray fathered those twins. He never slept with that woman. She claims he was drunk, but if I know Ray Russo—and believe me I knew his body, his heart, and his soul—if he'd been drinking, nothing but sleep would have occurred that night."

I drew in a breath to ask another question, but before I could, she went on speaking, getting louder with each word. "How dare you come in here and accuse me of killing my husband? Are you so desperate to salve your guilty conscience you'd throw your own mother under the bus?"

She stood up and threw her electronic pencil across the room. Her usually smooth pale skin was blotchy and the muscles in her throat were clenched so tight they looked like ropes. She stomped to the door of her office. Tears stained her cheeks.

"Get out. Don't come back until you're ready to apologize."

I hate having people angry at me. Apologizing right away is what I would do most times, but the vehemence of her reaction made me think twice about crossing her off the suspect list so soon. Was she fooling herself the twins weren't Ray's? They looked just like him, and Ray must have had a reason to believe they were his children. I'd have to think this through and talk to her about it more when she'd had time to get over the heartbreak of Ray's death. I stood up to go.

She slammed the office door as soon as I was out in the hall, another reaction unlike my serene mother.

Instead of going back to my office, I stopped into my lab to see Rosie. I hadn't been by to work with her since Ray's death. I hoped she hadn't been lonely all alone in her aquarium. Most octopuses are shy loners, but Rosie seemed to thrive on the attention I paid her.

I tapped once lightly on the glass and Rosie peeked out of her shell to see what all the commotion was about. When she recognized me standing there, she oozed over to greet me. "Hello, sweetie," I said. "I've missed you."

As was her way, Rosie said nothing, just watched me through her enigmatic eyes while she swirled her tentacles in the gentle current created by the tank's aerator. It took me a moment to realize she was waiting for a treat, but as soon as I made the connection, I dropped a clam into the tank. She flashed her thanks and went back inside her cozy shell.

Restless and on edge, I couldn't concentrate on work, struggling with remorse about fighting with my mother. The taste of the bitter words we'd exchanged was acid in my mouth. I was pacing around my office when I saw Maddy heading down the dock toward her personal boat, the *Sea Princess*. Her fins and mask were slung over one shoulder, and she carried a scuba tank in each hand. It never failed to amaze me that as tiny as she is, my mother is as strong physically as she is mentally. I admired her independent spirit and the iron will that propelled her to the top in the two old boys' clubs of diving and underwater exploration.

Having fought her way to the top with grace and professionalism, I could imagine how angry she must have been when her equally high-profile husband made her look like a fool by cheating on her with a one-night stand and presenting her with adult twins from his indiscretion.

I watched her stow her dive gear on the *Sea Princess* and start the engine. She cast off and headed out to sea.

The ocean was her happy place, and she'd be calmer when she returned. I'd apologize when she got back and ask if she'd help me rule out some of the other suspects. Maybe we'd uncover the real killer and I could stop the nagging worries swirling through my head.

CHAPTER THIRTY-THREE

THE SUN SETS LATE in the Caymans, and it was still a little over an hour from sinking below the horizon. I hadn't seen my mother return, and I was starting to worry. She should have been back by now. Two tanks meant two hours of diving, plus a one-hour surface interval between dives. Twenty minutes to the dive site and twenty minutes back. Maybe some time for a snack or a sandwich, although she hadn't been carrying a cooler when she left. Whatever, she should have been back well before this. Her cellphone went straight to voicemail every time I called, so I knew either she was ignoring my calls, or she was so far out to sea she had no cell coverage.

I hurried through the marina in case I'd missed her return. Maybe her boat was there, just not in her usual slip. The *RIO One*, *RIO Two*, the *Maddy*, the Zodiacs we used for rentals or quick trips, and several other boats belonging to the staff were in their assigned slots, but there was no sign of the *Sea Princess*. Frustrated and frightened, I paced the length of the pier several times before hopping onto the *Maddy*.

I used the radio to check with the Coast Guard. They had no reports of wrecks or maydays. The hospital hadn't admitted any accident victims. I called Theresa and Gus. Then Alec. Even Newton and Cara. Nobody had seen or heard from her all day.

By now my heart was hammering. Something had happened to her. I knew it.

I untied the *Maddy* and backed her out of my slip. I'd cruise by a few of Maddy's favorite dive sites to see if the *Sea Princess* was moored on one of them.

I headed east past Bodden Town, swinging by Prospect Reef. I looked for the *Sea Princess* while cruising past Bat Cave Reef, Elmo's Wall, Iron Shore Garden. Nothing.

No sign of her at Lighthouse Wall or Grouper Grotto.

Changing to a more northerly heading, I swung by Dragon's Lair and Chubb Hole. Still nothing.

After clearing the East End, I headed west by Delwin's Delight, Top Secret, and Northern Lights.

She wasn't at Babylon, either.

That was one of her favorite sites.

After not finding her at any of the expected locations, I was at a loss. She couldn't have just vanished. Realizing I had to be more methodical, I decided to do a slow cruise all the way around the island and if I still hadn't found the *Sea Princess*, I'd call in the Coast Guard. I throttled back the engine and started my search pattern. I steered the boat with one hand and used the other to hold a pair of binoculars to my eyes. I swept my gaze across the ocean's surface and stopped about every hundred yards to do a complete 360-degree sweep of the surrounding area and the far horizon. I'd been at it for over an hour. Visibility was getting worse because of the ripening darkness.

I eased up on the throttle. One more sweep and I was turning the search over to the Coast Guard. I peered in all directions looking for the *Sea Princess*, but I didn't see any sign of her. I was about to put the binoculars down and reach for the radio when I saw something out of the corner of my eye. I swiveled back.

There, just ahead and to my port side, was a barely visible skinny red column sticking up out of the water. A scuba sausage. My heart leaped. There was no sign of her boat, but I prayed the distressed diver was my mother.

I reengaged the *Maddy*'s engine and spun the wheel in the direction of the sausage. I held the wheel with one hand and grabbed the microphone with the other. "Ahoy, scuba sausage. Do you need help?"

A head popped out of the water. The swimmer held up both arms in the scuba distress signal. I raced the *Maddy* in that direction, and when I got nearer, I jammed the engine into idle and rushed to the deck. The boat's rescue ring hung on the side of the cabin. I threw it, yelling "Maddy, is that you?"

The life buoy landed close enough that with a few strokes she was able to drape an arm over the ring. As soon as she signaled it was secure, I began reeling her in. It didn't take long before I recognized my mother despite the neoprene hood covering her distinctive blonde hair.

When I helped her up the ladder in the stern of the boat, her lips were blue, and she was shivering. I unfastened her BCD and stowed it in the rack, then I unzipped her diveskin and pulled it off her shoulders. After I wrapped her in a big fluffy towel for warmth, I folded her into a bear hug. Our tears mingled as she whispered. "Thank you. I knew you'd find me."

Hearing her words was like a soothing balm on a mosquito bite. My mother still had faith in me. I was elated. I had failed

Ray when he needed me, but against the odds, I'd managed to save my mother.

I led her to the *Maddy*'s bench and helped her to sit. I knelt and lifted one foot and then the other to remove her fins before pulling her diveskin the rest of the way off. I used another towel to dry her legs.

I brought her below and draped a blanket from the bunk around her and lifted her feet to help her lie down. She was still shivering so I made her a cup of hot coffee in the galley to warm her up. I placed a pile of pillows behind her so she could drink it. She held the steaming mug with both hands, struggling to steady her shriveled fingers enough to hold on. When she was ready, she took a long drink, then another, but she was still shivering.

"Hungry?" I asked. Even in the warm waters around the Cayman's, the thermal drain of a long submersion saps a body's energy stores, leaving the person ravenous.

"Starving."

I found a box of crackers in one of the cabinets and I dropped a handful on a plate. Maddy ate them all. After the second plateful disappeared, I handed her the box. "Thanks," she said, her mouth full of stale crackers.

"Will you be okay alone down here? I don't want to leave you, but I do want to get you home where I can take better care of you," I said.

She nodded and handed me the empty cracker box before rolling over. "I'll be fine." She was asleep before I was out of the cabin.

I started the *Maddy*'s engine and tore across the waves back to RIO's marina. By the time I'd finished mooring the boat, she'd emerged from below. She stood barefoot on the deck, wrapped in the blanket with her long damp hair hanging down her back. Anyone else in her condition might have looked piti-ful, but my mother looked beautiful. Strong and brave. Still, I'd wait to ask what had happened until she was safe and warm at home.

I helped her off the boat. She was barefoot, so we stayed on the grass beside the crushed shell path to RIO's parking lot to protect her feet from the sharp edges of the shells. Because her hands were still stiff with cold, I opened the door to my car and buckled her seat belt for her. She fell asleep within seconds and slept the whole way to my house.

She walked in on her own. I settled her on the couch in the living room and covered her with a crochet afghan she'd given me years ago. Although the ocean might be the last thing she wanted to think about at the moment, the afghan's soothing blues and greens always reminded me of the sea. I noticed the deepest blue threads matched her eyes, and I smiled at her, shuddering at how close I'd come to losing her too. I loved her so much. "What would you like to eat?"

"Whatever you have. Don't go to any trouble." She yawned.

I left her with her eyes closed while I went to the kitchen to see what culinary delights I could whip up to tempt her. Most days my kitchen held a vast assortment of half empty take out containers and little else. Neither of us expected me to whip up a gourmet repast.

I was proud when a few minutes later I carried in a tray covered with two plates of thick grilled cheese sandwiches and two bowls of hearty cream of tomato soup with a few flakes of dried parsley floating on top to hide the fact the soup came from a can. I set the tray down on the glass coffee table in front of her.

"I'm impressed," she said, reaching for her spoon. "I wouldn't have believed it if I hadn't seen it with my own eyes.

You're like Betty Crocker, Rachel Ray, and Martha Stewart all combined into one beautiful daughter." It wasn't funny, but we laughed from sheer relief that she was safe.

I tucked a napkin on her lap before I sat in the Windsor rocking chair set catty corner to the couch. I reached for the other bowl of soup and a spoon of my own.

Maddy had finished her soup and most of her sandwich before I'd taken more than a few bites of soup. "Here," I said, pushing the other sandwich toward her. "Take this one too. I'm not very hungry, and you must be starving. It takes a lot of energy to spend that long in the ocean without succumbing to hypothermia."

"Thanks," she said. She popped the last bit of the first sandwich in her mouth with one hand while her other hand reached out for the second sandwich. I was amazed to watch my ninety-five-pound mother pack in the food like a lumberjack, and I sent up a silent thank you to whatever in the universe had led me to her before the ocean had done her in.

At last, the hot food did its work, and she stopped shivering. I piled the dirty dishes on the tray and took it to the kitchen. When I got back, she was asleep again. I was dying of curiosity about what had happened to the *Sea Princess* and how she'd ended up so far out at sea all alone.

My curiosity could be put aside till morning, but my guilt wouldn't wait. Maddy had taken her boat out alone because I'd accused her of murdering her husband. My sane, careful, and rule-abiding mother had gone diving alone, without telling anyone where she was going, or when to expect her back. If I hadn't happened to glance out the window when I did, I wouldn't have seen her take the *Sea Princess* out. I might never have gone looking for her, and it might have been too late to save her even if I did. She was in bad shape as it was. She wouldn't have survived an entire night or even a few more hours in the water.

My fault again. I'd driven her to this. By accusing my mother of killing Ray, whether by accident or intent, I'd given her more than she could bear. I'd almost lost her, and I wouldn't have been able to handle the guilt if I had.

CHAPTER THIRTY-FOUR

I GOT up every hour to check on Maddy, but she slept peacefully through the night. Just before sunrise, I put on a pot of coffee. When the coffee was ready, Maddy joined me at the kitchen counter, still wrapped in her afghan. Despite the solid night's sleep, dark circles rimmed her eyes, but at least she wasn't shivering and blue with cold.

"Hungry?" I asked.

She blushed and laughed. "I'm starved. I can't believe it after all I ate last night, but I could eat a horse."

"You had a tough experience. It takes a lot out of you." The last of my bread had gone into the sandwiches last night, meaning toast was out of the question. I peeked in the refrigerator to see what I had. A few eggs. Some milk. I knew I had some instant oatmeal and a package of frozen sausages around too. We were good to go.

A few minutes later I slid a big bowl of oatmeal in front of her, along with milk and some ancient raisins. While she ate her oatmeal, I scrambled the eggs and divided them onto two plates with the sausage. I poured more coffee for each of us, then sat down. Her plate was already empty, and she blushed again when she saw me notice.

"Had enough to eat?'

She nodded and sipped her coffee. "Thank you."

"If you feel up to it now, can you tell me what happened yesterday?" I asked her.

"I wanted to dive on High Top because it reminded me of Ray. We set the mooring there ourselves years ago," she said, after taking another sip of coffee. "I was stupid, because it gets so little traffic and I didn't tell anyone I was going there. Anyway, I must have messed up when I moored the *Sea Princess*, because when I surfaced after my first dive there was no sign of her."

I was certain my mother had never once slipped a mooring in her entire life. She was meticulous in the extreme. I frowned and said, "You think you messed up when you moored the boat? Really? I find that hard to believe. Tell me more."

"Well, at first I assumed I'd surfaced in the wrong spot, but the only possibility is she slipped her mooring and drifted away. High Top isn't one of the usual dive sites, and it doesn't get much traffic at any time of day. I'd seen a few sharks in the area on my dive, and I didn't want to be out there alone all night. I inflated my scuba sausage and started swimming for shore. I didn't expect to be rescued. Thank you for coming after me. I might have made it back, but it would have been tough."

"You were miles from shore when I found you," I said. My voice cracked. "Thank goodness you had the presence of mind to inflate your scuba sausage or I never would have seen you." I decided not to mention how close she'd come to losing her life. She wouldn't like hearing my opinion on the topic.

I did, however, still have questions about the *Sea Princess* slipping her mooring. "Did you hear or see any boats while you were diving, or after you surfaced? Could someone have taken the *Sea Princess*?"

"Pirates?" She smiled. "I doubt it. I didn't hear anything, and all I saw while I was diving was those sharks, a blenny, a spotted drum, and a tarpon at a cleaning station. Oh, and a spotted eagle ray."

"Lucky you saw the eagle ray. They're a good omen."

"This one sure was a good luck charm, bringing you to me. She hopped off her stool and brought her dishes to the sink. "Mind if I shower?"

"It's all yours," I said. "I'll find something for you to wear." As soon as the water was running, I called the Coast Guard to report the *Sea Princess* missing.

It was still early when we arrived at RIO. She kissed my cheek when we parted in the hallway near her office. "Thank you again," she said. "I always knew you'd find me."

It was mid-morning when I glanced out the window and saw a Coast Guard cutter towing the listing *Sea Princess* into our marina. I went to get Maddy, then we walked out to the dock to talk to the officers and assess the damage to the *Sea Princess*. I could see Oliver and Lily among the crowd of RIO employees watching the boat and murmuring about the visible damage.

We were still a couple of hundred feet away when the officer called out to us. "Hey, Dr. Russo. We brought your *Princess* back for you. She's a little the worse for wear. What happened, anyway?"

Maddy's hand flew to her mouth when she saw her boat leaning halfway over. She ran the rest of the way to the dock and stopped short when she saw the gaping hole in the boat's hull. "What happened?"

The officer shrugged. "We were hoping you could tell us. It

looks like someone tried to scuttle your boat. You wouldn't know anything about that, would you?"

Maddy had a puzzled look on her face, not understanding what he was getting at. I took him aside and explained what had happened, how I'd found Maddy alone in mid-ocean trying to swim for shore.

"Uhuh. How much does she owe on the boat?" His voice was bored. Cynical.

He must deal with people trying to collect on their boat insurance all the time. "Nothing. She's owned the *Sea Princess* forever. We had a fight earlier and she went diving to calm down. Something happened to the boat while she was under."

"You didn't call us for help?" he asked.

"I was sure I could find her myself. And I did."

He gave me a long look. "Yes, you did, didn't you?" He paused a moment. "How bad was the fight? She's had it tough lately with Ray's death and all. Could she have been trying to hurt herself?"

I opened my mouth to blast him for even suggesting such a thing, then paused to consider the idea. "No. No, I don't think so. She had her buoyancy control device and sausage inflated. She was swimming hard when I found her."

"People sometimes change their minds about suicide," he said. "But she's safe and that's what counts. Keep an eye on her though, just in case." He flipped his notebook closed and stuck his pen in his pocket. "Well, the boat's back. Have a good day." He walked away.

There were too many accidents and suspicious occurrences, and every time something happened, the police questioned me. Their suspicion made me think they still suspected me of killing Ray, and they didn't seem especially interested in questioning anyone else. It was still up to me to find Ray's killer. But I'd learned my lesson when asking if she'd killed Ray made Maddy so angry it almost drove her to her death. I'd keep my investigation a secret from everyone, especially the people I love. As far as they'd know, I considered Ray's death a tragic accident. Nobody's fault.

I had to find the killer before he or she struck again, but my search for the truth wasn't worth the pain it could cost the people I loved.

CHAPTER THIRTY-FIVE

IT WAS LATE AFTERNOON. I wanted nothing more than for this day to be over. I packed up my things and then took a detour by RIO's marina to pick up the logbooks Ray had left to me along with the boat. I wasn't up for any creative work. All I wanted was to read about Ray's adventures from his early days. I planned to spend the rest of the day at home reading the logs.

Approaching the slip where I moored the *Maddy*, I had a premonition something was wrong. Nothing seemed amiss from where I was, but still, I broke into a run and vaulted aboard while I was still several feet away.

Someone had searched my boat, and they hadn't been subtle about it. The mess was shocking, even more so when juxtaposed with my memories of how fanatical Ray had been about keeping everything ship shape. All the cupboards were open, and food, dishes, pots, and pans littered the galley floor. The door to the locker where Ray stored charts and maps had been wrenched open, and the vast accumulated collection lay strewn across the floor. Some were torn while others lay in the mess of food thrown from the cabinets and refrigerator.

The furniture had been destroyed, and the cushions on the daybed were sliced open. Handfuls of white stuffing tumbled back and forth across the floor in unison with the rocking of the waves. Most of the delicate electronic instruments had been ripped from their housings and smashed into glittering shards. The few items of clothing I kept aboard had been thrown to the floor.

My hand flew to my mouth to hold back a sob until I remembered the speargun. Ray'd kept it hidden behind a panel in the head. Owning a speargun is illegal for most people in the Caymans, but Ray had a license for his. I'd been meaning to turn it in to the police, because I was not one of the very few people who'd been granted licenses. I flung open the head door and breathed a sigh of relief. The panel was intact. Thank goodness I wouldn't have to explain to the police that not only had I been in illegal possession of a speargun, but it was now missing.

I was leery of reporting the break-in to the police. They were already suspicious of me, and then there was the matter of the speargun. I decided to deal with the mess on my own. Blinking away salty tears, I knelt to begin the cleanup. Less than a minute later, I heard a surprised whistle.

"Wow, I hope you never get this mad at me." Newton Fleming stood on the pier looking down at the destruction aboard the Maddy. "What happened?"

"Dunno," I said. "Looks like someone tossed my boat, looking for something or maybe just trying to hurt me. Why would anyone do this?"

"I can't imagine, but maybe I can help you swab the decks or something. Whatever you need. Permission to come aboard, Captain."

I waved him aboard and noticed he left his shoes on the pier without my having to ask. He learned fast.

Newton grabbed a plastic trash bag from an open box on the counter and knelt on the cabin's deck beside me. He picked up a map and slid the cracker and cereal crumbs that covered it into the bag. He pulled a handkerchief out of his back pocket and dusted the fine particles off before he folded the map along its original creases. He placed it on the galley table, then he picked up another chart and followed the same process, pausing every now and then to meticulously tape the ones that were torn back together.

Because most of the charts were dirty but not wet, there'd been little real damage done to them. I couldn't say as much for the daybed cushions and the chairs. Everything soft, even the life vests, had been slashed and destroyed.

While Newton concentrated on the charts, I was picking up wads of fluffy white stuffing from the daybed cushions and the larger pieces of broken glass or pottery. Any undamaged crockery, I placed in the sink. We worked in silence for several minutes before he said, "How long have you been living aboard the *Maddy*?"

"How did you know?"

"Your clothes are here. Fresh fruit and milk. Lavender scented candles," he said, holding a broken taper in his hand. "It's your boat now, and none of this stuff looks like it was left over from Ray's time."

I sniffed back a sob. "I miss him. He was my father." Then I caught myself. "I mean, like my father."

"No, you were right the first time. He was more father to you than I ever was. I hope to be better at that in the future if you'll let me, but in your heart, Ray will always be your father. I'll have to learn to accept that."

Because I couldn't argue with that even if I wanted to, I just went back to work. Newton stayed with me, and he worked hard. We had the mess cleaned up in no time. As far as I could tell, nothing was missing.

All the maps and charts were back in place, and we'd put most of Ray's logs in the cabinet where they'd always been. I stuffed the last of my clothes, which were covered with milk, syrup, and assorted crumbs into a laundry basket, and added a plastic bag containing several of the earliest of Ray's logbooks to the top of the pile. I planned to start reading them in chronological order to get a picture of Ray's life before I knew him. Finished packing, I hefted the basket and turned to Newton. "Thanks. This would have taken a lot longer without your help."

He smiled. "Glad I could be here. Need a hand taking that stuff to your car?"

"No, thanks. I'm good." I didn't want to sleep alone on the *Maddy* tonight.

"See you around," he replied. He put his hands in the pockets of his khaki shorts and strolled across the lawn.

Bemused, I watched him go. I would never have thought the great Newton Fleming would get down on his hands and knees to sweep up crushed Cheerios. Or painstakingly tape torn charts back together. I liked this version of the man. If I didn't know better, I'd say he'd acted like a real dad.

CHAPTER THIRTY-SIX

ON THE WAY to Rum Point, I stopped at a convenience store and grabbed some laundry detergent and a pre-made sandwich for my dinner because, as usual, there was nothing to eat at home. After carrying my bundles inside, I put a load of laundry in the machine and picked out the oldest of Ray's logbooks to read while I ate my turkey sandwich sitting at my kitchen counter. Anything to stop obsessing about the destruction to the *Maddy*. I loved that boat, and for me, it was a permanent reminder of Ray.

Like him, Ray's logs were fun. They were as much personal journals as they were ship's logs, and Ray was a witty and engaging writer. Several times I laughed out loud at some of the antics he, Gus, and Stewie had pulled off in their younger days. Getting to know Ray this way made me feel closer to him, and before I realized it, the sky had grown dark and the moon was setting. Tomorrow—or today, really, since it was after midnight —was a workday. It was past time for bed.

I brushed my teeth and got into one of the comfy oversized tee shirts I like to wear when I sleep. I wanted to read one more adventure from the logbook before I called it a night. I picked up the book I'd been reading and snuggled under the covers.

Before I turned the next page, I wondered if the *Maddy* had been trashed by someone looking for the treasure's location. Maybe that's why they'd pulled out all the maps and charts but, other than dumping the logbooks on the floor, they'd been unharmed. Everyone who knew of Ray's bequest to me seemed sure the location of the Queen's Tiara was hidden somewhere on the boat, but the only thing in these logs was a collection of rollicking good stories about his adventures on the high seas with his buddies Stewie and Gus. They made me feel closer to Ray, and I loved reading them. I realized I might have to protect the logbooks until the treasure fever died down. They were too precious a reminder of Ray for me to risk losing them. I decided I'd keep them with me until I thought of a place where they'd be safe.

CHAPTER THIRTY-SEVEN

THE SUN WAS BARELY UP the next morning when I pulled the basket of clean laundry out of the trunk of my Prius and piled Ray's logbooks on top. It was a heavy load to carry across the parking lot and the lawn to the marina, but I planned to drop the *Maddy*'s linens and my clean clothes on the boat before I started work for the day.

I came around the hedge that separated the parking lot from the lawn and saw a small group of people aboard the *Maddy*. I dropped the basket and ran to my boat, shouting, "Hey, whoever you are. Get off my boat."

The entire group froze, but they didn't get off the *Maddy*. Just before I reached the end of the pier, Newton came out of the cabin and stepped onto the dock. He held his hands up in a slow-down motion. "Whoa. I didn't expect you here this early, but it's okay, Fin. They're with me."

"What do you think you're doing on my boat? Get off right now." I was panting from anger more than from the run.

"I wanted to surprise you," he said. "We've been here all night. If you don't like anything, you can change it, or we can put it back the way it was. I only wanted to help." He handed a wad of bills to the leader of the group. "Thank you. A splendid job, and I appreciate the quick turnaround. I'll be sure to recommend you to my friends."

The five people who'd been on the boat with Newton gathered up toolboxes, buckets, and brushes and left, heads down.

Hands on hips, I confronted Newton. "What have you done?"

"I had a team come to clean up the mess and repair your instruments. While we were at it, I had them make new cushions for the day bed and replace all the chairs and life vests. Everything's new, right down to the forks in the drawers. If there's a single detail you don't like, just say so, and I'll have it changed."

I pushed by my father to the cabin of the *Maddy*. It was spotless. Everything shone, from the light fixtures to the handles of the drawers to the gleaming floors. The old daybed sported plump new cushions covered in the soft aqua color of the Cayman seawater. Newton's team had replaced the ruined electronics with brand new equipment, all the latest top of the line models. Not only was the *Maddy* as good or better than new, now it looked like me. Like a place I would want to spend all my time. I had to admit to myself I loved the changes.

Newton spoke softly from the dock. "I hope I didn't overstep. I could see the destruction upset you a lot, and I wanted to do something nice for you..."

My father is the CEO of a major global financial conglomerate. His companies only invest in environmentally responsible enterprises. He's a top-shelf corporate lawyer, although he doesn't practice law anymore. He's rich and powerful. He's been interviewed on TV and by business magazines and newspapers. He was named one of *Human Magazine*'s most eligible bachelors for years. I hadn't believed the great Newton Fleming could do nervous, but if it had been a lesser mortal in front of me, I'd have been certain that's what I was seeing.

His demeanor took me by surprise. My whole life I'd considered my father to be a hard, cold, uncaring person, yet since we'd met, he'd shown me an unexpected soft side. I decided to give him a chance. "I love it. Thank you."

Newton beamed.

"But how would you feel if I just snuck into one of your homes and redecorated the whole thing without even consulting you?"

"If you ever want to redecorate one of my homes, be my guest," he said. "I'd take your efforts as a welcome sign you cared about me."

I always felt off-balance around Newton, trying to reconcile the cold man I'd thought he was with the caring man I was beginning to know. I blew out my breath in a sigh and turned away to get the basket I'd dropped on the lawn.

I knelt in the grass to refold my tee shirts. Newton stooped to pick up a towel. He shook it out to get rid of the dust and grass clippings, folded it, and placed it in the basket. Then he did it again, working beside me without a word until everything was back in the basket.

He carried the logbooks to the Maddy, while I managed the laundry basket. He didn't come aboard the boat, just leaned over and placed the three books on one of the benches inside the gunwales.

I brought the basket to the cabin below. I could sort out my things later. Right now, I wanted to talk to my father. I went back on deck. "Newton, do you want a coffee or..." He was already halfway across the lawn, his head down and his hands in his pockets. I watched him go. He looked sad and lonely. The sight brought a lump to my throat, and I felt a pang of longing to know this complex man with all his contradictions.

CHAPTER THIRTY-EIGHT

LATER THAT MORNING, I stared out my office window at the ocean, trying to get back in the zone. My concentration broke again when I heard an unfamiliar voice behind me.

"Miss Fleming, may I have a word, please?"

I turned around to see the Royal Cayman Islands Police Service Detective Superintendent standing behind me. I knew him by sight from various fund-raising events over the years. "DS Scott. Come in. Have a seat. What can I do for the RCIPS today?"

"I came by for a chat with you, Miss Fleming. I have some questions about the incident with the *Sea Princess*."

"Good. I'm very concerned about what happened to my mother."

He sat in a visitor's chair in front of my desk. "Did you get cold feet this time?"

That was confusing. "Cold feet? What are you talking about?"

"Your stepfather died under suspicious circumstances. At first, we classified it as death by misadventure, but we're starting to think it was murder. We haven't forgotten your confession after his funeral. That would make you the chief suspect in the case."

My face flushed but I forced myself to hold his gaze. "I see. Is that what you wanted to talk about today?"

He stared at me. "It has come to my attention somebody tried to kill your mother yesterday, and you were involved."

I opened my mouth, but all that came out was a squeak.

He held up a hand to forestall my response. "Once again, you look like the chief suspect to me. Someone towed your mother's boat from its mooring and smashed the hull with an ax. That someone left your mother alone and adrift in the sea, miles offshore. It had to be someone who knew her. Knew where she liked to dive. Knew she would be there alone, that day, at that time. Who could it be? One person comes to mind. I must ask again. Did you get cold feet this time? Was that why you didn't end up murdering your mother like you murdered your stepfather?"

My mouth went dry and there was a roar in my ears. I couldn't be a murder suspect. I stood up, wobbled. Put a hand on my chair to keep myself upright. "No, you're wrong. I..."

"Don't say a word, Fin. Let me handle this." Newton Fleming pushed by the chief and stood beside me. "I'm her lawyer as well as her father. What happened to Madelyn yesterday was an accident. Ask her yourself."

"Wishing doesn't make it so, Mr. Fleming, and a mother's love can make a woman blind to the truth. Someone hacked a hole in your ex-wife's boat yesterday. If it wasn't Finola here, who could it have been?"

"I believe it's your job to find that out, sir," said Newton. "My job is to make sure you don't make a mistake and ruin my daughter's life."

The chief's eyes glittered. He turned to leave without another word.

Newton watched the chief walk down the hall to RIO's lobby. He crossed to my desk and picked up the phone. When the guard answered, he said, "This is Newton Fleming. Please do not allow the police to enter the building again without a warrant unless you contact me first." A pause. "Yes, that's right. Finola Fleming's father." He hung up.

"What gives you the right..."

His ears turned red. "But..."

I picked up the phone to call security, but before dialing, I put the handset back in its cradle and turned to Newton. "Thank you for sending him away, but please stop telling people you're my lawyer. And please don't tell RIO employees what to do. You have no authority here."

"Maybe we should discuss this with your mother."

"Sure, but nothing will change. She'll back me up. Let's go."

We didn't speak on the way to Maddy's corner office. She was sitting at her desk, working on her computer when we looked inside.

Newton cleared his throat. "Maddy, are you up to talking?"

She turned around. "Not really, Newt. It's been a tough few weeks."

"I agree, but Fin needs our help...and some answers."

Maddy sighed. "I guess you're right. Sit down."

We all sat at the small round conference table in her office.

I started. "Newton keeps telling the police he's my lawyer, even though he's not. And he told the security force not to let the police in without talking to him first. I don't know where he gets off..."

She interrupted me. "He's been your lawyer since you were a baby. He's the chief trustee of your trust fund. He's on RIO's board of directors, and he's our largest donor if you add up the gifts from all his corporations and trusts. He's always been involved in RIO. In fact, in the early days, he bought the *Omega* and leased it back to me until I could afford to buy it outright."

That stopped me cold. As far as I knew, my father had been gone for good since before my fifth birthday and had never contacted us since, except for those impersonal birthday cards and gifts. "Why didn't you ever tell me, Maddy?" I turned to Newton. "Why didn't you ever try to see me?"

Maddy went pale. "My fault," she said. "Newton travels most of the time for his businesses, and you were just a baby when Ray and I fell in love. Newton's schedule was crazy, and he had to cancel a few times at the last minute. And other times he'd show up with no warning after being away for weeks. I didn't like it, and it was confusing for you to have Newton popping in and out of your life while Ray was trying to establish his own place.

"Newton didn't believe you'd be better off without seeing him, but he agreed to try it my way. The arrangement was supposed to last a few months—a year at most. But things came up, and time slipped away. It never was the right time to reintroduce your father. Before we knew it, you were a teenager, then a young adult. I'm sorry." She didn't meet my eyes, and I could see her clasped hands were shaking.

"No, I'm the one who's sorry." Newton reached over to touch my arm. "I should never have agreed to the plan, but since I did, I should have stuck to the schedule. I was weak and selfish. If you're angry—and you have every right to be—you should be angry at me. I'm the one who let those years slip by. After a while, I realized how much time had passed, and I was afraid to talk to you. I was terrified you'd hate me. That's why I was such a jerk the day we met. I was scared." I could hear the tremor in his voice. His eyes, so much like mine, were wide with fear. Tears gathered in the corners and threatened to spill.

"Back when you were little, your mother and I did what we thought was best. She was a good mother to you, and it pains me to say it, but Ray was a better father to you than I would have been. I failed you in every possible way. But I'd like to try to make it up to you if you'll let me." He saw me notice his hands shaking, so he placed them flat against the table. "Please."

All I could feel was anger and regret at their selfishness and stupidity. Anger at how they wasted time. Time we could have spent together.

Instead of having too much love, I'd always felt unloved, thinking Newton didn't care. The idea that my father had abandoned me eroded my self-esteem. Made me settle for people like Alec who used me. Was it possible my parents never noticed how much they hurt me?

I left Maddy's office and got in my car for the drive home. How could two people who were as brilliant in their work as my parents be that clueless when it came to raising a child? I would have been capable of loving both Newton and Ray without getting confused about who was my father. And when it comes to children, there's no such thing as too much love.

I could have a had a real family. With a brother and a sister to hang out with. Two fathers who loved me. Maybe even two Maddys, if Cara was in the picture. Why not? Other people did it.

Instead, I spent my life as an only child. I grew up at RIO and on the *Omega*, exploring the world and learning about the sea and its mysterious inhabitants. I never had a chance to make friends my own age. I'd loved that time. I knew it was a unique and valuable experience, but I wondered how much more I would have appreciated it if my whole family had been part of my life.

In the past, I would have talked to Ray about my feelings. He always took the time to listen, and he offered brilliant advice. I could hear him in my heart.

"Fin," he would have said, "people do the best they can. Sometimes they make bad decisions that hurt the people they love. But when that happens, you need to ask why they did what they did. Was their act meant to hurt you, or was it done with good intentions? It's the intentions that matter. If there's love behind it, you forgive, no matter how much their actions hurt you. And always remember, you are my daughter, and you are loved."

Oh, Ray.

I missed him so much.

CHAPTER THIRTY-NINE

THE NEXT MORNING, the first thing I did was call a locksmith to inquire about having a safe installed in my house. I wanted a place to store Ray's logbooks. I couldn't keep carrying them around with me wherever I went. The locksmith promised to get right on it. That should have been reassuring, but I knew he worked on island time, which could mean anything. Still, his promise helped put my mind at rest.

That freed me up for other things, so I was hard at work when I heard a tap on my door. I looked up to see Cara Flores standing in front of my desk, dressed in a hot pink shift dress that set off her dark hair and eyes. The gold coin necklace was the only jewelry she wore. As always, her nails and toes were polished to a high shine, and her hair and makeup were perfect. She looked fabulous. Expensive and well cared for.

I wore no makeup, and I was drenched with sea water from feeding the fish in RIO's aquatic research lab. My ragged shorts were worn out and my tee shirt was faded. The frizz in my shaggy hair had reached monumental proportions from the relentless humidity. I'd kicked off my flip-flops earlier, so I was barefoot under my desk, showing the chipped and ancient polish on my toenails.

No doubt about it. Cara Flores could make me feel like a frump, despite being at least twice my age. "Hi, Ms. Flores. What's up?" I asked with a frown.

"It's Cara Russo. That's my name now. I feel I'm entitled to use it. But you can call me Cara." She smiled with tight lips and no eyes.

Her statement got my back up, but I had enough on my mind without getting into it with Cara Flores. Anyway, I think it's legal for people to use any name they want if there's no intent to defraud. I made a mental note to get Newton to follow up on that question though.

Rather than start a fight, I looked at her with a blank stare, but Cara continued anyway. "I need you to talk some sense into your mother. She won't give me what Ray promised me."

"That doesn't sound right. I heard her say as soon as you showed her some documentation, she would transfer funds..." It was odd Cara was so concerned about money. She was a well-paid executive. I couldn't believe she needed to badger my mother for money.

"Pfft. I don't have any paperwork. Who thinks about paperwork when you're young and in love? And make no mistake, Ray and I were very much in love when we conceived Lily and Oliver."

Yuck. I tried to keep my voice even when I replied. "Maybe you thought you were in love, but that's not the way Ray told it. Whatever you have that supports your claim would be good though. Did anyone else hear him say it, or..."

"Hmmm," she said. "It's hard to remember who was present that long ago, but maybe I can find someone who heard him." She tapped a finger on her cheek, testing this new scenario to see if it would bolster her story.

"I don't understand why you are trying so hard to get money from Ray's estate. You must have more than enough money to take care of whatever you need. And you're with Newton. He'd give you money if you needed it."

Cara was watching me so closely it was like she was trying to read my thoughts. A few nanoseconds later, she drew in a deep breath and blushed. "I don't like to ask him for money. You know how it is."

I'd caught her in a lie. She wasn't with Newton, but she tried to give the impression they were together. I could be naïve, but I recognized a scammer when I met one. I was impressed that she could blush on command though.

"I'm sorry. Unless you have proof that Ray promised you an inheritance, there's nothing anyone can do. Maddy is already being very generous with the twins, but she's not going to transfer any more of Ray's estate to you without paperwork showing you have a right to it. Talk to your lawyer. Maybe they have copies of something on file..."

She narrowed her eyes. "I told you I don't have any documentation. You owe me. You almost killed my Lily with your stupid poison tank."

I wasn't going to let her rewrite history to make me the bad guy in that story. "No, Cara. You're mistaken. I saved her life. If I hadn't acted as fast as I did, Lily would be dead, but it still wouldn't have been my fault."

She opened her mouth to speak, but I held up a hand to silence her. "And neither my mother nor I owe you anything unless you can show a legal reason why we do. For all we know, you came to the island just to shake Ray down. Maybe you even set up his death looking for a payout."

"I didn't kill Ray. I loved him. But he wouldn't leave your sea witch of a mother. She took everything from me, now I want something in return. I can't have Ray, but I'll settle for his money."

"I'll just bet you would," I said. "But I don't believe your story. You and Ray hadn't spoken in years. You never even told him about the twins. It sounds to me like you were jealous, and you came here just to kill him."

She looked at me like I was crazy. "I wasn't jealous. I wouldn't have taken Ray back if he'd crawled across broken glass to beg me. But I want what's mine, and half of Ray's money should be mine. My family and I will be heading back to New York as soon as your mother does the right thing and gives me my money."

"Uhuh. I think Maddy established Ray didn't leave much of an estate. And you have no paperwork proving your claim on what he did leave. But let's say I did believe you. It's out of my hands. It's a legal issue. You're not in the will, and you have no paperwork showing he promised you anything. So, if that's all you wanted to talk about, please excuse me. I have a lot of work to do." I put my hand on my mouse and went back to editing film.

Cara sputtered for a few seconds then turned to go, slamming the office door behind her as she left.

Good riddance.

CHAPTER FORTY

I SPENT Sunday evening flipping the pages of Ray's logs without being able to concentrate long enough to absorb any details. Exhausted, I went to bed early, but then I tossed and turned all night, getting very little rest. When my alarm went off before dawn, I dragged myself out of bed to start my day.

My face in the mirror was gray and haggard. My hair stood out in ragged tufts all over my head. Dark circles rimmed my eyes. I looked like a fading rock star who'd forgotten to remove her makeup before bed.

I put a hand to my cheek and ran a finger along my scar. My hope it would look like sexy crinkles near my eyes hadn't come to fruition. The flesh had healed in a raised ridge that puckered my eye and the corner of my mouth. It had faded a little, but it was a florid pink that stood out against my skin. I remembered Alec tracing the wound with a finger in the air the first time he saw it. His gesture had felt like a curse. Maybe that's why it hadn't healed well.

As much as I wanted to blame Alec, I knew it was much more likely any problems with healing were caused by my complete refusal to follow the doctor's instructions. I hadn't stayed in the hospital. I'd gone diving while the cut was still open. I hadn't used any of the antiseptic creams the doctor prescribed. I hadn't taken it easy and rested. Now it looked like I would be paying the price of my hubris for the rest of my life.

With a shock, I recognized the pattern. I was so smug—so convinced I knew better, so sure I could handle anything—I made mistakes. It was a continuing pattern, and it showed up in every area of my life.

I'd married Alec, believing I could overcome his raging temper and selfishness. That turned out not to be the case.

I'd almost lost my mother because of my poorly chosen words when I all but accused her of murdering Ray.

I'd delayed my rescue attempt when Gus didn't return on time from his practice dive.

I'd believed I could save Ray if he needed me.

Too many accidents and near misses had occurred on my watch. All the events must be connected, or it was too much of a coincidence. I knew I'd never forgive myself even though I hadn't set out to kill him. I wasn't his killer, but I was the person who'd let Ray die. I'd cut corners, missed key details, and Ray had died because of my carelessness.

And later, I wallowed in guilt instead of acting. That had to stop.

I would unmask Ray's killer and get justice for my stepfather. I'd get to the bottom of the other accidents, which I recognized as a pattern of deliberate malice. Gus, Me, Lily, Ray, Maddy. Too many accidents to be accidents.

I met my eyes reflected in the mirror. The person I saw there now was someone who took responsibility and solved problems, not a person who drifted along through sunshine and rainbows. For the first time in my life, my eyes looked hard and determined. The eyes of an adult, not a child.

I suspected Cara, and both Lily and Oliver. Stewie. Alec. Even Theresa. And despite the partial thaw in our relationship, I still distrusted Newton, my bio-dad. I decided to make him the next person of interest in my investigation. I'd either clear him or find out he really was the cold unfeeling man I'd always thought he was. To figure that out, I'd need to spend more time with him.

I remembered Newton saying I should get my scar fixed while I had the chance, because people would always focus on the scar and not the person behind it. I didn't listen to him back then, but I decided to ask him to help me get the scar fixed now, as much because it would be a chance to observe him up close as it would be to fix my face. I picked up my phone and dialed his number.

"Newton, it's Fin. I hope it's not too early to call. Can I come to your hotel? There's something I want to talk to you about."

"Good morning. Never too early to hear from my beautiful daughter. Come on over. I'll order up some breakfast."

I was about to turn down breakfast when my stomach gurgled. Breakfast did sound good. "Super. I'll see you as soon as I can get there."

I heard happiness in his voice when we said our goodbyes, and I was a little ashamed for deceiving him. But I had to either find proof he was behind the accidents or rule him out, so I shrugged and grabbed my keys.

The ride to the Ritz was easy so early in the morning. I pulled up in front of the hotel and Liam hustled over to take my car.

"Welcome to the Ritz, Miss Fleming. Er, Fin. Miss Fleming." His skin flushed under his golden tan.

"It's always Fin to you, Liam."

"It's hotel policy. I'm not allowed to call guests by their first names."

"It's my personal policy you are only allowed to call me Fin. I'll let management know."

He laughed. "That should solve the issue."

"It seems like you're here all the time. You work long hours."

"I have to. I never know when you'll turn up to brighten my day."

I smiled at him, feeling my face glow with happiness at his words. He was such a nice man, and I found myself hoping we could spend more time together. Soon.

Instead of telling him what I was thinking, I handed him the totes containing Ray's logbooks. "Will you watch these for me please? I'll get them on the way out." After the destruction on my boat, I didn't want to leave the logbooks where just anyone could access them.

"Will do," he said, smiling. "I'll guard them with my life."

I waved at the concierge in the lobby, and I saw her reach for the phone, probably to let Newton know I was coming. The elevator arrived at his penthouse just as a waiter with a room service cart was about to knock on his door.

Newton let us in, and I was startled when he hugged me. "I'm so glad you're here. From now on I'm going to do at least one thing each day to show you how much I love you. I'll spend the rest of my life working on it. Consider today's breakfast the first step in my campaign. And I know no matter what I do, it'll never be enough."

"If you're serious about making it up to me, you can take me to see your friend the plastic surgeon. You were right about the scar. I want to have it fixed."

He poured himself a glass of orange juice from the pitcher the waiter had placed on the sideboard before he left. "Funny. I was wrong about it being the only thing people would see. Now that I've gotten to know you, I don't even notice it. But as you told me before, it's not up to me. I'll set up the appointment right away. And maybe we can take in a Broadway show and get your hair done like I promised."

"What, no pony?" We both laughed.

"Don't worry about the travel arrangements. It'll be much more convenient to take my jet. And you'll have more privacy if you stay at my place in Manhattan instead of a hotel. I have plenty of room. I'll even arrange for a private nurse to care for you after your procedure."

Newton had fallen for my plan. I'd have to be careful, but while he was playing the doting father, I would be looking for the evidence I needed to nail him. "None of that is necessary, but it will make it easier for me. Thank you. This is all very considerate of you."

"It's no problem. The doctor will work around your schedule. I've had him on retainer since the accident. It's time I got something in return for my money." He picked up his phone.

"Sid? Newton here. I want to bring my daughter in for a consultation. I trust you can fit us in this week?'

That boggled my mind. My mother was rich, and I guess by extension, I was too. But even if we were rich, we'd never lived like we had a lot of money. Maddy and I treated people like equals, and we tried to be thoughtful and considerate of everyone around us. We had nice houses and always bought good quality things, but we didn't have servants and we didn't put on airs. The idea of keeping a renowned surgeon on retainer for weeks just to get your daughter to the top of the priority list whenever you wanted didn't seem right. I worried about all the people who'd been waiting their turns getting bumped for me.

Newton hung up, satisfied that things would fall into place

the way he wanted with no further effort. "We're good to go. Let's have breakfast." He went to the sideboard where the waiter had set up a buffet of juice, coffee, pastries, eggs, sausages, and bacon.

Now that I'd set my plan in motion, I was torn. I wanted to investigate Newton, but if he'd been trying to kill me and other members of my family, it might not be safe for me to be alone with him in New York.

Too late now. I was committed.

"Thank you. It looks yummy. Tell me about your friend the plastic surgeon," I said, loading my own plate.

Newton described the doctor's practice, his cutting-edge work with lasers, and even named some of the high-profile clientele who patronized him. When he ran out of things to say about the doctor, he said, "Tell me what it was like growing up here. It must have been an ideal childhood."

"It was. Maddy, Ray, and I had so much fun and a ton of adventures. Looking back, I can see my life was every kid's dream."

"And Ray? He was always good to you?"

I looked deeply into his eyes before nodding. I could see in his expression he needed to be sure I'd had a good life. I saw no hint of malice. "He was. He was the best dad anyone could have hoped for."

Newton winced.

"Sorry. I just meant you left me in good hands."

His eyes clouded over with regret. "The one thing I did right during that time. I'm glad it worked out for you."

"It did, but it would have been better if my other father had come around once in a while."

He nodded ruefully. "Duly noted. I sucked as a father, and it will always be the biggest regret of my life. You grew up to be such an amazing person, and I'm proud that you're my daughter—even though I had no hand in making you the person you are." He sipped his juice. "Anything else you need to get off your chest?"

"What about Cara? It still seems like there's something between you two."

He cocked his head. "No, I told you there's no romance anymore, although there was once, long ago. She's just a very good employee. She can sniff out a profitable deal the way a shark can sniff out blood in the water. She's been with me since before the twins were born."

"That's a long time to work together. You must rely on her a lot."

"I do. She's been good for the business. And speaking of the business, can I interest you in joining Fleming Enterprises? Name the position you want and it's yours. It'll come with a super salary and lots of perks."

"No thanks. I'm happy where I am. Anyway, I can't imagine not living on an island."

"Manhattan's an island..."

"But not my kind of island. Thank you for the offer but I'll stay where I am. And speaking of which, I need to get to work." I was reluctant to leave. I was learning to like my father. I put my dishes on the sideboard, gave him a brief hug, and left.

CHAPTER FORTY-ONE

EVEN THOUGH IT was in the wrong direction, I decided to go back to my home office to pick up some image files for the Harry video. I pulled into the drive and slammed on the brakes when I realized my front door was open.

I tiptoed up to the open door and peeked in. Alec was sitting at the desk in my home office. I was enraged at his nerve. Last time I'd seen him he swore he loved me and apologized for stealing my work, yet here he was, obviously about to do it again. I inhaled deeply to regain my composure. His selfishness and petulance had made him unbearable to live with, and I didn't have to put up with it anymore.

He didn't know I was there, and I watched him without speaking as he worked on my computer, fiddling with the mouse, clicking away, and mumbling to himself. "No. No. Not that one either. C'mon. She must have something I can use."

I cleared my throat. "Can I help you find what you're looking for?"

Alec looked up and the color drained from his face. "Fin. I didn't expect you back this soon."

"I could tell. What are you doing?'

He stood and came around the desk. The smell of alcohol on his breath was overpowering when he reached out to hug me. "I heard about what happened to the *Maddy*. And after Ray's death..."

I pushed his arms away. "What are you doing? You have no right..."

"I was looking for some new images for the lobby screens. We should have some pictures of Ray up there. Sort of a tribute to him."

"Not your concern. You don't work at RIO, remember?" Not only was Alec's story an obvious lie—it was a weak one. The hi-def monitors in the lobby were already filled with images of Ray. He'd been as much the face of the Institute as my mother. He was featured on multiple posters, mugs, refrigerator magnets, and assorted other tchotchkes all for sale in our gift shop. "Why are you here? What are you doing on my computer?"

He drew in a breath and raised his shoulders in a shrug. "I needed to find the images from that trip to Ningaloo Reef we took. They're easier to find on your computer. You're way more organized than I am."

"And why do you think I would have any photos you took on my computer? Unlike you, I never made a habit of commingling our work. Doing that leads to mistakes." I made air quotes with my fingers around the word 'mistakes.'

He had the grace to blush, and I felt sorry for him. At least I did until he started talking again. "I got an idea for an app. I was thinking of putting together our most spectacular shots along with facts about the animals and locations in the images. We could add new images all the time as we get them and charge our users a subscription fee. I think we could make some real money with it."

"But you were going to use my shots, not yours? What's up with that?"

"No, no, I wasn't. Well, not really. I was going to use your shots for the beta I'm putting together."

"Were you planning to run this idea by me? Get permission to use my stuff, maybe?"

"Yeah, I was. I just wanted to surprise you and I thought you'd be more receptive to working with me if the images were yours. I'd make sure they were all credited to you, of course."

"Of course. Given your history and all. I guess it didn't occur to you to ask my permission to use my stuff. Or to suggest we work on your project together."

"Like I said, I wanted it to be a surprise. A nice surprise. And I didn't think you'd work with me unless you saw it first."

"You got that right. And I think I'll skip your little venture anyway. You're not the kind of partner I want to work with. I learned my lesson the hard way."

"C'mon, Fin. You and Ray ruined my life. I can't get a nature photography gig anywhere, thanks to you two. What am I supposed to do? I can't stay here playing second fiddle to you for my whole life. I'm talented. I'm Alec Stone, for God's sake!"

"Yes. You are Alec Stone, and you are talented. You just take too many shortcuts. Try earning your way, for once. You always said I was coasting on my mother's hard work. Listen to your own advice and try working for success instead of stealing someone else's." I knew this would set Alec off, but in the moment, I was angry enough not to care.

Alec's lips tightened and I could see him struggling for control. He threw the computer mouse against the wall, where it shattered into tiny pieces. He keened a high-pitched whine that hurt my ears. "I hate you. I hate Ray Russo. I hate everyone at RIO. But most of all, I hate you."

It shocked me when he continued his rampage by ripping

the cables out of my computer and hurling it against the wall. Electronic components rained to the floor. He pushed my monitors off the desk, and they cracked with a sickening crunch. He knocked all my reference books out of the bookcase. The whole time he kept screaming, "I hate you."

I was rigid with fear. Alec had thrown lots of temper tantrums while we were married, but although the potential for violence always ran just below the surface, he'd never been as bad as this. It was terrifying. I backed out of the office into the hall and pulled my cell phone out of my pocket to call the security force that patrolled my gated community.

When there was nothing left in my office to destroy, Alec started kicking the wall. He was still kicking when the security team arrived. The two burly guards each grabbed one of his arms.

"C'mon, Mr. Stone. We'll take care of you now," said one of the men in a kind voice, trying to calm Alec down and stop his rampage. "Everything's gonna be okay if you come with us." He nodded as the trio passed me on their way out of my home office.

I surveyed the ruin of my office. I'd seen Alec angry before, but I'd never seen him this enraged. His hatred for Ray and me was frightening. I needed to be around people, so I grabbed a couple of RIO-branded tote bags from my closet, locked my door, and drove to the office.

When I pulled onto RIO's grounds, I walked to the dock where the *Maddy* was moored. I wanted to gather the rest of Ray's logbooks before anything happened to them. Plus I hadn't taken much time to examine Newton's renovations, and I was looking forward to spending some time on my beautiful, refurbished boat. Newton had been very thoughtful to arrange the cleanup and repairs. I knew I hadn't been as gracious as the gesture warranted.

I didn't want to discourage him from trying to get closer to me until I was sure about my own feelings, especially after he'd confided how difficult those years of estrangement had been for him too. I sensed he was trying to forge a stronger relationship. One generous gesture didn't make up for the past, but I wanted to find a way to show him his concern meant a lot to me—that is, if he hadn't been responsible for Ray's death.

I was feeling warm toward Newton, but the warm feeling dissipated like smoke in the wind when I stepped onto the *Maddy* and found him sitting below deck reading Ray's logbooks. I was certain Ray would not have wanted Newton to read what amounted to his personal journals. "What are you doing here?"

Newton gave a start and dropped the book he was reading. "I thought you were working. I didn't expect to see you."

"That's not what I asked." My voice was sharp.

"I was worried about you."

"That still doesn't answer my question. Look, I appreciate what you did to restore the *Maddy*, but that doesn't give you the right to come aboard without permission. If you think it does, I'll pay you back for whatever the repairs cost you. My father is rich, you know."

He laughed. "C'mon, Fin. You must know I had the repairs done to make you happy."

"I appreciate the gesture, but your concern came...oh, about twenty years too late."

"I'm trying to make amends for that. And I was worried. Because something on this boat or in these books is important and valuable enough for someone to tear the boat apart to find it. I'm afraid for you. What if the person came back again when you were here alone? You could get hurt."

"I can take care of myself. And if Ray had wanted you to read his logbooks, he'd have left them to you instead of to me.

Now get off my boat and don't come back aboard without an invitation."

He stared at me for a moment before closing the book he'd been reading. He gathered it and the other books on the bench beside him and slipped them into the bookcase. He walked past me, and nimble as a goat, he hopped up to the dock. He turned around. "I didn't mean any harm. I thought if I read Ray's books, I could learn how it's done. I just want to be a good father to you. I may be late to the game, but that doesn't mean I don't care." He turned and left, his head hanging down.

I didn't know what to feel. I'd spent my whole life being angry at my father for not loving me. Now here he was, trying to get to know me and learn how to be a parent. I didn't know whether to believe his words and his recent actions or the twenty years of neglect that came before. Maybe we were better off when we never communicated. At least then we knew where we stood.

I watched Newton's car pull out of the parking lot, shading my eyes against the intensity of the early morning Cayman sunshine. When he'd gone, I took my tote bags to the *Maddy*'s cabin and removed the rest of Ray's logbooks from the bookcase behind the captain's table. They barely fit into the three big canvas totes I'd brought. I placed the heavy bags on deck and went below to examine the renovations.

The tiny galley had been completely refitted, and everything sparkled and shone. A two-burner induction cooktop and a small microwave and refrigerator framed the kitchen area. A new set of lightweight plastic dishes in a delicate floral pattern replaced the broken crockery. Of course, the insulated coffee mugs shelved behind a carved wooden rail had the RIO logo on them. The crisp gingham curtains with deep aqua checks coordinated with the lighter colors of the new daybed cover and the seat cushions on the chairs. The walls had been repainted a soft

white, and all the teak woodwork had been polished until it
gleamed. Two white leather captain's chairs flanked the entry.
Drawers and cubbies filled every nook and cranny, providing
plenty of storage.

Newton had replaced the old depth meter, fish finder, and
GPS, along with the radio and emergency beacon. He'd
thought of everything. I'd have expected this much work to take
months, but he'd accomplished it all in a single night.

I loved what Newton had done to the *Maddy* for me, and I
wanted to spend some time enjoying it. I sat on the boat's
transom reading the logbooks and watching the waves sparkling
in the sun.

I was still reveling in the beauty of the surroundings and
my refurbished boat until I heard shouting from RIO's grounds.
I sprinted down the pier to see what was going on.

Oliver was standing toe-to-toe with Alec, their noses inches
apart, fists clenched at their sides. Alec must have come here
immediately after they released him from the security office in
my community. He was obvious he was itching to cause trouble
today. I hurried over to see what he was up to now.

"You take that back." Oliver was shouting at Alec, who
wore the infuriating bland expression I'd hated during our
married days. "He didn't know about us or he would have taken
care of us. I know he would have.'

"Sure," Alec said. "That's why he never bothered to call or
text or anything. Twenty years is a long time to let slip by. At
least Fin's real father sent her birthday cards every year."

Oliver raised a fist like he was going to punch Alec. While I
couldn't blame him, I knew a fight on RIO's grounds would get
him fired, even if he was part of the family, and even though
Alec was looking for a fight. I didn't want Oliver dragged into
his destructive orbit so I sprinted across the lawn. "Oliver, let it
go. Alec doesn't know anything about Ray or what he'd have

done if he'd known about you. Don't you see he's trying to hurt you?"

Both men turned toward me. Oliver looked like he was trying not to cry. Alec's eyes glittered like ice, and he took a swig from the bottle of spiced rum in his hand. I remembered how mean he could be when he drank too much. The wreckage in my home office was a harsh reminder. "Alec, get off RIO property right now. You aren't welcome here."

Alec took a step toward me. For a moment it looked like he was going to hit me instead of Oliver, but he stopped himself. He turned and stomped away without another word.

"I can handle my own problems. You didn't have to step in," Oliver said.

"I know you can handle yourself, but you're my family, and family sticks together. Alec was out of line."

At first, he didn't say anything, just shuffled his feet in the grass. "We were fighting about you."

"Me? Why would you be fighting about me?"

"That big jerk said Ray cheated on your mother, and he didn't want you or her to find out about it. He said that's why Ray never came to see us. Alec said because he loved you so much, he had nothing left over for his own children."

I reached out to touch his arm. "Oh, Oliver. That's so not true. Ray had the biggest heart in the world, and I know for a fact he loved you and Lily the minute he knew about you. Never doubt his love."

Oliver sniffed. "I just wish I'd had more time..." His voice cracked.

"We all do, Oliver. We all do."

CHAPTER FORTY-TWO

I WAS SITTING at my desk watching the clock on my cell. The digits seemed to be changing too slowly to be moving in real time. Luckily for me, the workday was almost over, and I could leave with a clear conscience. I was packing up my things to leave for the day when my desk phone rang, earning itself a frown for delaying my early getaway. "Fin Fleming," I said into the receiver.

"Good afternoon, Fin. This is Carl Duchette, Editor in Chief of *Your World* magazine. If this isn't a good time to talk, we can set up an appointment at your convenience. I think you are a talented underwater photographer. I'd like to talk to you about doing a feature for the magazine."

I swallowed. "Now's a good time."

"Brilliant. First, I owe you an apology. It has come to my attention that we attributed some of your fine work to someone else, and that was inexcusable. We should have checked the artist's credentials more carefully. We will be printing a full-page correction statement and an apology in the next issue."

"Full-page? That's nice, but not necessary. That much

attention will ruin Alec's reputation beyond repair." I didn't love him, but I didn't need to add to his pain. From his recent actions, it was clear he was already hurting.

"I didn't mention his name. But be that as it may, he should have considered that before he certified the work as his own. At any rate, we will print a correction and an apology. But that's not why I called you today.

"I've admired your work for quite a few years, which is another reason I'm embarrassed I didn't recognize it when it was submitted. I'd like to offer you an opportunity to create a five-page spread in the magazine, plus supply the cover photo for the same issue. Would you be interested in that assignment?"

I took a slow deep breath before responding. "I'd be interested, Mr. Duchette. What would the topic be?" I was dancing a little jig beside my desk.

"Please, call me Carl. And the topic is up to you. I won't bore you right now with details about our style and the kinds of things we cover, because I assume you're either already familiar with us, or you will be soon. Sometime in the next few weeks, we could meet in my office in New York to brainstorm some ideas, unless you have any ideas off the top of your head. We'll pay your travel expenses, of course."

"Um, no. No ideas. I wasn't expecting this."

"I thought you might have been expecting my call because Ray sent me an email before his death telling me what Alec had done and asking me to investigate it. Ray and I had a follow up meeting by phone the day before he died. I've tried to contact Alec to get his side of the story, but until today he wasn't returning my calls. To be honest, I'd already seen some of your work, and I'm a huge fan. This offer would have come your way sooner or later. Ray's email and Alec's duplicity made it happen a bit faster, that's all."

I wondered if Alec ever would have come clean with *Your World* if Ray hadn't beat him to it. "I didn't realize Ray had been in contact with you." I sniffled at the thought that even after his death, Ray was still looking out for me.

"We're old friends. I introduced Ray to your mother. She was looking for a lead diver for her first documentary, and the rest is history, as they say." He chuckled, and I laughed along with him.

Thanks, Carl. Do you have a date in mind for the discussions?"

"We can work around your schedule. I don't have a lot of time right now, so I need to hang up, but I'll have my assistant call you later today to schedule it. I'm looking forward to meeting you."

"Likewise," I said.

"Before we go, I want to offer my condolences on your loss. Your stepfather was a good man. His death was a tragedy. Please let me know if I can do anything for you or Maddy."

"Thank you. I will. See you soon."

We hung up, and I continued my little happy dance around my office. Thanks to Ray, at last I was on my way.

My phone rang again within seconds. It was Carl's assistant and we put together a plan for my trip to New York. I wanted to synchronize the trip with the visit to the plastic surgeon, so we left the dates tentative. I promised to get back to her by the end of the day.

CHAPTER FORTY-THREE

THE NEXT AFTERNOON, Maddy dragged me to Newton's hotel while she signed the paperwork on the trust funds she was setting up for the twins. She wanted another opportunity for me to get to know Newton better. Figure out he's not such a bad guy.

Trouble is, I'd already figured that out. God help me, despite his inept and neglectful parenting, I like him. At least, I do when he isn't prying into things that are none of his business —like Ray's logbooks. Or when I'm not suspecting him of murder.

I left my car with Liam. Once again, I checked the tote bags containing Ray's logs with him for safe keeping. I knew he always said Newton took care of tipping him, but this went beyond a valet's role. I resolved to find a way to repay him for his help.

We arrived at Newton's suite early, long before Cara and the twins were due to get there. I think both Newton and Maddy wanted to make sure everything relating to the trusts was in order.

As always, the hotel had supplied Newton's suite with plenty of food and drink. Because I hadn't eaten all day, I helped myself to a sandwich and some chips. Maddy nibbled on a cookie, and Newton poured a glass of single malt scotch from the decanter on the bar.

He sipped his drink. "You're sure you want to do this, Maddy? There's no obligation to do anything for those kids. It must have hurt you to learn about them."

"I was mad when Ray told me about the twins, but we worked it out. Ray told me he had no memory of Cara at all. He thought she was a gold digger. But he loved the twins right from the start. God knows, they looked like they were his kids..."

"That's because they were his kids, Maddy. Cara and Ray had a one-night stand when we were here once on business. She told me all about it soon after it happened. I'm not surprised he didn't remember her. She said Ray had been drinking and he woke up hung over with no memory of their night together. Apparently, he'd been so out of it he was lucky he remembered his own name."

"I don't think that's what happened at all, Newton." Maddy said. "Ray and I talked about it a lot, and he wasn't convinced he'd ever been with Cara. He admitted they'd had drinks, and he ended up in her hotel room. But he said he'd always loved me, and no amount of alcohol would ever tempt him to risk what we had together. I believed him."

Newton lifted his glass to his lips, but not before I saw the pain in his eyes.

"At first, I thought he was just trying to cover himself because he got caught having an affair. After a while, I realized he wasn't taken in by Cara's claim either. But even though he didn't believe they were his, he loved the kids as soon as he met them."

This statement caused me a twinge of pain. Ray always

said he loved me the minute he met me. I'd thought it was because I was special, but now I knew that's just the way he was. Still, he'd loved me, and I was lucky to have that. I put my jealousy aside and went back to listening to Maddy.

"I wasn't convinced Cara was telling the truth either. I asked Dr. Smithers to do a DNA test on Lily's blood after her accident, while she was in the chamber. The results just came back this morning. Lily and Oliver aren't Ray's biological children. Ray told me the truth. He was never with Cara.

"He said when he woke up in her hotel room, he was so upset he gave up drinking. He never touched another drop of liquor because he didn't ever want to be tempted and risk losing what we had together." She wiped a tear from her eye.

I breathed a sigh of relief at hearing the DNA results. I hadn't known about the test, but I'd hated thinking Ray would ever hurt my mother that way. Now I knew he'd been the good man I'd always thought he was.

Newton put his empty glass on the sideboard, his back to my mother. "If you're sure..."

"I'm sure. It's the right thing to do. Even if they weren't his biologically, he loved the twins. Just the way he loved Fin. He'd want them taken care of, and I can afford to be generous as long as Fin is okay with it."

I shrugged. "Fine by me. There's plenty to go around." I really was fine with Mom taking care of the twins financially. I have my own trust fund already, so this action wasn't taking anything away from me. I knew Ray had loved them, even though he'd only known them for a short time. This is what he would have done for them if he could have. Maddy and I both wanted them to have a good life for his sake, and Maddy has plenty of money. As far as I was concerned, she could do whatever she wanted with it.

"I'm not happy to learn Cara tried to dupe you and Ray.

We can still fight her claim if you want." Newton sat at the table again.

Mom smiled "That's just it, Newt. I don't want to fight it. Since Fin is okay with the plan, I want to do this for Ray's sake. Print out the papers, please. I want to read through them before they get here."

"But if you know they're not his kids..." Newton tried again.

"It doesn't matter to me if Ray was their biological father, any more than it mattered to him. He took those kids into his heart the minute he met them—exactly the way he took Fin into his heart the first time he met her. Ray loved Fin, and even though he only knew them for a short time, he loved the twins. I owe it to him to make sure they're taken care of the same way he always took care of Fin. Now please print the documents."

Newton sighed and pushed the print button on his computer screen. For a few moments, the only sound in the room was the soft whirr of the printer. Then he said, "Do you plan to tell Cara or the twins about the DNA results?"

Mom looked troubled. "I'll tell Cara. It's up to her whether she decides to tell the twins the truth. They've been hurt enough already,"

He handed the printed documents to Maddy and me. I put mine aside. The details were none of my business. I was just here to keep Maddy company.

Newton sighed. "Maddy, we can make this quick. The terms of the trust are almost the same as Fin's. Unless it's to pay for their education, they can't access the principal until they turn twenty-five, and even then, they can't withdraw more than ten percent per year. Gus, you, and I are the trustees, and if anything happens to any one of us, Fin is the designated replacement."

"Okay," she said, putting on her reading glasses. "Can you show me where ..."

I went out onto the balcony while they huddled together talking business. I looked up when I heard Maddy tap her copies on the table. "All looks good."

Newton set a fresh copy of the documents in front of each chair at the table, then he cleared his throat. "Before the others get here, there's something else I want to talk about."

"Sure. What's up?" Maddy smiled at him.

Newton's ears turned red and he looked like he'd swallowed his tongue. After a pause, his words came out in a rush. "With Ray out of the picture, is there any chance for us to start over? After you've had enough time, of course." His voice trailed off.

My mother's face went white as snow—or as white as I'd always heard snow could be. "I'm sorry, Newton. Really, I am. But I don't think I'll ever love someone the way I loved Ray. And you deserve someone who loves you like that."

The doorbell chimed, breaking the tension, and Newton rose to answer it. Cara, Oliver, and Lily came in. They were followed by Theresa and Gus, who was looking better than he had been for a long time. I was happy that he seemed to be recovering. Everyone sat at the huge round table.

Newton explained the terms of the trusts to them. "Any questions?" he asked when he'd finished. Both twins seemed stunned, but Cara had a triumphant smile on her face while he spoke.

"This is unexpected," Lily said. "Ray set this up before he died?"

No, he didn't," Newton said. "Ray didn't have anywhere near enough assets to support this generosity. Madelyn is doing this on her own because she knows it's what Ray would have wanted."

"Thank you, Mrs. Russo." The twins spoke in unison. Lily had a big happy smile on her face.

Oliver was pale, staring at his shaking hands. I assumed he was feeling guilty he hadn't been there when Ray needed him.

"If there are no questions, we can sign the paperwork and the trusts will be funded by the end of the day tomorrow. Ready?" Newton handed pens to everyone involved, and they all signed the documents.

"And for me?" Cara asked.

"Nothing. Why would you be expecting anything?" Newton glared at her over his reading glasses. It was obvious he wasn't happy with her attempt at conning Ray.

Cara's face fell, but she covered her disappointment with a crooked smile. "No reason except I'm their mother."

"Since this is such a happy occasion, let's have a drink together to celebrate," Maddy said, interrupting the start of Cara's familiar whine. She rose from her chair.

Cara put a hand on her arm. "Sit. Let us serve you. You've done enough for my family." She walked to the bar, followed by Lily and Oliver.

Theresa stood up. "Nothing for either of us. We can't stay. I need to get Gus home." She helped him to his feet.

Gus kissed my mother's cheek. "Goodbye. See you all soon." He and Theresa walked out together.

Nobody said anything when the door closed behind them until Cara broke the ice. "What are you having, Fin?" Cara asked, her back to me.

"Just water, thanks."

"Me too," said Maddy.

"I presume you're having your usual scotch, Newton?" she said, placing two icy glasses of spring water on a tray. She added two cans of soda for the twins, and two Baccarat crystal highball glasses, each containing two fingers of scotch.

Oliver picked up the tray and carried it to the table. Lily took the beverages off the tray and placed each one on a napkin.

"To a big happy family," Cara said, raising her glass in a toast.

I'm not sure Maddy had been planning to welcome Cara to her family, but she clinked glasses with everyone at the table anyway. After a few sips of her water, she rose. "I need to get back to work. Coming, Fin?"

CHAPTER FORTY-FOUR

AN HOUR LATER, I was sitting at my desk, on edge and unable to focus on work. I'd heard and seen how much Newton cared about my mother. The wistful expression on his face when she talked about how much she missed Ray...heartbreaking. Now I rued asking him to set up the appointment with the plastic surgeon so I could spy on him. My own father couldn't be trying to kill me. We should talk things over like real families do, instead of playing games to cover our true feelings. Starting right now. I grabbed my keys to drive to the Ritz to see him.

It wasn't long before I pulled up at the valet station, and Liam opened the door for me. "Fin," he said. "It's nice to see you again." I saw real pleasure in his eyes before he blushed bright red. "I mean, welcome back to the Ritz-Carlton, Miss Fleming. Do you need help carrying anything inside?"

I laughed. "Good to see you too, Liam. I'm fine, thanks. I'm just here to see my dad. I won't be long, but can you hold on to these again for me, please?" I handed him the tote bags containing Ray's logbooks.

He gave me that devastating smile of his. "Don't I always? Do you want the concierge to call to let him know you're here?"

"No thanks. It's a surprise." I handed him my keys along with some folded bills and took my ticket. "I'll see you on the way out."

"I get off at six-thirty," he said, handing me back my money as he always did. "In case you were wondering." There was a twinkle in his deep blue eyes. "In case you want to have dinner."

"I'd like that. I'll pick you up at six-thirty." I beamed at him. He smiled back, and we stood there staring at each other, grinning like fools. Finally, I shook my head. "I have to see my father," I said, turning to the entry.

"See you at 6:30," he said.

I felt his eyes on my back as I left, and knowing he was watching me almost made me forget how to walk. Fortunately, I made it into the lobby.

"Good afternoon, Miss Fleming," the concierge said when I passed her desk. "Would you like me to let your father know you're here?"

"No, thanks. It'll be fine." I saw her frown and knew she'd call him anyway. Okay by me.

The elevator doors opened with a hushed whoosh, and I stepped out onto the thick carpet. I could hear the melodious chiming inside the suite when I rang the bell, but I didn't hear anyone coming toward the door. "Dad? Newton? It's Fin. Can I come in?" I said, rapping the door with my knuckles.

The unlocked door swung open. It wasn't like Newton to leave his door unlocked. He was casual, yes, but also security conscious. I stepped inside the suite and looked around, calling out again when I didn't see anyone. "Newton? Are you here?" Curse my luck. He must have gone out. I turned to leave, but before I shut the door, I heard a faint sound. It was so quiet it could have been a fingernail tapping on the rim of a glass or melting ice shifting in the bucket, but I knew it wasn't either of those. I stepped further inside and looked around.

I found him lying on the floor outside his bedroom. His glass of scotch had fallen out of his hand and the liquid soaked the rug beside him. He must have hit his head on the wall when he fell, because a heavy stain of blood marred the pristine white paint. His lips were blue, and his skin was cold and clammy when I put my hand to the pulse in his neck. I was shocked at how fast his heart was beating.

Newton had been fine when we left not that long ago. I turned him on his side so he wouldn't choke. "Hang on, Dad. I'll get help." If it wasn't a heart attack or a stroke, it looked like a suicide attempt to me. I was afraid my mother's refusal to consider getting back together had put him over the edge.

I rushed back to the main living area and picked up the phone. "This is Fin Fleming. Please get an ambulance and send the EMTs up to my father's suite. He needs medical assistance. Fast. Please hurry."

I raced back to Newton's side. If anything, he looked like he'd gotten worse in the short time I'd been on the phone. His lips were a deeper blue, and his breathing was labored and thready.

I grabbed one of his hands. "Don't die on me, Dad. We have a lot of time to make up for. I just found you. Please don't go."

One eye opened. "Won't. Go. Help." He could barely speak.

"Help is coming, Dad. Hang on." I chafed his wrist, fretting. If we'd been on a boat or underwater, I'd have known what to do. On land, I was useless.

After what felt like a year, a paramedic tapped my shoulder. "We've got him now, Miss. We'll take it from here."

I ran out to follow the ambulance to the hospital. Liam had my keys ready for me. I grabbed them and ran to my car without stopping to exchange our usual pleasantries.

After two hours at the hospital, the doctor came out and told me Newton had taken an overdose of pills, but he would be fine.

"No," I said. "He wouldn't do that. Someone did this to him."

The doctor patted my arm. "Sometimes even families don't realize what's going on. Don't beat yourself up over this." He continued his status update. Newton was asleep and would stay asleep through the night, under a twenty-four-hour suicide watch.

Since I was exhausted myself, I went home. There was nothing I could do until Newton woke up.

CHAPTER FORTY-FIVE

GETTING up before dawn was becoming a habit, but I wanted to see Newton and make sure he was okay before I got into my day. When I arrived at Cayman Islands Hospital, it was long before official visiting hours. I'd planned to sneak in, but his private duty nurse opened the door for me. "He's awake and anxious to see you."

I was shocked by Newton's appearance. It wasn't just the presence of the usual hospital paraphernalia—all the tubes and the buzzing and beeping equipment. He looked terrible. The skin of his sunken cheeks was ashen, and his lips were bloodless. The nurse had said he was awake, but his eyes were shut. Rather than disturb him, I started to back out of the room on tiptoe.

"Don't go." Newton lifted the fingers of his right hand. "Please."

I crossed the room to the chair beside his bed. "I thought you were asleep." I grasped his hand. "But yesterday I thought you were a goner, so I guess that's better."

He squeezed my fingers and tried to smile. His fingers

lacked strength, and he looked like he hadn't slept in days. "Not easy to get rid of." His voice was raspy and hoarse.

"I just found you. Why would I want to get rid of you? But they told me this was a suicide attempt. I heard you ask Maddy about getting back together. Is that what made you try to kill yourself? Tell me the truth, Newton."

"I swear to you I did not try to kill myself. I think the same person who did this killed Ray and they've been after you and Maddy. Be careful, Fin."

I sighed with relief that he wasn't suicidal, but then then the rest of his words sank in. Someone was after my family. "I thought it was you."

He opened his eyes wider at that. "Never," he said, struggling to sit up.

I looked into his blue eyes so much like my own and knew he was telling the truth. "I'll find the person who did this to you," I said. "You just rest. I'll be back later." I tucked his hand under the covers and left.

CHAPTER FORTY-SIX

AFTER I LEFT my father in the hospital, I went to RIO. I needed to think about who could be responsible for my father's overdose but I also needed to buckle down and get some things done before my trip to New York. I raced down the hall, but I stopped short when I saw the mess in my office. Everything in it had been demolished.

My new computer lay smashed on the floor. My monitors and backup drives were also smashed, and all the books and manuals from the bookcase were in the pile, many with pages torn out and crumpled. The contents of my desk drawers had been dumped on the floor and trampled. The desk had been upended and the bookcase overturned. The seats of my desk chair and all the guest chairs had been slashed. The vandal had poured soda, ice cream and maple syrup over everything.

Worst of all, the enlargement of the picture of Maddy and the great white had been ripped to shreds. The frame was twisted and the glass was broken. Along with everything else in my office, it was a total loss.

Where had security been while all this was going on? It

was true we only had a skeleton crew at night, but strangers couldn't enter the building unless someone let them in. The only people who wouldn't need the security team to open the doors for them were the people who worked here. But I couldn't imagine anybody who worked here would do this.

I was staring at the wreckage when Stewie came down the hall.

"It's a mess, huh?" he said. "Somebody must really have it in for you."

"Yeah. Who would do this?"

"Looks like someone was looking for something. Maybe Ray's map to the location of the Queen's Tiara?" He stared around my office and whistled. "What a mess. I just dropped in to say hello, but I'll help you clean up."

"Thanks for the offer, but I'll get maintenance to do it. See you later, Stewie." He shuffled off down the hall, hands in the pockets of his baggy cargo shorts. While I waited for maintenance to come with trash bags and bins, I filled out a requisition for yet another new computer.

When the maintenance team arrived, Stanley, the younger of the two men, looked around and whistled through his teeth. "Wooee. What a mess."

Eugene, the head maintenance manager, gave him a look that made it quite clear he thought Stanley should keep quiet. "I'm sorry about the mess." He looked around. "But it won't take us long to clean it up."

"I can handle it myself. Thanks, Eugene."

"Nah, we'll do it, Fin. You have enough on your plate. It's our job anyway."

I smiled at him with gratitude. "Thank you. I appreciate it.

I walked down the hall to Maddy's office. She looked at the requisition I slipped onto her desk. "Again?" she said when she'd read it. "What happened this time?"

"Talk to security. Too many people who have no business being in the RIO offices wandering around at all hours. First Alec trashing my home, then fighting with Oliver, now this. It must be someone we know."

"I'm certain nobody we know would do this, but I'll speak to security about making sure people don't come in except during business hours, okay? No matter who it is, they don't come into the office area without an escort unless they work here."

I nodded. "Good. Thanks."

"Try to make this computer last more than a few days, will you?" She grinned at me after she signed off on the purchase. "We are a non-profit organization, you know. We have better uses for our funds than buying new computers for you every few days."

I shrugged. "So, about my desk. And my chair. And the guest chairs that used to be in my office..."

She groaned. "Really, Fin? What's next?"

CHAPTER FORTY-SEVEN

LATER THAT DAY, while driving along East Church Street to go back to the hospital, I had the idea to stop in at Sunset House to see Theresa first. I hadn't talked to her much lately. That was no way to treat a best friend.

I strolled across the sunlit parking lot and down the hill past the dive shop to the bar. It was a relief to get out of the sun and under the bar's thatched roof.

"Hey, Fin. It's been a while. What'll you have?" For once the bar was empty, and Brian, the bartender, was polishing glasses instead of hustling at top speed to keep a steady stream of Stingray beers, mudslides, and margaritas flowing.

"Just a cola, Brian, thanks. Say, have you seen Theresa today?"

"She worked the breakfast shift in the main restaurant today. You just missed her," said Brian. "But I think she'll be back for the dinner shift." Like many people in the hospitality industry, Theresa worked hard.

"Thanks," I said, accepting the frosty mug he handed me. I

took a deep drink before I claimed a shady table near the wall. I unfurled the umbrella before sitting down with my feet up and gazed out to sea.

But instead of focusing on the view, I remembered the last time I'd been here. I'd been with Alec, a few days after my accident. It was the night I met Lily. A lot had happened since that evening. It was hard to believe that was only a few weeks ago.

As though my thoughts had conjured them up, Alec and Lily ambled into the bar. Lily was laughing at something Alec said when she caught sight of me. "Fin, I've been meaning to call you." She sat down at my table. "The usual," she said to Alec. He nodded and left to get her a drink.

Interesting. They must have been seeing a lot of each other if Alec knew Lily's usual. Funny, neither of them had mentioned it to me. Of course, they didn't have to. I wasn't in charge of their lives, but it still seemed strange.

"What are you doing here in the middle of the day, Lily?" I asked, noticing her wet hair. "Been diving?"

"Yes, we did the shore dive. Even with all the beautiful dive sites in the Caymans, I think the shore dive here is one of my favorites. We saw a southern stingray, a sea turtle, and a nurse shark sleeping under the wreck. We even saw the tourist submarine come by while we were admiring the mermaid statue. Something interesting is always happening here."

"Yup," I agreed. "It's a special site. Have you and Alec been doing a lot of diving together?" I tried to sound casual, but the look she gave me said I hadn't succeeded at fooling her.

"We haven't been dating, if that's what you mean." Her voice was cool.

"None of my business, anyway. You're welcome to him, but you should know what you're getting into. He's a complicated man." I sucked on the last sliver of ice in my drink.

Alec came over with a mudslide for Lily and a bottle of Stingray for himself. He looked at my empty glass. "Sorry. Did you want something, Fin? I should have asked. I can go back..."

"No, thanks. I was just leaving. See you guys around." I rose and strode out of the bar.

CHAPTER FORTY-EIGHT

INSTEAD OF GOING to the hospital to see my dad, after seeing Lily and Alec together I went for a long drive. It wasn't that I wanted him back, more like I didn't want him dating my sister. He was not a good man, but it wasn't my place to set Lily straight about Alec. It was late afternoon by the time I cruised back to the hospital, and afternoon visiting hours were over. Disappointed, I went back to RIO.

Eugene and Stanley had finished cleaning up the mess in my office. They'd put all the furniture back in place, but my papers were all in the wrong folders and the books were out of order in the shelves.

I spent the next few hours putting all the books to rights, sorting papers, and rearranging the folders in the desk drawers. Organized at last, I sat down to work. Except my desk wobbled, my chair had three wheels instead of its previous four, and my shattered computer was nonfunctional. I wasn't worried about my files or the draft of my thesis because everything was backed up to the cloud, but I was feeling guilty about how little time I'd put into my job lately. It was now after five, and I worried about my lack of productivity. To make up for it, I decided to do some work with Rosie in the lab.

Before I could leave my office, June, Maddy's assistant, poked her head in the door with a question about the requisition for new office furniture. She and Maddy had come up with the idea I should move into Ray's old office, or barring that, move his furniture into my current office rather than buy a new desk and chairs. That would save us from spending money unnecessarily until we decided whether to replace Ray as CFO and head of diving operations. With no documentary to bring in new funds this year, our budget would be tighter than usual.

Either of their ideas worked for me, but I liked the view out my windows. I decided it was best to move Ray's furniture into my office. June called Eugene, who said he and Stanley would take care of it right away. I was grateful for their dedication. It meant I'd be able to get right to work in the morning. I wrote a note to bring in my home computer in the morning and stuck it to my car's key fob and put the keys in my purse.

Then I unpacked all the folders in my desk drawers again and stacked the books on the floor in the hall. By the time I finished unpacking everything I'd just put away, Stanley was there with a dolly to move the damaged furniture out.

Eugene was right behind him with Ray's desk on another dolly. Together they shuffled the furniture in and out, until at last, everything was in position. I refiled my folders in the desk drawers and stacked the books. It was after nine P.M. by the time I finished, but I wanted to stop in and see Rosie anyway.

The lights were off in the lab when I got there, which was odd. Since the flashing of lights going on and off could disturb the sea creatures who lived in the lab, we kept it dimly lit all the time. Even during the day when the scientists were working, the overhead lights provided just enough illumination to let people see what they were doing. I'd never had to use the light switch in all my years at RIO, so I was groping around looking for it.

I stepped further into the pitch-dark room feeling for the switch when I noticed cool wetness licking at my old flip-flops. That was alarming. The floor shouldn't be wet unless something had happened to one of the tanks. My heart started beating faster, and I couldn't catch my breath. What could have happened? At last, I found the switch. Light flooded the room. It was a disaster.

Every aquarium and tank had been smashed, the sand and gravel strewn on the floor. Fish food and supplies had been knocked off the shelves and lay in sodden heaps. Lab reports and research papers were everywhere, turning into wet, soggy lumps of papier-mâché that would never be readable again.

The worst sight of all was the misery inflicted on the lab's inhabitants. Hundreds of fish and exotic sea creatures lay on the floor, many already dead and dried out from lack of water. Others still lived, gasping out their final breaths. Tears rolled down my cheeks.

It was a nightmare. I screamed for help, but nobody came. After nine P.M. was too late for people to still be at work. I would have to do what I could to save these helpless creatures all on my own. Because we never knew when we might adopt a new inhabitant and what sort of environment the new occupant would need, we had dozens of aquariums in our supply room. I rushed there and turned the knob. It was locked.

I had a key, but my keys were in my office. I ran down the hall and yanked open the desk drawer where I stored my canvas purse. My shaking hands fumbled around in the purse's cavernous depths searching for my keys. Kleenex. Chapstick. Wallet. Pen. Sunglasses. Phone. Where were the keys?

Frustrated, I dumped the purse's contents out on my desk and heard the telltale jingle of keys tumbling to the floor. I knelt, reaching under the desk to retrieve them, pulling them to me with trembling fingers. I ran back to the supply room to grab the aquariums, but time stretched out so far it seemed like I was running underwater.

Back in the lab, I slipped on the slick tile floor and fell, cutting my knee on a shard of glass. I ignored the bleeding and swept debris from shattered aquariums off the nearest table. I placed the two large aquariums I'd brought in the cleared space before realizing these helpless creatures would not survive immersion in tap water. I had to get sea water into the tanks. In desperation, I looked around for some way to save the fish.

A small stack of buckets we used for feedings in the public aquarium stood in a back corner on the far side of the room. I grabbed one in each hand and looked around to see if any of the fish looked like they wouldn't survive the few extra minutes it would take me to bring back bucketsful of sea water. I gently picked up a few who looked close to extremis and put them in the pails.

I sprinted out of the lab and across the lawn toward the marina. When I passed the dive shack, I saw lights shining through the windows. I screamed "Help me. I need help."

I kept running. These poor fish didn't have a moment to spare if I wanted to save their lives.

When I reached the pier, I knelt and submerged the buckets in the water. Within a few seconds, the fish began to revive. Since I was intent on watching the fish to make sure they would make it, I didn't hear Oliver come up behind me.

"Are you all right, Fin? I was filling tanks when I heard you shouting for help."

I almost jumped out of my skin. When I caught my breath, I said, "Someone destroyed the lab. Fish dying. Can you run up there and grab a couple more buckets?"

His mouth dropped open. "That's awful. Who would do that?"

I shrugged. "Hurry. Put any fish that look like they don't have much time in the buckets and bring them here to revive. When they're strong enough, we can bring them back and put them in a new tank. I'll bring these guys up and we can use the sea water in the buckets to fill some aquariums.

He grabbed the pails out of my hands and was already halfway across the lawn, running at top speed despite the heavy buckets of water and fish. "On it," he shouted.

I ran after him. The rescue process would go faster if we worked together.

Oliver passed me at the door on his way back to the ocean. He carried a bucket in each hand. One bucket contained dozens of small fish, the other a large tarpon, his body hanging listlessly over the rim on each side of the handle.

I had to admire his strength. Tarpon are big fish, weighing anywhere from fifty to three hundred pounds. The one he carried was not yet full grown, and I estimated it weighed one hundred pounds, but Oliver carried the bucket with one hand.

I reached the lab and tipped the sea water from the first set of buckets he'd carried up into the waiting aquariums. Then I looked for more fish who seemed bad off and put them in the newly filled tanks, overcrowding them but careful not to mix predators with prey. Meanwhile, Oliver had returned, grabbed two more buckets, added some dying fish, and headed back on another trip to get more water.

I poured the water from the latest buckets into aquariums and added more fish. The fish begin to revive as soon as their gills touched the salty water. I looked around for more specimens to save and started putting them in empty pails for Oliver's return trip. I was at the door of the lab ready to run back to the dock when I bumped into him. I grabbed the buckets from his hands.

"I'll take these. You get more buckets. They're heavy when they're full, and you can move quicker and carry more weight than I can. It will go faster if I stay here and set up the aquariums while you get the water. Together, we can save more of the fish."

Without another word, he grabbed my buckets and tore off across the lawn. Most days I'd have been annoyed at his assumption he was stronger and faster than me, but I had to admit he had completed the trip back from the dock carrying those heavy buckets faster than I could have. I was grateful for his help as we worked together to reduce the destruction.

I pushed the debris off another of the lab's worktables and rushed to the supply room for two more aquariums. When I got back, I dumped the water Oliver had brought into the new tanks and looked around the floor for creatures who seemed to be at the most risk. One by one, I picked up each fish with gentle hands and sorted them into the tank where it would be safest. I ran to the supply closet for more aquariums. Then I triaged the floor for the next batch of near-dead fish for Oliver to take back to the sea with him.

I had the buckets loaded with the worst-off fish when he came through the door with fresh pails of sea water and reviving fish. "I'll take those." He grabbed my buckets and ran back to the dock.

I rushed to get more aquariums. I lost count of the number of desperate trips we'd made, the fish we'd saved, and the fish we'd lost.

My body was so tired it seemed like we'd been working for days when Oliver entered the lab and dumped sea water into the last two unfilled aquariums. We picked up the fish still on the floor and placed them in the tanks.

But our work still wasn't done. Since the fish populations in the tanks would soon deplete the oxygen supply unless we were able to replenish it, we needed to set up an aerator and filtration system in each tank to keep them from suffocating. My back ached and I was bone tired, but I had to keep working.

I looked at Oliver. He was bent over with his hands resting on his quadriceps, panting, and a mixture of sweat and sea water dripped from his head to the floor. His shorts and tee shirt were wet and covered with dirt, fish scales, and blood where he'd wiped his hands when the weight of the full buckets caused the wire handles to cut into his palms. A rush of fondness and gratitude to Oliver swept through me. Losing the lab would have been one more loss in my life, and I had to admit, I wouldn't have been able to recover as anywhere near as many of the valuable specimens without him.

"Can you stay a little longer? Help me get the filters set up?"

He nodded, still panting too hard to speak. Then he went to the sink and washed his hands. When they were clean, he cupped them and brought water to his mouth. After he drank, he wiped his face. "That was quite a workout. But those poor fish..." I saw the unshed tears pooling in his eyes before he turned away.

I knew how he felt, but the longer we delayed the more fish would perish. "C'mon. Let's get started." We trotted back to the supply room to grab the first few filtration setups. While we were there, Oliver hoisted a heavy sack of white aquarium gravel to his shoulder.

Back in the lab, I started assembling filters while Oliver stood at the sink rinsing the gravel to remove any dust or impurities. "Which one first?" he asked, when the rinse water ran clear.

"We can't pour the gravel in while there are fish in the tank.

We'll need to set one up, and then we can move the fish around from tank to tank. We'll have to clean the used tanks before we can refill them, and sort the fish before we put them back to make sure we don't put natural enemies in together, and ..." My voice broke. I was tired, disheartened, beaten. I wasn't sure I could even stand up long enough to refit all the tanks. It felt like the world had been working against me ever since Gus's accident, and I didn't like the feeling one bit.

I turned away to hide how upset I was, but Oliver seemed to know anyway. He leaned against the table I was working at and handed me a cup of fresh, cold water. "Drink this. You'll feel better, and the fish will be fine for a few minutes while you take care of yourself. You won't be any good to anyone if you keel over."

I took a big gulp, blinking back tears. While I'd been feeling sorry for myself, Oliver had gone back to the supply room to grab more tanks and now he positioned them on an empty lab table. Then he went back to the dock with two empty buckets while I scooped in clean gravel and set up the filter. I poured sea water from the last pails he'd brought up, just as he returned with more.

As we finished setting up each new aquarium, I used a net to move fish from the other tanks. This time, I looked for fish that could cohabit in peace rather than selecting them by how close to death they looked. We had just finished putting the last fish—a young purple tang, one of my favorites—into his new home when Oliver said, "You were amazing. You worked hard to save them all."

"It was a team effort, Oliver. I couldn't have gotten this far without your help. Thank you." I was shaking with exhaustion.

"Who would do a thing like this?" he asked. "It's so senseless. The poor fish didn't hurt anyone." He looked around, his gaze lingering on the pile of fish that hadn't survived.

I sighed with weariness. "We may teach diving and have fund raising events, but our real work is research and studying the ocean. Every one of those fish was important to our mission. It may take us years to get the research program back where it was."

I was embarrassed when my voice cracked, but Oliver nodded and put a hand on my shoulder. "You'll come through. You always do." He looked around. "Say, where's that little octopus of yours? I've heard a lot about her, and I've never even seen her."

Oh my God. In the rush to save as many of the sea creatures as possible, I'd forgotten about Rosie. I didn't remember putting her in a bucket or in a tank. "Are you sure you haven't seen her?"

He shook his head. "Let's check the tanks. Maybe she's hiding."

He started at one end of the room and I went to the other. We peered into the corners of every tank, but we didn't see Rosie. We hadn't had the bandwidth to put in plants or shells yet, so none of the tanks had a place she could hide.

I looked at the pile of dead fish we'd made while trying to save the ones we could. I didn't think Rosie was in the pile, but I had to look. I held a bag open while Oliver lifted each body and placed it inside. It took a long time, but we reached the bottom of the pile without finding Rosie. I searched the room for drains, exits, or small crannies that might have looked like sanctuary to a tiny, frightened octopus.

"I'll get started cleaning up while you keep looking for Rosie, okay?" said Oliver. He left to find a push broom and a dustbin.

I still hadn't found her when he returned. He had the push broom over his shoulder and was towing a wheeled trash bin behind him. He pulled on a pair of leather work gloves he'd taken from the maintenance closet and started picking up the large pieces of glass from shattered tanks.

He picked up a small pink shell that'd been partially submerged in the spilled water. When he shook it, Rosie tumbled out into his palm. "Found her." He passed her to me. I cradled her in my hands. "Oh, Rosie. Oh, sweetheart." She was in a bad way. Her skin was dry and leathery, and her eyes were filmed. Her mantle expanded and contracted, with a gasping whistling sound when she tried to breathe, but without water, she couldn't get the oxygen she needed. I estimated she had, at most, minutes to live.

I looked at the overcrowded tanks, filled beyond their normal capacity with hungry and frightened fish. We hadn't had time to put in plants or coral to make the fish comfortable. Not a single aquarium had the secluded refuge my shy little Rosie needed to feel safe. We could put in her shell, but Rosie would still be at the mercy of all the fish in the tank with her.

I shook the last drops of tap water out of my cup and dipped it into the nearest tank to scoop out some seawater. I placed Rosie—shell home and all—into the cup, but the oxygen in the little cup wouldn't be adequate to keep her going for long. I would need to do something right away if I were going to save her.

I did a quick mental run down of the aquariums we'd worked so hard to set up, and which fish were in each. None was a safe harbor for Rosie. We had no more unused aquariums. I knew what I had to do. To save her, I'd have to set Rosie free.

I raced out of the lab, down the hall and out the door to RIO's lawn. Slipping on the early morning dew, I rushed across the grass to where the ocean lapped against our shore. I plunged into the water beside the dock, still holding Rosie in her cup. I sat down and held her beneath the life-giving water.

For a moment, she didn't move. Her mantle didn't pulse with her breathing, and her tentacles weren't exploring her surroundings. I sobbed.

But after a few more seconds, one of Rosie's tentacles began moving. She reached out with a light touch against my palm. Her mantle expanded as she pulled in seawater to extract the oxygen she needed. Slowly, her mantle pulsed again. Another tentacle moved. Rosie was alive.

I held the cup until she was fully revived, then I waded out in the water to a grouping of coral heads on the shallow bottom. I held my breath and ducked under, examining the coral. I had to surface for air three times before I found what I was looking for. It was a small indentation in the coral, just the right size for Rosie to be safe and sheltered. Sobbing my goodbyes, I was about to place her inside when I heard Oliver shouting.

"Wait, Fin. I found a tank for Rosie in the gift shop." He was brandishing a small glass aquarium like kids used for goldfish. It would work for now.

He dipped the glass bowl into the sea water and I splashed over to him to put Rosie and the pink shell inside. She settled in and looked up at me with inscrutable eyes, her tentacles swirling around her. After a moment, she flashed pink. I wiped tears from my eyes and waded slowly back to shore.

We were crossing the lawn when I had a thought. "How did you get into the gift shop?" I asked Oliver.

He shrugged. "I broke the door. You can dock my pay."

"Not a chance," I said. "You saved my Rosie."

We entered the lab and I placed Rosie's new home on one of the racks. I set up a filter and an aerator while Oliver finished cleaning up the lab. We stopped by Maddy's office and I left a note on her desk explaining the destruction and the steps we had taken to save the fish. I knew it would have been better to call her, but if I did, I'd end up staying to help organize the repair efforts. I couldn't face it. Oliver and I had worked through the night, and I was too tired and disheartened to be of much help.

The sun was rising when Oliver and I went our separate ways. I contemplated the way the senseless destruction of the lab mirrored the problems that had dogged my life. I realized I'd acted instinctively to rectify the problem in the lab, and I'd accepted the help I needed when it was offered. That proved I could do it if I wanted to. When I reached my home, I slept like a baby for the rest of the day.

CHAPTER FORTY-NINE

I AWOKE at sunset and checked my phone. Maddy had left several messages, but I was still too shaken to talk about what had happened. I decided to give my report to Maddy tomorrow and spend the evening working on my Harry video instead of answering questions.

I queued up the film clips, not realizing the one that ended with me getting struck by the Jet Ski was in the mix. When it began to play, I watched myself hit and thrown aside. I saw the bright blood that had seeped from the wound in my head. I saw myself drifting toward the ocean floor. The water wasn't very deep, but it was sure deep enough that I would have drowned if Lily hadn't rescued me.

The RCIP had never identified the boy driving the Jet Ski. It was unlikely he was a local, more probably a tourist, and long gone by now. After all this time, the chances he would ever be identified must be close to zero.

I wasn't sure how that made me feel. This person was roaming free after almost killing me. Yes, some of the blame fell to me because I'd ignored safety rules, but he should have at least stopped to see if I was okay. I didn't want him punished. Just scolded.

I reset the clip and watched it again. And again. I couldn't look away. I lost count of how many times I watched the video, and the room grew dark around me. I turned up the brightness on my monitor, and the contrast with the glowing screen made the colors in the video stand out. If I hadn't been watching in the dark, I never would have noticed the clue.

The Jet Ski banked as the driver turned around after hitting me. The toes of one foot were briefly visible just below the water's surface. The dainty toenails were painted with bright pink polish. The knowledge washed over me like a tsunami. The driver had been female, not a young boy as Lily had reported.

I wondered if she'd lied about what she'd seen or if she'd made an honest mistake. Since Lily had said she jumped in to rescue me right away, it was possible she hadn't caught more than a glimpse of the driver. She'd been far away from the scene, on shore, looking into the sun. I'm sure the accident happened fast, but I still couldn't fathom how she could have been so mistaken about the Jet Ski's operator.

And given what I now suspected—that I'd been targeted— was it possible Lily had been the person driving the Jet Ski? No, that didn't make sense. Why run me down only to rescue me? Maybe it had been Cara, and Lily hadn't wanted to rat her out. That made much more sense.

I decided to show Lily the clip next time we were at RIO to see if I could get her to tell me the truth.

CHAPTER FIFTY

LILY CALLED LATER THAT EVENING. "Can we go diving together tomorrow? I'll feel safer with you there as my buddy."

I was surprised Lily wanted to dive with me again, since despite what she'd said, I was sure she was seeing my ex. I needed to ask her about the details of my accident. Even though I knew she wasn't his biological daughter, Ray had loved her just as he'd loved me. I wanted a close relationship with my almost-sister. I said yes. "Meet me at the marina at 7:00. We'll beat the cattle boats from the local dive shops."

"Sounds good." She chuckled. "That's early, but I can do it."

"See you tomorrow." I hung up and went off to check the gear in my dive bag. I'd sign out tanks in the morning, and this time, nobody but me would touch them.

After I had everything packed and prepped for the morning, I changed into an old tee shirt I often wore to bed because it was soft and cool. I planned to read Ray's dive logs for a few minutes and then go to sleep early. I didn't want to be late to meet Lily.

I went to the foyer where I usually dropped my stuff when I got home, but the tote bags with the logbooks weren't there. They weren't in the breezeway or in my car. I didn't think I'd left them at work or on the *Maddy*, but where else could they be?

I retraced my steps several times from my car to the various rooms in my house looking for them, but even I couldn't misplace three large tote bags full of heavy books

I wondered if someone who was convinced the books held the secret to Ray's treasure had taken them. I considered everyone who'd asked about Ray's map to the mythical prize. The list was long. Stewie, Theresa, Newton, Cara, Lily, Alec. Even my mother, although she was the only person who hadn't been interested in the money. I decided I'd go to RIO even earlier than I'd planned. I wanted time to search the *Maddy* and my office for the books. I turned out the light and tried to sleep.

Once again, I was out of bed before the sun rose. After a quick shower and a bowl of stale cereal, I loaded up the car and was on my way. When I got to RIO, I brought my gear bag to the *Maddy* and stowed it under one of the benches. I searched every inch of the boat, looking in every drawer and cubby. The tote bags were not on board.

I hurried inside to check my office, but the totes weren't there either. In desperation, I checked the Lost and Found, a tiny closet near the maintenance room. I found a handful of paperback books, an umbrella, three baseball caps, a lovely cashmere sweater, and several odd shoes. Some were men's shoes and some were women's shoes, but all were for a left foot. I pondered this mystery while running out to pick up the tanks for the day's diving. I had to have a clear head. I'd resume worrying about the logbooks when we returned.

I'd just slipped the last tank into the rack when Lily called

out from the pier, "Ahoy, Captain. Permission to come aboard."
She giggled.

"Permission granted." I went over to take her dive bag and
offer her a steadying hand while she stepped down from the
dock. She stowed her bag under the bench across from mine.

We were setting up our regulators on the tanks when I
asked her if she remembered seeing the tote bags with Ray's
logbooks anywhere. She froze for a moment, closing her eyes
and looking up at the sky. "Nope. I remember seeing the bags
once, but I can't remember where or when. Sorry." She went
back to her task.

I watched her attach her regulator with practiced ease.
Either she was a natural or she'd had stellar training. I chose to
believe my training had a hand in her skill.

"Where do you want to dive today?" I asked her. "Is there
any site you'd like to try?"

"Anywhere you want to go, as long as we won't run in to a
bunch of other divers. I'd like to do a wall if we can. Maybe
Black Rock Drop Off?"

"Sounds good. Let's do it."

When we were ready to go, I climbed up to the flying
bridge, while on the lower deck Lily held the mooring ropes.
The colorful streamers on the bridge's rails flapped in the
gentle ocean breeze. The boat's engines purred to life and we
glided out of the marina.

The happiness surging through me was a surprise. I must
have needed this relaxation day more than I realized, and I was
looking forward to a fun day with Lily. Once we were out of
the 'no wake' zone, I kicked the engine up a notch, and we sped
off to the site.

After I'd moored the boat, Lily stood at the *Maddy*'s
transom waiting for me to gear up and make my way forward.
Like a good buddy, she checked to make sure I had my weights,

that my tank was secure, and that my air was turned on. I did the same for her. She made a giant stride entry, surfaced, and gave the okay sign. I made my own entry, and we began to descend.

The dive site consists of a level reef at about 60 feet that drops into a wall that goes down a mile or more. We swam to the edge of the drop off and continued our descent. We'd planned to go down to about 100 feet and cruise along the wall, before gradually coming back up and spending most of the dive on the reef top. I looked at my dive computer to check my depth and tank pressure. I noticed the pressure reading bounced up and down with my inhalations and exhalations, a classic sign the tank valve wasn't open. I was annoyed by my carelessness, but I knew how to handle the problem.

I reached behind me to turn my air on, but I couldn't find the valve. I turned my head and saw my tank had come loose from my buoyancy control device. The tank floated loose behind me, connected to me only by the regulator in my mouth.

This was my own fault. I knew Lily was inexperienced and I should have taken more responsibility for my own predive check. I was irritated at myself for screwing up, but there was no reason to panic. I would remove my BCD, reattach the tank, and slip back into the buoyancy device—all without letting the regulator out of my mouth. I unfastened the BCD's waist strap and slipped it off my shoulders to begin the process.

It sounds scary and complicated, but it's simple if you stay calm, and easier underwater than it sounds. I'd done it thousands of times during practice sessions. Ray had drilled me until I could do it quickly, even at night, in low visibility, or in a heavy current. But Ray had never prepared me for what happened next.

Lily took hold of my tank and wrenched it hard enough to

pull the regulator out of my mouth. At first, I thought she was panicking and trying to help.

I made the slow down hand sign before snagging one of the BCD's Velcro straps. I held on, trying to regain control. Lily didn't relinquish my gear, and she was swimming straight down and toward the edge of the reef, dragging me and my survival gear with her. Once she was well out over the drop off, she wrested the equipment away from me and let go. I watched in disbelief as my tank and buoyancy device fell away toward the ocean floor.

On most dives, I carry at most one or two pounds of weight in my BCD, but my gear was sinking fast, like it had been heavily weighted.

I hadn't noticed the extra weight. I was comfortable enough underwater that without thinking about it, I compensated for weight and depth with my breathing. The weight in my BCD was pulling my gear down, making it tough, but not impossible, for me to catch up with my tank, which was now attached to the BCD only by the snap on connection to the octopus regulator.

I would be safer in the water with my buoyancy vest and scuba tank than without it, and even if my gear sank beyond my reach, I knew I could still get to the surface because the compressed air in my lungs would expand as I rose.

No reason to panic either way, but I wondered what had gotten into Lily, because rather than helping me, she headed for the surface, swimming hard.

I assumed she was going to get a new tank. Not the best solution to the current situation, but Lily didn't have the years of experience and rescue training I had. She must have panicked.

I was torn. Go after my gear or go for the surface?

I went for the gear. I snagged it by the still-attached octopus regulator's hose and pulled the tank and vest to me. I used the thick Velcro straps to reattach the tank to the BCD, then I slipped the vest and tank over my head. While I was securing the Velcro cummerbund at my waist, I looked up at the surface and saw Lily climbing the ladder to the *Maddy*.

If I hadn't been wearing a dive mask, I'd have slapped my forehead in frustration at my own stupidity. Lily had to be the killer. I still had a few details I needed to work out—like why she'd let me give her the poisoned tank or why she'd saved my life after striking me with the Jet Ski—but no one else made sense. Especially given that it looked like she'd just tried to drown me.

I took a deep, unhurried breath and let myself rise to the surface at a slow but steady pace. I should have hovered at fifteen feet for the recommended five-minute safety stop, but I didn't. I approached the boat's ladder without breaking the surface. I tugged off my fins and clipped them to my vest, then attached the whole thing—vest, tank, fins, and all—to a D-ring on the *Maddy*'s stern hull. I stood on the bottom rung of the dive ladder and watched Lily who was facing the bow.

She'd placed her gear in the rack and pulled a soda out of the cooler on the deck. She walked away from me into the cabin and took a long slug from the can before she reached for the radio. She shouted, "Help. My sister is drowning. Please help me." She panted and gasped, doing an outstanding imitation of a helpless, panic-stricken sister. She was good. I'd give her that.

She released the radio button and took another swig of soda. I ducked behind the boat's stern when she came out of the cabin to climb the ladder up to the flying bridge. I heard the *Maddy*'s engines roar to life.

She grabbed the radio mic on the bridge. "Help. I can't find my sister. She's underwater. I'm afraid she's drowning. We're at the Arch dive site."

We were nowhere near the Arch.

She put down the mic, took another sip of her soda, and laughed.

Long. Loud. Ugly.

I climbed aboard the *Maddy* as quietly as possible, leaving my gear still clipped to the boat to avoid alerting her with the clang of a tank sliding into the rack. I crept along the deck in my bare feet. They didn't make a sound against the vinyl-clad deck or while I climbed the ladder to the flying bridge.

Lily was sitting in the captain's chair facing away from the ladder, looking out over the bow. She was blasting some tunes, tapping her feet to the music while attempting to punch some coordinates into the GPS system. I assume they were coordinates for the Arch. When the Coast Guard arrived, she'd need to at least be in the vicinity to make her story believable.

She jumped when I grabbed her arm. "Going somewhere?" I asked.

"Oh, Fin. Thank God. I was so worried." She was startled but regained her cool so fast I almost missed the shift in her facial expression. She put down her soda can and rose to her feet, holding out her arms as though she meant to hug me. "I'm glad you made it to the surface. I was just about to go back for you with a fresh tank."

"After you finished your soda?" I knew Lily was lying. I saw now she'd tried to kill me more than once.

She shrugged. "I was scared. My mouth was dry. I was afraid I would choke under water. Then where would you be?"

"You were more afraid of choking from thirst than about leaving me in a hundred feet of water without a tank? Your concern for me is heartwarming." I shook my head in disgust. At her for thinking she could fool me, and at myself because she had fooled me for so long.

She smiled, her face all innocence. "I knew you'd be okay.

How'd you get back to the surface, anyway? That's unbeliev-able. You surprise me every time."

"You mean I surprise you every time you try to kill me."

Lily took a slug of soda before she responded. "I wasn't trying to kill you. We're practically sisters. How did you manage to make it back anyway?"

"I had exceptional training. Ray made me practice my self-rescue skills constantly." I was stalling for time, trying to find a way to gain control of the situation.

Her eyes were darting around, and for the first time showed the madness she carried inside. "God, I was worried sick about you. I didn't know you had that kind of training."

"Worried enough to send the rescue team to the wrong site? We're not on the Arch, and you know it. You picked the site, remember? Cut the crap, Lily. Why are you trying to kill me?"

I missed the telltale tensing of her muscles that foretold her lunge, but my reflexes were still good enough that I managed to grab the railing around the flying bridge instead of falling.

I hung on, my legs dangling over the side, flapping in mid-air.

Lily was pounding on my fingers. "Let's see how you handle this, you witch. Did Ray train you for this, too?"

With the way she was pummeling my hands, it would only be a matter of time until I had to let go. Without a doubt, when I let go I would either crash onto the deck below or fall in the water. I chose the water. It's my natural element. I knew I'd be fine.

I pulled my legs up and placed my feet flat on the wall of the cabin, knees bent into a crouch position with my back to the water. I pushed with all the power I had while at the same time letting go of the railing. I hovered in mid-air long enough to see Lily's satisfied smirk. I waved my arms around like Wile E. Coyote, pretending I was in a panic.

I fell, taking a deep breath on the way down and deliberately making a big splash when I hit the water.

Once I was under, I sank down to about 15 feet. From where she sat on the flying bridge, Lily wouldn't be able to see me swimming to the stern of the boat. I climbed the dive ladder and snuck barefoot across the *Maddy*'s deck. I could see her back. She was still on the flying bridge, sitting in the captain's chair, her feet propped against the dash. She drained her soda and tossed the bright red can overboard and shoved the boat into gear.

The sound of the engine hid any noise I made when I went into the cabin and opened the weapons safe hidden behind the false panel in the head. Since nobody ever goes in there if they can avoid it, a marine head makes an ideal hiding place for anything you want to keep safe and secure.

I pulled out Ray's ancient Champion speargun. It was the one speargun model allowed in the Caymans, which regulates spearfishing to protect its pristine marine environment. I'd meant to turn the gun in to the police when I found it after the break-in on the *Maddy*, but I still hadn't had a chance yet. Now I was glad it was still on board.

I carried the speargun with me as I climbed down the ladder to the engine compartment. I studied the engine until I saw what I was looking for. The kill switch. I flipped it to the off position, and the engine died. The *Maddy* stopped moving.

"Dammit," Lily said. Her voice was audible in the sudden stillness. "Now what?"

I exited the engine compartment and grabbed a coil of rope from one of the lockers before climbing the ladder to the flying bridge. I peeked over the rim to make sure she couldn't see me while I was vulnerable on the ladder, but I didn't need to worry. Lily was turned away from me, flipping switches, and pushing buttons, hoping to find a miracle that would restart the *Maddy*'s engines.

I stepped onto the bridge and pointed the speargun at her. "It won't start. I made sure of that."

She whirled around. "Where did you come from? I've been going around in circles looking for you..."

"Cut the crap, Lily. You were hoping I was gone for good and we both know it." I tossed the rope to her with one hand, keeping the speargun trained on her with the other. "Now stop talking and tie your feet to the chair, then loop one hand to the rail. Make it tight. Don't try anything funny or I'll shoot you."

She laughed. "Pretty dramatic, but I'm your sister. You won't shoot me."

She was right, but I waved the speargun with a look of menace just to worry her.

A nasty sneer flickered across her face. She lunged at me to try to wrest the speargun out of my hands. I stepped aside and smacked her wrist with the broad side of the speargun's barrel.

"Stop fighting, Lily, You're done. Now do as I say and tie yourself up."

She raised her chin and glared at me, but the sun gleaming on the wicked barb of the spear pointed at her heart must have made her think twice, because she picked up the rope and started tying her feet.

"Make it real tight," I said. "No slack, and don't try anything. Ray trained me in spear fishing too. I'm a better aim than you might think."

Now there was no missing her scowl.

She finished securing her feet to the chair, and after she'd looped the rope around her hand, I reached over and grabbed the boat keys out of the ignition and threw them in the water. I knew where the set of spare keys was, but I didn't think Lily did.

I picked up the radio mic. "Mayday. Mayday." I gave our estimated location and then draped the radio cable over the console away from Lily. I reached over and wrapped her free wrist in the trailing end of the rope and pulled it tight. I tied the rope to the railing on the other side of the bridge. I tested the knots on her feet, tightening them a little where I'd noticed she'd left the rope slack enough to escape. I observed the hot pink polish on her toenails and knew for sure I'd found the person who'd tried to kill Gus, my mother, and me; ransacked my boat and my office; and destroyed RIO's lab. I knew she'd killed Ray too.

When I was certain she was securely tied, I swiveled her chair around to face the *Maddy*'s stern and sat on the floor of the bridge. I kept the speargun trained on her.

"It was you, wasn't it? On the Jet Ski."

She smirked. "Took you long enough to figure it out."

"Call me stupid if you want. I trusted you. But one thing I don't get. Why did you run me down and then rescue me?"

"I wasn't done with you yet. I wanted to see you suffer. Suffer at my hands like I suffered at yours."

"I see. And how did I make you suffer?"

"You had my father. You don't know what it's like not to have a father's love when you know he's right there. Loving someone else. Not loving you."

"I do know what that's like. Newton's my biological dad, but I didn't know my own father until after my accident. And Ray never knew about you and Oliver. If he had, he'd have loved you. He was a very loving man."

She glared at me. "You don't understand." Her voice cracked when she spoke.

"Oh, I understand all right."

I took a breath. "I just could never figure out how it could be done, so I concluded it was just bad luck and nitrogen narcosis. But you were the diver who tried to kill Gus, weren't you?"

She laughed. It was an eerie sound. "Yup. I meant to grab Ray, but I lost count of who was diving. It wasn't hard to hold Gus under long enough for him to lose consciousness, and you guys never suspected a thing. It was even easier than I thought it would be. Since he was freediving, he didn't have enough air left to fight me."

"You were on scuba? Down that deep? What about oxygen toxicity? Why didn't we see your bubbles?'

She made a face like I was too dumb to live. "Rebreather. Heliox."

I nodded. "You're not a beginner, are you?"

"Pretty sharp, Fin. And here I thought you were too stupid to notice. Shame on me." She grinned, baring her teeth and gums.

"What about the carbon monoxide tank? Why did you dive with it? You could have died."

"That was a big mistake. I knew the bad tank was on your side of the boat and I was trying to act natural. I wasn't watching while you set up the tanks. It never occurred to me you could do two dives on one tank. Next time I'll know better."

"And Oliver? How much of this was he in on? Did he help you?"

She sneered. "Oliver? That wuss? He's a total chicken with a soft heart. He never would have done anything to harm you or Ray. He worshipped you both. The only reason he agreed to learn to dive was because I promised I'd take the class with him, even though I was already certified."

I heard the Cayman Islands Coast Guard approaching. A voice through a loudspeaker bellowed, "Put down your weapons. We're coming aboard."

I put the speargun down and raised my hands in the air. "It's Fin Fleming and Lily Russo. We're on the bridge. Nobody else is on the boat."

The Coast Guard vessel tied up alongside the *Maddy* and several members of the crew leaped aboard. They didn't carry guns, but they had plastic handcuffs. One stopped and used a net to scoop Lily's discarded soda can out of the water. Another man took my speargun and carried it onto their vessel, while an officer I knew from dive training classes at the Institute used plastic handcuffs to secure my wrists. "Sorry, Fin," he said. "It's the rules." Another officer used his handcuffs to subdue Lily, which was all I cared about. I knew I'd be free in a couple of hours, but I hoped she'd never be free again.

The officers helped her down the ladder. I could hear her saying, "She was trying to kill me, I swear it. She's crazy."

"That true?" asked the officer behind me. I remembered him from a dive class.

"Nope, Officer Ebanks, it's not true. I can show you the proof, but let's talk about it when we get back to dry land."

He smiled sympathetically. I'd grown up on the island and he knew me. "Mhmm. Yeah, okay. Everybody has their side of the story. We'll straighten this out at the station. Meanwhile, I don't see a key in the ignition, so I guess we'll have to tow your boat back to shore."

I shook my head. "No need. There's a spare key taped to the bottom of the top drawer in the galley."

"Bitch," Lily said. "I didn't know you had a spare key."

Officer Ebanks laughed. I could tell he knew I was telling the truth about what had gone on.

Two police cruisers waited for us at the dock in George-town. The police placed Lily in one and me in the other. At the station, we were seated in separate rooms for questioning. It took hours, but they let me go when Lily finally gave in and confessed. They told me later it was more like bragging than a confession. She was proud of every dirty trick she'd pulled on me and my family.

"What will happen to Lily?" I asked the officer at the desk where I waited to get my dive computer back.

"I can't say," he said. "Sign here, please."

I walked out to the lobby, still wearing my diveskin and bare feet. My mother and Newton rose from a bench along the wall where they'd been waiting for my release. Maddy rushed over and enveloped me in a hug. "Thank God you're okay,"

Newton took my hand. "I was so worried."

"If you're that worried, you might want to try hugging me," I said.

He looked startled, then with a shy smile, he pulled me into a tentative hug.

"I won't break, Dad. Give it your best. This has been a long time coming."

His arms tightened around me and his tears were wet on my cheek. Or maybe they were my tears on his cheek. Let's just say both of us were teary eyed.

"Let's go home," he said. "You must be tired."

Newton's Mercedes was parked on the street outside the station. He unlocked it and drove us to the Ritz-Carlton. Before getting in the car to park it, Liam stopped me with a hand on my arm. "Do you want your tote bags now, or should I keep holding on to them?"

I broke into a rapturous smile. The logs weren't lost after all. I'd forgotten I'd given them to Liam to keep them safe the day Newton was poisoned. "I'll pick them up on my way out, Liam. Thanks for taking such good care of them."

"No problem." He smiled his brilliant smile.

CHAPTER FIFTY-ONE

THE THREE OF us were sitting on Newton's balcony, enjoying the ocean breeze and the stunning view. Room service had brought us iced teas and snacks. I took a deep breath and sank back into the plush cushions of my lounge chair. I hadn't felt this relaxed since the day of the first accident—when Gus nearly died.

Newton raised his glass. "To my brave and beautiful daughter. You solved the mystery and brought Ray's killer to justice. Brava."

"I was lucky, that's all," I said.

Maddy laughed. "Lucky is better than good, remember?"

Newton put his tea on the glass table beside his chair. "I have some news."

"Spill it," I said.

"I bought a condo on Grand Cayman. I'm moving the company's headquarters here. Effective immediately."

Maddy raised her glass to him. "Congratulations. It will be wonderful for us to have you nearby."

"Yeah. Wonderful," I said, but I was hurt. If he could move

to Grand Cayman just like that, why hadn't he done it years ago, when I needed my father? I didn't want to start a pity party today, so I changed the subject."

"Where's Cara?" I asked. "Not working today?"

Newton paused a moment. "I don't know. I think she left the island. After what she tried to pull on Ray, I had to let her go. I can't have a con artist working in my company."

I was startled by his announcement. "I thought she was your top executive. What are you going to do without her?"

"Everyone's replaceable. Except you two." He smiled. "I offered the job to Gus. He'll be coming on board as a divisional VP as soon as the doctor gives her okay."

Once again Newton had surprised me. I pivoted between anger and adoration every time he spoke. It would take a lifetime to learn the ins and outs of his personality. Luckily, we had a lifetime ahead of us to work on it. I let go of my pain and relaxed into my comfortable seat.

CHAPTER FIFTY-TWO

THE SUN HAD JUST RISEN when I arrived at the beach at Rum Point. I watched the gentle waves and the shore birds cavorting for a few minutes. I hadn't felt such peace in a long while. Lily's trial would be starting soon, and meanwhile, she was in jail where she couldn't hurt anyone else. As I crossed the beach, my heart soared because the ordeal was over. The remaining members of my family were safe, and Gus once again had a good future ahead of him.

When I was ready to dive, I squirted defogging drops into my mask and waded into the warm salty water. After slipping on my fins, I dove, swimming under water until I reached the line of buoys that marked the swimming area. I blew out my snorkel and kicked along the water's surface, scanning the sandy bottom.

I saw the outline of a Southern Stingray's wings in the sand below me, and the sight reminded me of my beloved Harry. The stingray saw me too, and he lifted off from the sand, waggling his wings to dislodge any errant grains of sand. Then he swam toward the wall, graceful and majestic, leaving me hovering.

I didn't want to frighten him, or worse yet, drive him into the jaws of a hammerhead shark, the way Harry had died. I just stayed where I was, watching him go. Before he glided out of sight below the wall, he stopped, turned back to me, and dipped his wings. It was like he was saying goodbye, and it brought tears to my eyes.

I kicked my way back to shore, thinking about Ray and how much I missed his humor and his love. He'd been the best father a girl could ever hope for, and I would feel his loss every day for the rest of my life. But now I knew I would survive. Ray had trained me well.

ACKNOWLEDGMENTS

Nobody writes a book alone, even though you have to be alone to write a book. During the years it took me to learn how to write a book worthy of publication, a lot of people helped me along my path.

Thank you to my writing group, including Mary Beth Gale, Kate Hohl, Andrea Clarke and Stephanie Scott-Snyder. You make me happy and you make me strong. I couldn't do it without you.

Extra special thanks to C. Michelle Dorsey for the conversations and encouragement.

Thank you a million times to Sterling Watson, a most excellent writing mentor and a terrific author. You taught me a lot, and I think about your teachings every day when I sit down to write.

Thanks to Hallie Ephron, one of the greatest writing teachers ever. I thank my lucky stars for that class at Yale Writer's Workshop. And in Tuscany. Both the food and the instructor were superb.

Thanks to Hank Phillippi Ryan for early encouragement.

Edwin Hill, you make it look easy.

Brenda Buchanan, thanks for the early critique of In Deep.

I was lucky enough to work with a great editor, Kristen Weber. She provided insights that led to a major breakthrough and vastly improved the book. Thank you.

Dan Milauskas, who taught me to scuba dive and love the underwater world. Thank you.

Mom, I finally did it. Wish you could have seen it.

Jack, you are and always have been the best husband anyone could want. Your belief, encouragement, and yes—nagging—helped immeasurably. Love you totally.

ABOUT THE AUTHOR

Sharon Ward is an avid scuba diver. She was a PADI certified divemaster and has hundreds of dives under her weight belt. Wanting to share the joy and wonder of the underwater world, she wrote In Deep.

She lives on the south coast of Massachusetts with her husband, Jack, and Molly, their long-haired miniature dachshund. Guess who's in charge?

Made in the USA
Middletown, DE
08 September 2021